ROBERT GOLD

NINE HIDDEN LIVES

SECRETS ONLY SURVIVE IN THE DARK

SPHERE

SPHERE

First published in Great Britain in 2025 by Sphere

1 3 5 7 9 10 8 6 4 2

A CIP catalogue record for this book
is available from the British Library.

Hardback ISBN 978-1-4087-3061-4
Trade Paperback ISBN 978-1-4087-3062-1

Typeset in Garamond Pro by M Rules
Printed and bound in Great Britain by
Clays Ltd, Elcograf S.p.A.

Papers used by Sphere are from well-managed forests
and other responsible sources.

Sphere
An imprint of
Little, Brown Book Group
Carmelite House
50 Victoria Embankment
London EC4Y 0DZ

The authorised representative
in the EEA is
Hachette Ireland
8 Castlecourt Centre
Dublin 15, D15 XTP3, Ireland
(email: info@hbgi.ie)

An Hachette UK Company
www.hachette.co.uk

www.littlebrown.co.uk

Robert Gold is the *Sunday Times* bestselling author of the Ben Harper series, which includes *Twelve Secrets*, a Richard and Judy Book Club pick, *Eleven Liars* and *Ten Seconds*. Originally from Harrogate in North Yorkshire, Robert Gold began his career as an intern at the American broadcaster CNN, based in Washington DC. He returned to Yorkshire to work for the retailer ASDA, becoming the chain's nationwide book buyer. He now works in sales for a UK publishing company. Robert lives in Putney and his new hometown served as the inspiration for the fictional town of Haddley in his thrillers.

For my sister, Katie.
And for Pamela.

NINE
HIDDEN
LIVES

WHO KILLED ALAKA JHA?

*Unsolved mystery of murdered journalist still
haunts Haddley residents thirty years later*

BEN HARPER
18 September

Thirty years ago, an unknown killer bludgeoned to
death *Richmond Times* journalist, Alaka Jha. The
case remains unsolved today.

Late on a Friday evening, Alaka stopped her
car in a small layby on Haddley Hill, a little
more than two miles from her home in Oreton.
She switched off the engine, removed the keys
from the ignition and slipped them into her jacket
pocket. Later, police found no mechanical fault,
but for some reason Alaka climbed out of her
Nissan Micra.

Concealed in the woodland at the side of the
road, her killer was waiting. When the killer
struck, Alaka fell backwards, through the open
driver's side door, into the front seat of her car. She
died from blunt trauma wounds to her head, most

1

likely inflicted by a wrench or tyre jack. Despite extensive searches, police never recovered the murder weapon. Her purse was found with her body, its contents apparently untouched. There were no indications of sexual assault.

Alaka was thirty-five. She was survived by her husband, Professor Manish Jha, and their daughter, Uma.

This week, on the thirtieth anniversary of her mother's death, I met with Dr Uma Jha, at the offices of the *Richmond Times*. She is still seeking answers to the many questions that remain about her mother's death.

'I will never give up hope of finding the truth,' she told me. 'After so many years, I want this to be the moment I find justice for my mum. I believe, even after all this time, that somebody must know something. Thirty years ago, it might have been difficult for them to come forward but it's never too late to do the right thing.'

Sam Hardy, the paper's editor, joined us. 'Alaka worked for the *Richmond Times* for eleven years, winning numerous awards and rising to become the paper's senior reporter. In the year before her death, she shone a spotlight on the case of Fiona Nicholls. The killing of the former naval recruit, at the hands of her long-term partner, Evan Littlewood, sent shockwaves across our southwest London community.'

Convicted of murder, Littlewood died two years later in a prison knife fight.

'After the case, Alaka found herself inundated with heartbreaking letters from other women who lived in fear of their partners,' Hardy continued. 'When Alaka came to me and said the most dangerous man a woman encounters is her husband, I was shocked. The tragedy is it's still true today. Alaka resolved to champion women whose husbands governed and regulated their existence. She gave voice to lives lived in silence and fear.'

Alaka conducted a pioneering series of anonymous interviews with women who were suffering abuse and coercive control at the hands of their partners. The articles she wrote received national attention. On the afternoon of her murder, she conducted one final interview with an anonymous Haddley woman.

Uma Jha is urging anyone with any information to come forward. Did a family member arrive home late unexpectedly that night? Or did a friend appear dishevelled and distracted? No detail is too small and may help to shed light on a case that has baffled police for thirty years.

'It terrifies me that my mum may have sacrificed her life in her efforts to help other women,' said Uma Jha. After living much of her adult life away from southwest London, Dr Jha returned with her husband, Edward, early last year to help nurse her ailing father. 'Growing up without a mother affected me enormously. Her murder thirty years ago impacted not only me but also countless other people. Time and again, I ask myself if a witness has knowingly or unknowingly concealed the identity of my mother's killer for the past three decades. That idea still tortures me almost every day. I feel certain that same secret must torment other lives.'

One

Uma Jha

'To Uma it felt as if nothing existed for him outside of his study, not even her.'

She stood in front of the bathroom mirror and pressed the gentle lines that lately had appeared at the corner of her eyes. Next month she'd be thirty-five, the same age as her mother when she died. Did she have lines like this? Uma struggled to remember. Her father might know, and if Manish Jha had been a different sort of father, Uma might have asked him. Throughout her childhood, Manish had struggled to even speak his wife's name. Consumed by grief, he'd retreated into an academic world where he found his only solace. To Uma it felt as if nothing existed for him outside of his study, not even her. Her only comfort came from the time she'd spent with her Aunt Hema, helping her to raise her two youngest cousins.

Uma turned away from the mirror and walked into her bedroom. Hidden beneath the bottom of the window blind was the gold key used to wind her ornate antique clock. Each morning, she carried out the ritual of seven turns, until the clock was fully wound. With its vibrant colours and hand-painted face, the family heirloom came as a gift from her aunt, following her marriage last summer. There had been no note with it, no other acknowledgement of the ceremony that her Aunt Hema hadn't been invited to. After a decade together, neither Uma nor Edward had desired an elaborate celebration. From her family, she invited only her father. When she briefly contemplated a larger gathering, the idea of a party with aunts, uncles, cousins and their various offspring terrified her. A week after receiving the gift, she penned a handwritten letter to her aunt, but in the year since she'd not heard from her again.

When she'd lived away from London, it had been easy to forget about her past – her childhood, her family, her mother's death. At eighteen, Uma had fled from her hometown. After studying in Edinburgh, she'd spent two years as a newly qualified doctor at a practice in the highlands of Scotland. With Edward, she'd moved to his hometown of Leamington. But then, at the start of last year, her father's cancer diagnosis had arrived, and Uma's family loyalties proved surprisingly strong.

She turned the small, gold key over in her hand. Returning to London to help care for her father, she'd slowly tried to fill the gulf in their relationship. At the same time, she'd discovered a new resolve to face up to all that had gone before. With that came an intense determination to uncover the truth about her mother's death, whatever the truth might mean.

FRIDAY

CHAPTER 1

'You don't think it'd be easier if we went into your office?' asks Sam, leaning over my shoulder as we sit together at my small kitchen island.

I raise my eyes from my laptop but say nothing.

'Nobody expects you to be the tech guy, Ben,' he continues.

Lying on the old sofa at the back of the room, my girl-friend, Dani, laughs. 'Leave him alone, Sam. He's doing his best.'

'I'm perfectly capable of uploading an article onto the site.'

'As long as you're sure. We don't want anything to go wrong while you're running the show.'

For the next two weeks, I'm managing the UK's biggest online news site. Last week, my boss and Sam's daughter, Madeline Wilson, checked herself into the Priory hospital for a period of treatment. After drinking a bottle of Yamazaki Japanese whisky in a single day, she recognised her life was spiralling out of control. She left with a warning not to make myself too comfortable in the boss's chair.

Managing multiple deadlines throughout the day, and sometimes through the night, I've already realised there's very little chance of that. And with Dani about to give birth to our first child, I'm already counting the days to when I can hand back the reins.

'Don't worry, everything's under control.' I enter my security code, upload the article, and click to publish. 'If you look on your phone,' I say to Sam, 'you'll see it's live.'

'Already?' he replies, refreshing his screen. 'You're right, it's there. You're amazing.'

'When you're the boss, things happen very quickly.'

Dani laughs again. 'Sam, don't let the power go to his head.'

'Look, it's really there,' he replies, holding up his phone before passing it to her.

'The *Richmond Times*'s very first global story,' she says.

Sam is the owner and editor of our local newspaper, a position he's held for over forty years. He's an old-school journalist and his desire to tell the very best story has never waned.

'We do have our own website,' he tells Dani.

'Of course,' she replies, glancing in my direction, 'but this is the first *Richmond Times* article on Madeline's site.'

He smiles at Dani and whispers loud enough for me to hear. 'I never think of it as real journalism unless you can hold it in your hands. This is a decent article, but it definitely needed to begin its life in print.'

Two days ago, I wrote a front-page story for the *Richmond Times* on the murder of the paper's senior reporter, Alaka

Jha. Three months ago, Alaka's daughter, Uma, contacted him asking for his support in using the thirtieth anniversary of her mother's death as an opportunity to seek new evidence in the crime. Sam, who has always said he will one day uncover the truth of what happened to his close colleague and friend, agreed. He asked for my help, and as our news site's main investigative reporter, I was happy to take up the challenge. Having spent many hours with Uma in recent weeks and seen her determination to seek justice for her mother, I now share in her and Sam's commitment to uncovering the truth. Our hope is that the publication of the article, first in the *Richmond Times,* and now globally on our site, will bring forward new witnesses to the crime.

'No more than a *decent* article?' I ask Sam.

He holds up his hands. 'It's pretty good, I'll give you that, but let's see what kind of response it elicits. Madeline reckons we might see a response pretty much as soon as we publish.'

'She does, does she?'

He sits on the arm of the sofa. 'I might have mentioned it to her last night when I was visiting. Only in passing, no more than that,' he quickly assures me.

'You know the rules: no work chat with Madeline. Your visits are meant to be a time for family support, not an opportunity to talk news.'

Six months ago, Madeline suffered at the hands of a brutal kidnapper, who held her hostage for over seventy-two hours. Sam and I worked desperately during those hours to free her. After her escape, despite her initial bravado, insecurity and fear seeped into her life; alcohol became her only way of operating. And although he would never admit it, his daughter's suffering has had a lasting impact on Sam. He's begun to slow down. He's seventy-five, and still passionate about his work, but I've seen how tired it now makes him. Still, he refuses to take a step back.

'Maddy likes to know what's going on,' he says. 'She lives for her work.'

'She's not the only one,' I reply. As I do, Dani closes her eyes and grimaces. Twisting onto her side, she presses her hand against her lower back. I jump to my feet. 'Let me get you another cushion.'

She waves me away. 'A couple of kicks, nothing more. The baby will settle down in a second.'

'Yes, stop fussing, Ben,' adds Sam, with a wink.

'Don't you try and change the subject.' Estranged from my own father for as many years as I can remember, I've gradually adopted Sam as my surrogate dad. He gave me my first job more than a decade ago and we've stayed close ever since. In Madeline's absence, I feel like it's up to me to look out for him.

'It's all right you telling me no more work chat,' he says, 'but what am I supposed to do when Madeline starts quizzing me about what's happening?'

'Tell her Ben has everything under control,' replies Dani.

'I'm glad someone believes in me.'

There is a knock on the front door of our house. 'I'll go,' says Dani, pushing herself up onto her feet. Our first child is two days overdue. While both of us are nervous and excited in equal measure, Dani is now desperate for the baby

14

to put in an appearance sooner rather than later. 'I need to stretch my back,' she continues, crossing the kitchen with Sam following behind her.

'Where are you going?' I ask him.

'You come as well,' he replies, with a glint in his eye. 'I have a feeling this might be for you both.'

Dani opens our front door to be met by Madeline's driver, Vlad. Sam nudges me in the ribs. 'Maddy said I could use him whenever I like; otherwise, he'd only be sitting at home all day playing *Mario Kart*, or out moonlighting as an Uber driver.'

Vlad carries a shiny new pushchair into our hallway. He heads back outside, only to return with a carrycot, car seat and even a matching rucksack.

'It's from us both,' says Sam. 'Me and Madeline. She paid for most of it, but then again, she can afford it.'

Dani hugs Sam and kisses him on the cheek. 'It's too generous but thank you.'

When he steps back, I drop my arm around his shoulders. 'You shouldn't have, either of you, but give Madeline a hug from me.'

He turns away, wiping his hand across his eyes. 'It's the least we could do. Without you, she wouldn't be here today.'

I carry the boxes through to the kitchen, and Sam's head is buried back in his phone. 'When do you think we'll see any comments?'

'I only posted the article five minutes ago.'

'Every time I see Maddy, she tells me she has over thirty million readers.'

15

'We do, but they don't read every article the second it's live.'

Sam's shoulders drop and he slips his phone into his pocket. He's kept in touch with Uma throughout the last thirty years. I know how much this means to him.

'We'll get something soon,' I reassure him, 'but you have to give it a bit of time. We all want to know what happened, but there are no guarantees. There are a lot of crazy conspiracists out there. It's not impossible all the article does is bring them out of the woodwork.'

Sam nods slowly. 'As long as we try. I owe it to Uma. And Alaka.'

CHAPTER 2

Uma raised her face to the bright sun filling the sky above Haddley Bridge. Ahead of her on the embankment path, morning rowers carried their boats down to the water's edge, while from the small Haddley pier, boats ferried commuters down the River Thames to the City of London. Opposite the pier's gated entrance was the Boathouse café. Uma watched as the barista handed a cup of steaming coffee and a chocolate muffin to the man at the front of the line.

'Healthy breakfast,' she said, coming up behind the man and gently touching his arm.

'Uma!' Dinesh, her youngest cousin, turned and smiled.

'Eat too many of those and the girls won't love you any more.'

'I barely have time for them to love me. I'm working fourteen hours a day.'

She laughed. 'Did you think your City bank would pay you an exorbitant salary and not expect you to earn it?'

'I even worked on Saturday.'

'Welcome to the club.' They walked to the water's edge and looked across the river. 'It's good to see you,' she said.

'And you.'

'Have you moved into your own place yet?'

'Two weeks ago.'

'My baby cousin all grown up.'

'Mum's still going to come around each week to clean up after me.'

'Why doesn't that surprise me?'

'Saves me paying for a cleaner.'

She slapped his arm. 'You're better than that.' Her cousin sipped his coffee. 'Thanks for your message,' she continued. Two days earlier, on the anniversary of her mother's death, Dinesh's kind words were the only ones she'd received from her family. Realising how much she still missed him, she'd replied suggesting they meet.

'I'm not completely thoughtless,' he replied.

'I never said you were. For my sixteenth birthday, you made me a necklace out of your mum's gold beads.'

'I was only six, but I don't think she's forgiven me yet.'

'I still have the necklace.'

He broke off a piece of muffin. 'Why didn't you get in touch, when you came back to London?'

'Your Uncle Manish hasn't been well, and what with work, and Edward and I still running our business in Leamington, travelling up and down the motorway each week ...' She was making excuses. When Dinesh looked at her, she could see that was exactly what he was thinking.

'How's your mum?'

'Still fussing.'

'You told her I'm back?'

'She still buys the local newspaper every week.'

Uma realised her aunt would've read Ben Harper's article two days earlier. 'Is that how you remembered the date?' she asked.

'No,' he replied, 'although it might just have jogged my memory.' He offered her a piece of muffin, but she held up her hand. 'Uma, why are you doing this? Don't you think it's better to let everything lie? Aunt Alaka died before I was born.'

'She's still my mum. Think how close you are to Aunt Hema. How would you feel if it was her?'

'But putting the story back on the front page of the *Richmond Times* won't help anyone.'

'Is that you or your father talking?' Dinesh turned away and gazed down the river. Uma sighed. 'Look, I'm sorry.' Throughout her childhood, she'd found the views of her uncle, Rakesh, suffocatingly traditional. Of all her cousins, Dinesh was the one who understood.

'Mum would love to see you, even if you didn't invite her to your wedding. She'd never admit it, but she misses you. It would be nice for her to have another woman around every now and again.'

'Please send her my love.'

'She should hear that from you.'

'I know,' she replied, softly. 'Maybe in time.'

Walking loops of the embankment path, Dinesh reminded Uma of how, years before, his mum had dragged them both to see *The Sound of Music* in London's West End. She laughed at herself.

'As a cool sixteen-year-old, it was the last thing I wanted to do. I was in a strop all day.'

Childhood memories were a safe space. Uma remembered rushing out to buy the winning single from *The X Factor* and Dinesh squirmed at dancing to Peter Kay's 'Amarillo'. She asked briefly about his brothers, and Dinesh hoped to meet her husband sometime soon. Both avoided any further mention of his parents, or hers.

'This is me,' said Dinesh, when they arrived back at the pier. He leaned forward to give Uma a brief hug.

'Good to see you,' she said. 'Let's try and keep in touch.'

She stood and watched him jog down the walkway to board the boat. He sat at the back and, from a distance, she could just about see him take the remains of his muffin from the paper bag. He'd always had a sweet tooth. When he was a toddler, she would feed him chocolate mousse and he would scream until he could lick the plate clean. She waved, but he didn't see her.

CHAPTER 3

'The blue crate is for cardboard,' I call to Sam. He is standing in the narrow alleyway outside the back door of my home, shoving the flattened boxes from his gifts in with the rubbish.

'You don't actually believe they separate out all the recycling, do you?' he replies, moving back inside the kitchen and closing the door. He pushes himself up and precariously balances on a high stool beside the island. 'It all goes into the same landfill in the end. I wrote a story on it a few years ago.'

'Whatever,' I reply, raising my eyebrows. 'Perhaps things changed after your exposé.'

He laughs. 'You'd be surprised how far my influence goes.'

'What time did you say to Uma?' I ask.

He looks at his watch. 'I thought she'd be here already. I said to come over first thing, so she'd be here when we published the article. I hadn't counted on you being such a techno whizz.'

'Why don't you drop her a message?'

'You mean a text?'

'Yes, I mean a text,' I reply, rinsing our coffee cups before wandering through to the living room.

'How are you doing?' I ask Dani, as she stretches herself out on our new oversized, cushioned corner sofa.

'If it wasn't for my back, I'd be doing cartwheels.'

I lie beside her and take hold of her hand. 'You and me and our very own family,' I say, quietly. 'Can you believe that this time next week there'll be three of us living in this house?'

She twists again. 'I bloody well hope it is only a week, and if Sam doesn't stop popping round, there'll be four of us.'

'Shh,' I say. 'He misses Madeline.'

'He only saw her last night.'

'He worries about her.'

'I know,' replies Dani. 'She's lucky to have him.' Dani's father, Jack, passed away three years ago, and she often thinks of him. He raised her alone, and she desperately wishes he'd lived to meet his first grandchild. 'Have you messaged your dad?' she asks me.

I rest my head on her shoulder. 'Perhaps once the baby's arrived. I couldn't deal with him now.'

'He might surprise you.'

'I doubt it,' I reply. My father left my childhood home when I was only three years old. In the thirty years since, I can count on one hand the number of times I've seen him. 'Sam's more of a father to me than he'll ever be.'

Dani runs her fingers through the back of my hair. 'That

22

doesn't mean you can't still build a relationship with him. He'll be the only grandparent the baby has.'

I hear Sam coming down the hall. 'Maybe in time,' I say to Dani, kissing her on the cheek.

'What's going on in here?' says Sam, entering the room. He stands at the front window. 'I'm not sure lying on the sofa counts as covering for Maddy.'

'Conducting editorial oversight gives me a lot more flexibility than writing my own articles.'

Sam looks out onto Haddley Common. 'Two minutes and she's here.'

Dani nudges me in the ribs. 'Who?' she mouths.

'Uma Jha,' I whisper.

Dani immediately shifts herself upright and pushes me off the sofa.

'What are you doing?'

'Dr Jha told me to keep active. I don't want her to find me lounging around on the sofa.'

Dani registered with the St Marnham village surgery when she moved in with me six months ago. It's only a twenty-minute walk away, and Uma Jha has helped see her safely through her pregnancy.

'She's here. I'll open the door,' says Sam, hurrying out into the hall.

'How long's he known her?' asks Dani, her voice quiet.

'Pretty much from the day she was born. From what he's said, Alaka brought Uma into the office when she was no more than a few weeks old.'

'Parental leave not quite what it is today?'

23

'Definitely not if you were working for Sam. Within a couple of months of Uma's arrival, Alaka was back writing front-page stories.'

'I'll tell you now, I will not be going back to the station after only a couple of months leave.' As a newly promoted detective sergeant in the Haddley Police, Dani has already informed the station's senior officer of her intention to be away from work for the next twelve months.

We hear Sam step outside.

'I'm not coming in,' says Uma, as he greets her.

Dani gets to her feet and accompanies me out to the front garden.

'All well?' asks Uma, when she sees Dani.

'Still waiting,' she replies, 'but fine.'

'The article is live on site,' Sam tells her, interrupting Dani and excitedly reaching for his phone. He shows Uma the post.

'Are you sure you won't come in?' I say.

'No, I'm on my way back to St Marnham and am only stopping by as I promised Sam I would.'

'Look,' he says, not listening to our conversation, 'one hundred and thirty-two comments already.' We stand together as Sam flicks down the page. Almost every comment is an expression of sympathy. 'However well-intentioned, pity won't solve this crime,' says Sam.

I catch Uma's eye. 'I'm sure they all mean well,' she adds.

'I'm not saying they don't, but—'

'We all said this might take time,' I say. 'We need to be patient. I'm sure somebody knows something that will help

24

us understand why Alaka stopped on Haddley Hill that Friday evening.'

As she leaves our garden, Uma tells us she has a full list of patients at the surgery this afternoon. 'I've a couple of house calls to make early this evening. If you're around, I'll try and pop by.'

'That would be great,' replies Dani, 'unless of course I'm in labour by then.'

'I promise you, it won't be long.'

Dani and I stand with Sam at the side of the common and watch Uma walk back towards the river path. As she disappears out of sight, Sam steps back and sits on our garden wall. Dani perches beside him.

'Have you always kept in touch with Dr Jha?' she asks.

'Always,' he replies. 'I mean, some years that might have been little more than a birthday card and a gift at the holidays, but I never forgot. Every year on the anniversary of her mother's death, I send Uma a bouquet of pink carnations.'

'That's lovely.' Dani squeezes his hand.

'I need the truth almost as much as she does.'

'You shouldn't blame yourself, Sam.'

'I can't help it. On the day of Alaka's murder, late in the afternoon, somewhere after five, she phoned me at home. I cut her off; told her I was too busy working on something I thought was far more important. I've no idea now what that was. I should have listened to her, but instead I asked her to call me later in the evening, said I'd have time to talk then. Of course, she never called. She was already dead.'

25

CHAPTER 4

After passing St Marnham village high street, Uma left the embankment path and crossed onto the narrow pavement, which ran alongside the river road. She walked beneath the railway bridge and stood to one side as a young mother wrestled with a pushchair. She smiled at the woman, who in response mouthed a *thank you*. As she waited, Uma felt in her pocket for her car key. She would drive the three minutes from her flat to the surgery so that she'd be ready to leave for her house calls as soon as she'd seen her last patient. But her pocket was empty. Uma swore softly. She must have left the key at home.

As she turned to retrace her steps, she glanced across the road, and noticed a young couple seated on a wooden bench on the embankment path. Both were wearing black hooded anoraks and Uma's first thought was how warm they must both be on a beautiful sunny day. She watched the woman reach towards the man and press her finger into his chest. He raised his hand in response. Uma paused again, and wondered if she should cross until she saw the man turn his back on the woman.

Uma stepped out from under the bridge and hurried along the footpath, until she reached her home; a Georgian mansion block overlooking the Thames. She pushed open a small wrought-iron gate, and from a flowerpot at the building's paved entrance she stooped to retrieve a crushed beer can, dropped by a thoughtless passerby. As she let herself in, she turned to look again at the couple on the embankment. She saw the man reach across and yank the woman's hood off her head. The woman slapped his hand away and turned her back to him.

Riding the building's ancient elevator to her fifth-floor apartment, Uma's thoughts kept returning to the couple on the bench. She remembered sitting on the very same bench with her husband, Edward. Only two weeks earlier, on a lazy Sunday morning, they'd enjoyed drinking coffee in the late summer sun. Last week, there'd been a father and his young son sitting there, watching rowing crews race down the river. The following day she'd seen an elderly couple, still holding hands after fifty years together, while away the hours, and yesterday, a woman sat alone with her thoughts. How many different lives that bench must see.

She hurried into her flat, grabbed her car key and caught the lift back down before it had the chance to trundle away. Outside, traffic gathered on the approach to the nearby roundabout. She walked along the footpath, away from the village, but when the traffic cleared, she stopped. The woman from the bench was on her feet, shouting at the man, the hood of her anorak now pulled down. With the noise of the passing traffic, it was impossible for Uma to hear what she was saying, but looking at her now, without her hood, she recognised her instantly. Although not a patient, Cheryl Henry was someone she'd tried to help on numerous occasions. Only last month, she'd found a place for her in a community-based drug recovery programme. The programme organiser called her to say that Cheryl had stopped attending after only one meeting.

The man pulled his hood further across his face, pushed himself up from the bench, and turned his back on Cheryl. He began to stride away, but Cheryl ran after him and grabbed hold of his arm. He spun around, but as he did, she swung her right arm and hit him full in the face. Uma winced as the man staggered backwards, his hand raised to his mouth. Cheryl didn't wait for him to retaliate; instead, she turned around and hurried away.

'You fucking bitch,' he yelled, his angry voice rising above the traffic. Ignoring him, Cheryl kept walking in the direction of St Marnham high street. Uma waited, worrying the man would charge after her, but instead he turned in the other direction, tramping along the river path.

Uma looked at her watch and realised she risked being late for her appointment, so she made her way down the side road where residents battled over a small number of reserved parking spaces. But as she retrieved her car key, a prickling on the back of her neck made her glance over her shoulder. From the embankment path, with his hand still pressed against the side of his face, the man looked directly at her. Was he watching her?

She hurried on, not looking back until she'd reached the

car. As she jammed at the unlock button, she looked again towards the river. The man was gone. She blew out her cheeks and slipped into the car. It wasn't until she pressed the button to start the engine that she spotted the note trapped beneath one of the windscreen wipers. *Who's grumbling about parking spaces now?*, she thought, before climbing back out of the car. She pulled the note out from beneath the wiper blade and unfolded it.

STOP ASKING QUESTIONS
WHILE YOU STILL CAN.

DON'T MAKE THE SAME MISTAKE
AS YOUR MOTHER.

CHAPTER 5

Pamela Cuthbert stood beside the flower stall that overlooked St Marnham village pond. She smiled at the florist
who was busy hand-tying a bouquet of bright red roses,
while a late middle-aged man, wearing jeans that were a size
too small for him, paced anxiously next to her. Pamela saw
him look impatiently at the time.

'I'll be with you in a minute,' called the florist to Pamela,
as she worked skilfully at the back of the stall.

'Don't rush on my account. I'm in no hurry,' she replied,
breathing in the bright floral scents. She wandered slowly
around the stall, enjoying the late summer blooms. 'What a
striking display,' she said, as the florist wrapped a giant bow
around the bouquet.

'They're for my mother,' the man replied, instantly. He
put two twenty-pound notes on the counter and snatched
hold of the flowers.

'So unusual to see cash these days,' said Pamela, as the
man pushed past her. He didn't reply and strode away
towards the village. She could see a champagne bottle

protruding from the top of his shoulder bag. Men could be so foolish.

She turned back to the florist. 'Those pink dahlias are delightful. Could you make me up a small spray, just half a dozen?'

Two minutes later, Pamela slipped the flowers into her shopping bag and crossed the road. The bright afternoon sun reflected off the village pond. A small group of children dashed out of the local primary school, and Pamela watched them chase a flock of waddling ducks around the edge of the pond. She glanced at the time. With only five minutes until her appointment at the doctor's surgery, she told herself not to linger.

The surgery stood on the opposite side of the pond and approaching the entrance she waited briefly to allow a small blue car to turn in front of her. A woman wearing a black anorak and torn jeans caught her eye. She was leaning against the whitewashed wall, which ran in front of the surgery car park. Pamela feared the holes in the woman's clothes were anything but a fashion statement. When the woman spotted Pamela looking in her direction, she pulled up her hood to hide her face, despite the warm afternoon sun.

Inside, other than the man who'd arrived in the blue car, the waiting room was empty. Pamela chose a seat by the open door, which looked directly out onto the reception area. She didn't want to miss the chance to say hello to anyone she knew. The walk from her home on Haddley Hill, past the boathouses and along the winding river path, was one she'd made hundreds of times throughout her life.

What once took her little more than thirty minutes took her close to an hour these days. She was seventy-five now. Her feet ached, her ankles swelled and the lumps in her hands flared up almost every other day. But she told herself she was lucky to still be able to enjoy the walk. And she knew Dr Jha would be pleased with her for keeping up her exercise.

Pamela heard the main door to the surgery swing open and, leaning forward, could see the woman in the black anorak standing in the entrance hall. Pulling off her hood, the woman looked around, but with nobody manning the reception desk she hesitantly approached the digital check-in screen. With a need to enter your date of birth, postcode and appointment slot, the first time Pamela had used the screen she'd found herself asking for assistance. That, she knew, only came after a ring of the bell on the reception desk. She rubbed the back of her leg. Her sciatica was playing up. She'd mention it to Dr Jha, but only in passing as the doctor was sure to ask her if she'd been doing her back stretches. Then she'd mention the lumps on the palms of her hands. When she'd examined them before, Dr Jha had said she could consider a steroid injection or even surgery, but Pamela didn't believe the lumps had got any worse. Still, there was no harm in the doctor taking a look. In reception, she could hear the woman tapping on the screen with increasing frustration. She didn't like to stare but looking over she could see the woman was yet to pass the first check-in screen. Pamela did begin to wonder if she even had an appointment.

The main reason for her own appointment with Dr Jha was that she'd read in the local paper earlier in the week that it was thirty years since the murder of her mother. Over the last twelve months, Dr Jha's compassion and care towards her had been unflinching. When Pamela had spent four weeks on remand, guarding her daughter Jeannie's dying secret, Dr Jha had been among the first to visit her. The kindness she'd shown Pamela felt far greater than any support she'd received from many of her supposed friends. Pamela could guess all too well how much Dr Jha would be suffering now. The appointment gave Pamela the opportunity to let the doctor know how much she was thinking of her.

The woman slammed her hand against the check-in screen. Pamela sat bolt upright. The woman hit the screen again, and then, clearly sensing Pamela's eyes on her, turned to look in her direction. Pamela quickly dropped her gaze to her phone. After a moment, shifting slightly in her seat, she was able to see the woman rush towards the deserted reception desk. A moment later, the tinny sound of the reception bell sounded repeatedly throughout the waiting room. Pamela felt certain that next to the bell was a short notice, taped to the counter. It read *Please Ring Once*.

A minute later the receptionist appeared from behind the screen that divided the reception area in two. Her name was Linda and Pamela often found her to be overly officious. 'Can I help you?' she asked, in a clipped tone.

'I want to see Dr Jha. Now!' said the woman, raising her voice.

'Have you got an appointment?'

'No, I just want to see her.'

Without an appointment, Pamela knew there was no chance of that. She'd booked the last slot of the day online. She always tried to book the latest possible time to stop the doctor hurrying through her ten minutes by using the excuse of other patients waiting. Whenever she booked through Linda, the receptionist always tried to push her into an earlier appointment. One thing Pamela knew for certain was the woman standing in front of Linda would get short shrift, and she was right.

'Are you registered with us?'

'I want to see Dr Jha.'

'Once you're registered with us, you'll be able to make an appointment with one of the practice doctors.'

'I'm entitled to see Dr Jha. I'm in the NHS.'

Pamela narrowed her eyes and observed the woman more closely. She was right. The holes in her jeans weren't a fashion statement but the result of wear and tear. She could have darned the holes with a patch, but she doubted the woman would have thanked her.

'I can give you the necessary forms to fill in or you can register online.' Linda's voice was monotone, and Pamela struggled to think of a time it had been anything other.

'It's an emergency.'

'In what way?'

The woman didn't reply. Instead, she took a step back and began pacing agitatedly around the reception area.

'If you have a medical emergency, I suggest you attend the A & E in Oreton.'

'What if I need a prescription?'

'The hospital will be able to help you with that.'

The woman didn't answer. She'd run out of ways to argue with Linda.

'Here are the forms if you'd like to register with us.' The receptionist held out the papers.

It took Pamela a moment to comprehend what happened next. One moment, the woman was reaching forward to snatch the forms out of Linda's hand, the next, she'd grabbed hold of the receptionist's wrist and was forcing her head down onto the desk.

'I want to see Dr Jha!' the woman yelled.

CHAPTER 6

Pamela recoiled at the sight of the woman's spit landing on the side of Linda's face. On the opposite side of the waiting room, the man who'd arrived in the blue car had put down his phone but was making no move to intervene.

'I think you might need to do something,' she said, aiming for a tone that was both polite and firm. The man was only young, perhaps in his mid-forties. For a moment, Pamela found herself wondering why he was there, he looked perfectly healthy, but quickly she brought her mind back to the matter in hand. 'Linda needs help,' she said, trying to instil urgency into her voice.

The man got to his feet only to stand in the doorway and block Pamela's view. She moved to stand behind him. She was about to push him forward towards the fight, when an ear-piercing alarm filled the surgery. With her free hand, Linda had reached beneath the reception desk and hit the panic button. The woman released her immediately, staggering backwards in shock.

'I want to see Dr Jha!' the woman yelled again, above the

noise. Her face was a burning red, and Pamela concluded the woman must be an addict. She'd read about the millions of people addicted to painkillers in America and felt certain one day the same thing would happen in London. She'd even cut back herself, taking only half a Nurofen at night, just to be on the safe side.

'The police are on their way,' replied Linda, her voice calm. Whatever run-ins they'd had in the past, Pamela could only admire her now.

The mention of the police seemed to have an effect. The woman stared at Linda furiously for a moment longer, before racing towards the exit. Just as she reached the door, she stumbled. Her hand smacked against the glass pan-elled door. A pane smashed. Pamela winced as the woman dragged her bloodied arm back through the shattered glass, her skin shredded. But the woman didn't stop, just yanked the door open and disappeared outside.

Linda reached down behind the desk and shut off the alarm.

'Shall I go after her?' the man asked, hesitantly.

'I wouldn't bother,' replied Linda. 'We'll have her on CCTV.'

The door to Dr Jha's office opened. 'Linda, what's going on?'

'Everything's fine. Nothing out of the ordinary.'

Pamela couldn't stop her face registering her surprise. If this was nothing out of the ordinary, she needed to visit the surgery more often.

'Are you sure?' asked Dr Jha.

'I'll get a brush and sweep up the glass.' Linda crossed the reception area and pulled open a corner cupboard. 'We'll have somebody here this evening to fit a new pane.'

'What was the issue?' said Dr Jha, standing beside the reception desk.

'An addict wanting a prescription; fell over her own feet on the way out. I'm sure she'll get what she needs at A & E.'

Dr Jha shook her head and a moment later turned towards Pamela. 'Mrs Cuthbert, how lovely to see you. Would you like to come through?'

As she followed Dr Jha into her office, Pamela turned and looked at Linda. She had nothing but admiration for her calmness in a crisis. But she was less convinced by the receptionist's powers of perception. It wasn't a prescription the woman wanted, it was to speak directly with Dr Jha.

CHAPTER 7

I sip on a cup of coffee while sitting on the sofa at the back of our kitchen. Hunched over my laptop, I scan through a number of articles still to be posted on our news site tonight. The evening light is fading, and I reach behind me to flick on an overhead lamp.

Sam looks at his watch. 'I should head off. Friday night is fish-and-chip supper at the Cricketers.'

Dani wanders into the kitchen. 'Are you sure you don't want to stay and eat with us?'

He shakes his head. 'They'll be expecting me at the pub.'

'Ben's cooking dinner.'

I lift my eyes from my screen but say nothing.

'However tempting an offer that is, I should go. I'll visit Madeline straight afterwards.' He stands up as Dani sits beside me.

'Ben, it's nearly six o'clock and you're still drinking coffee. I don't know how you do it.'

'Last cup of the day.'

'You'll never sleep.'

'I'll be able to keep you company.'

Her laugh lights her bright blue eyes. Over the last two months, she has rarely slept more than a couple of hours without the baby disturbing her. How she maintains such good humour I'm not sure. I close my computer.

'Anything more in response to the article?'

'Six hundred and thirteen replies,' says Sam, holding up his phone. 'I'll read through them all tonight.'

'Remember, be patient,' I say.

Dani rests her chin on my shoulder. 'What are you making us for dinner?'

'I stopped at the fishmonger in St Marnham and picked up some prawns. I could rustle up a salad.'

'Is that it?'

'I definitely must get going,' says Sam, winking at Dani.

'What about those pies Pamela dropped off?' she asks.

'Chicken and bacon?'

'That's more like it.'

'With mashed potatoes?' adds Sam.

'I thought you'd gone,' I reply.

There's a knock on our front door. 'I'll go,' says Dani. 'Don't want to hold up your dinner preparations.'

From the hallway, I hear Dani and Sam offer greetings, and then Uma Jha's voice. Sam tells her he's leaving.

'Can you hold on for two minutes?' she asks. 'I've something I think you should see.'

Hearing the unease in her voice, I walk quickly into the hall. 'Uma,' I say, 'what is it?'

'Somebody left this on my car windscreen. I found it earlier this afternoon.'

She hands me a folded scrap of paper.

Stop asking questions while you still can.

Don't make the same mistake as your mother.

I see the immediate concern on Dani's face.

'Did you notice anyone by the car?' she asks.

'Nobody.'

'Can you remember when you last drove it?'

'Tuesday afternoon. I popped over to Oreton to see my father.'

Dani turns to me. 'And your article was published in the *Richmond Times* on Wednesday?'

'Yes,' interrupts Sam, before I'm able to answer. 'Forty-eight hours on and this is our first serious response. Somebody is definitely spooked.'

'It's probably nothing,' says Uma.

'It's not nothing,' replies Sam. 'We've caught them off guard and now they've shown themselves. This might give us a real breakthrough.'

I can hear the excitement in his voice, and so can Dani.

'I don't think you should necessarily view this as a good thing,' she says, before turning to Uma. 'You need to be careful.'

'It could just be a copycat seeking attention,' I say. Three weeks before her murder, Uma's mother received the first in a series of threatening notes.

There is a moment of silence.

'What do you mean copycat?' Dani frowns at me.

41

'For that very reason, we kept the threats out of our article,' says Sam to me.

'We did, but it wouldn't take much googling to find the reports from thirty years ago.'

'Tell me about those threats,' Dani says, interrupting.

I wait for Sam.

'In the weeks before her death, Alaka received a series of scribbled threats, telling her to stop writing her series on local women.'

'What did she do?'

'Largely, she laughed them off. Alaka was convinced they were nothing more than insecure men responding to what she'd written. With each letter I became increasingly concerned. I pleaded with her to go to the police but she point-blank refused.' Sam's eyes glaze over. 'A week before her death, a letter arrived at our offices.'

'How did she respond?'

'She remained resolute, no police. I felt I had to act and the following day I went to the station.' Sam glances at Uma, then looks at the floor. 'A week later, Alaka was dead.'

CHAPTER 8

'Do you think we should go to the police?' I ask Dani.

'No,' says Sam, quickly. 'It's one torn piece of paper. Haddley Police are hardly going to jump into action in response to that.'

'I thought you said this was a real breakthrough?'

'For us, not the police,' he replies, snapping at me.

I glance at Dani. Uma's safety must be our overriding concern.

'Sam's probably right, but please do be extra vigilant,' she says to Uma, 'just for the next few days.'

'I will,' Uma replies. 'And don't worry, Sam, I'm not stopping now.'

Sam disappears out of the house and I go through to the living room and stand by the window to watch him walk towards his car.

'How did the police respond to Sam, after the letter arrived at the *Richmond Times*?' asks Dani, sitting on the sofa. Uma hovers behind her.

'Not quite in the way you'd hope they might today,' I reply.

'A detective dismissed all the threats as nothing more than a consequence of the *calculated risks* journalists choose to take when writing *provocative* articles. He even went so far as to suggest if Alaka hadn't *shit stirred* into other people's lives, she wouldn't have found herself in such a position.' I look uncomfortably at Uma, but she doesn't flinch. She knows all this.

'What a cunt.'

'Bloody hell, Dani.'

'Well, he was. I'm still astonished by some of the attitudes in the Met Police during the nineties.'

'Better today?' I say, sitting beside her.

'Yes,' she replies, slapping my arm, 'although with some work still to do.'

'Sam regrets not hiring someone himself, to protect my mum,' Uma says quietly.

Dani shakes her head. 'He couldn't have known. Whoever made the threats had a sick mind.'

'And now?' asks Uma.

'It is only one scribbled note. It might be nothing more than a few kids trying to be clever, or a copycat, as you say.'

'Or,' I say, 'it tells us there is somebody running scared. Somebody who knows something.'

Dani's gaze locks onto mine. 'When I said be careful, I didn't mean just Uma.'

'I'm always careful,' I reply, a grin creeping over my face.

'I mean it, Ben. If you get yourself in too deep, you might find I'm a little too busy to bail you out.'

'As if.'

'Aren't you meant to be cooking dinner?'

'On my way,' I reply, jumping to my feet. I am about to close the front door that Sam has left open, when I see Emilie, our midwife, walking up our garden path. 'Dani's in the living room,' I call. 'Go straight through.'

In the kitchen, I click over to our news site. Comments on the article are quickly approaching one thousand. I scan over them but there's nothing of immediate interest. For a genuine breakthrough, we need somebody to come forward with real information. I dig the pies out of the fridge, switch on the oven and hurry back into the living room.

'Baby's clearly very contented,' says Uma, when I sit beside Dani. 'You might have to wait a few more days.'

Dani wrinkles her nose.

The young midwife loops a blood pressure cuff onto Dani's arm. 'You're still feeling fine in yourself?' she asks.

'A little tired, but that's only from broken sleep.'

Dr Jha smiles. 'You might have to get used to that, both of you.'

'Ben can sleep anywhere,' says Dani, 'even after seven cups of coffee in a day.'

'Seven!' replies Uma. 'In one day?'

'Very rarely is it more than five,' I say.

Dani squeezes my leg. 'Liar.'

'Okay, occasionally six.'

'And the rest.'

'I've a lot of work on.'

'Four should be plenty,' says Uma.

'Four!' exclaims Dani. 'He has that by ten o'clock each morning.'

45

'We'll do Ben's blood pressure next,' says Uma to the midwife.

'Keeping up your exercise?' the midwife asks Dani.

'A couple of walks a day.'

'A couple!' I say, laughing.

'Definitely one good one,' she replies.

'Ignore him,' says Dr Jha. 'Right now, do what you feel like, but it is good to keep moving.'

'Dare I ask, when do you think?' says Dani.

'If you get to ten days overdue, we'll talk about options.'

'That's another week!'

'Hopefully something will happen sooner,' replies Uma, smiling and getting to her feet. 'I've promised to pop in and see Alice Richardson. She lives two doors down?'

'Three,' I reply. My six-year-old goddaughter spent a night in Great Ormond Street hospital at the start of the week, after having her tonsils removed. 'I think you'll find a patient fully recovered,' I say. 'She managed to chase a football around the common yesterday evening.'

'Young children are very resilient. Alice was just unlucky with her tonsils.'

'She inherited them from her dad.' Alice's father, Michael Knowles, was my very best friend from our first day in school. A car accident tragically took his life whilst he was still in his twenties. Before I met Dani, Alice and her mother, Holly, were the closest thing I had to a real family. 'I remember him missing two weeks of school to have his tonsils out.'

'I'm sure Alice will be fully recovered long before that. She's such a little character.'

46

'She absolutely adores Ben,' adds Dani, now standing beside Uma. 'If you're heading up the road, I'll walk with you. A little exercise while Ben finishes his dinner preparations will do me good.' Dani winks at me as she leaves the room.

Back in the kitchen, I drop onto the sofa and close my eyes. Ever since I was eight years old, when my brother was murdered, I've never allowed myself to think of the future. After Nick died, it felt as if everything good in my life was temporary, and it would only be a matter of time before it was snatched away. I lived my life as an endless series of single days. Dani has helped me see the world in a different way. Waiting for the arrival of our first child, I find it almost impossible to contain my anticipation and joy. For the first time in my life, I feel like I'm the luckiest man alive.

CHAPTER 9

'Give me two seconds to pop to my car,' said Uma.

Dani leaned against the garden wall, as Dr Jha crossed the road and clicked open the passenger-side door of her green Mini Clubman. As the sun dropped behind Haddley Woods, Dani closed her eyes and let the fading rays warm her face.

'Such a beautiful evening,' continued Uma, returning to Dani. 'It's just the two of you, you and Ben, as a family?'

Dani opened her eyes. 'We've got some good friends, but really, yes, it's just the two of us.'

'Ben's talked about losing his mum,' she tells Dani. 'I'm not stupid enough to think his main interest in my mum's anniversary isn't discovering a great story, but I feel some of his determination to help me find answers comes from his own loss.'

'He was twenty at the time of his mum's death. Years later, he uncovered the truth of what happened to her.'

'It was still important for him to know?'

Dani nods. 'He'd love to do the same for you.'

'And how about you?' asked Uma. 'Most new mums need a little bit of support, even if it's only to give you ten minutes to sit in the sun.'

'My Auntie Pamela won't be able to keep away. She loves children.'

'You don't mean Pamela Cuthbert, do you?'

'Yes,' said Dani, smiling. 'Do you know her?'

'She's one of my regulars. The most thoughtful patient I see. Perhaps a little lonely, with a tendency to interfere, but she has a sharp mind and a heart of gold.'

'Very true,' replied Dani. 'She's not really my auntie. She helped raise me when I was small, once my dad was on his own. We lost touch for a long time, but Ben's brought us back together. I'm glad he did.'

Across the common, at a narrow entrance to the woods, a man pushing his way through the overgrown bushes caught Dani's eye. Rarely did walkers battle through the thick bracken and out onto the common, not when there was a pathway directly from the woods onto the Lower Haddley Road. In the dim light, Dani strained to make out the man's form, until she saw a spark of a flame. He'd stopped at the far edge of the common to smoke a cigarette.

'Shall we head up the road?' she said, getting to her feet. Walking beside Uma, she noticed the copy of Roald Dahl's *Matilda* she held in her hand. 'I loved that book when I was at school.'

'Our receptionist organised a book sale in the surgery at the start of the week. I thought of Alice as soon as I saw it.'

'She loves her books. In fact, she's already told me she's

going to teach the baby to read.' In the middle of the common, the man with the cigarette was now passing beneath a Victorian streetlamp. Dani could make out a rucksack thrown across his back.

Uma kept talking. 'As a child, I can remember rushing upstairs after dinner to read my Roald Dahl books. I had a set in a little box and would read almost every night under my duvet. The stories transported me to a whole other world.'

Dani smiled but she was barely listening. As they walked, the man's gaze followed them up the road. She quickened her step. 'Alice will be off to bed soon,' she said. 'I'll call in and say hello, if that's okay with you?'

'Of course,' replied Uma. 'I'm sure Alice is fine. I'm only popping in as I promised I would.'

Arriving at Alice's house, Dani pushed open the garden gate. But, before she followed the path up to the front door, she stopped and looked back across the common. The man was hurrying towards them. Dani saw the aggression in his stride. Instinctively, she grabbed Uma's arm and pulled her into the small front garden.

'What is it?' asked the doctor, stumbling forward.

'I want to talk to you,' yelled the man.

Dani pushed the garden gate closed.

'Holly!' she called, hoping her friend might hear.

His step slower, the man walked across the road. From the stench in the air, Dani realised it was skunk he was smoking, not a cigarette. The smell turned her stomach.

'I said I want to talk to you,' he shouted, pointing his finger at Uma, his hand shaking.

Dani moved in front of her, pushing her backwards towards the house.

'Bang on the door,' she said, instructing Uma, before turning back to the man. With the hood of his anorak pulled over his head and a scarf wrapped high around his neck, she could barely see his face. 'I'm Detective Sergeant Dani Cash of the Haddley Police,' she called, standing behind the closed gate. The man paused in the middle of the road, and she felt for her phone. She held it out in front of her. 'I can have a colleague here in two minutes.'

'It's not you I want, it's the Indian doctor,' he bawled back.

Behind her, Dani was relieved to hear the front door open. 'Uma, get inside,' she said. She took a step back towards the house but, as she did, the man moved forward. She tried to get a better look at his face beneath the hood of the anorak. Did she recognise him?

'You've had your warning,' he yelled.

Turning her head, Dani saw Uma standing in the doorway with Holly.

'But just like your mother,' he continued, 'you didn't listen – and now you'll regret it.'

CHAPTER 10

'Who the fuck was that?' asked Holly, as Dani slammed the front door closed.

'I'm calling the station,' she replied, opening her phone.

'No, please don't,' said Uma, reaching for Dani's hand.

'He was threatening you. He might still be outside.'

'I think Dani's right,' added Holly, as the three women stood together in her narrow hallway.

'Ben said we might attract a few crazies. I think that's all he is.'

Dani shook her head. 'No, his tone was aggressive. Whoever he was, what he said was real. Uma, he was threatening your life.'

Holly stood on her toes and peered through the stained-glass window at the top of her front door.

'Is he still there?' asked Dani, her phone still in her hand. 'I can't see.'

'He'd obviously been smoking something,' said Uma. 'He was off his head. I don't think we should take him seriously. I'll be more careful, I promise.'

'This wasn't your fault,' replied Dani. 'Even if it turns out to be an empty threat, the police need to know.'

'Let me look out of the front window.' Holly hurried towards the living-room door, but a tiny figure suddenly appeared, blocking her path.

'I heard you say the F-word,' Alice said, her eyes wide with astonishment.

'Let Mummy get to the window,' she replied, edging her daughter to one side. 'Max, come away,' she continued, lifting her daughter's best friend away from his prime viewing spot.

'I was looking outside for my mummy,' he said.

Alice giggled.

'Your mummy will be another half hour,' replied Holly, scanning the common. 'I can't see any sign of him.'

Dani came to stand beside her. 'There was something familiar about him, but I can't quite put my finger on it.'

'His hood and scarf made it almost impossible to see his face,' said Uma, perching on the arm of Holly's sofa.

'Dani, you were very brave,' said Alice, taking hold of her hand. 'You shouted at him, and he ran away. I hope it didn't scare the baby.'

Dani smiled. 'I'm sure the baby is fine.'

'You should have arrested him.'

'I think he might be too quick for me right now.'

'Max and I could catch him,' Alice immediately replied.

'Super Max!' said Max, jumping to his feet from the living-room floor, where he'd returned to continue building an *Iron Man* Lego figure.

'Super Alice!' his friend replied. Both began to laugh before charging out of the room and racing upstairs.

Uma stared out of the window. 'The police are not going to find him now. He'll be back in the woods.'

Dani eased herself into an armchair. 'You're probably right. And if I'm honest, it'd be another couple of hours before anyone attended. I do still think you should make a report in the morning.'

Uma nodded. 'If you really think it's necessary.'

Dani stretched her back. 'I'm sure I recognised him.'

'He knew you, Dr Jha,' said Holly.

'I'm the Indian doctor,' she replied. 'I'm pretty recognisable, and I guess an easy target.'

Dani's stomach lurched. That was exactly what she was afraid of.

CHAPTER 11

Alice stood at the top of the stairs. She turned to Max and pressed her finger on her lips.

'No talking,' she whispered, in the quietest voice she could muster.

'I need my shoes.'

Alice repeatedly tapped her finger on her mouth. 'I said no talking. The man came to my house. That means I'm in charge of the investigation. You have to follow me.' Reaching up to hold the banister, she crept slowly down the stairs. On the bottom step she stopped and turned to Max. She pressed her finger to her mouth so hard it turned her lips white. In response, Max slapped his hand over his mouth and the pair tiptoed through to the kitchen.

Sitting on the kitchen floor, Max pulled on his trainers and Velcroed them closed. Alice pushed her feet into her wellington boots before dragging her coat off the peg by the back door.

'Your coat's on the top peg. My mum put it up there.'

Max stood beneath the coat and jumped up. 'I can't reach it.'

Alice folded her arms and thought. 'We can get a chair from the table, but we'll have to carry it across the room, so we don't make any noise,' she said.

In silence, the pair carried a wooden chair across the kitchen. Max climbed up and pulled down his coat. He clambered off the chair and began to drag it back towards the table. It screeched over the tiles, and Alice shushed him fiercely.

'We can put the chair back later,' she whispered. She reached up and clicked open the back door. For a moment Max hesitated. 'Come on, or he'll get away.'

'It's getting dark,' he replied.

'You're not scared, are you?'

'No, I'm Super Max.'

'Come on, then.'

The pair crept out into the alley and walked along the back of the terrace row.

'That's Ben's house,' she said, as they passed his back gate. 'Dani lives there now and she's having a baby.'

'I know!'

'I hope it's a girl,' said Alice. 'We've already got enough boys with you and Ben.'

The pair hurried to the end of the alley. For a second, they stopped before sneaking around the corner and facing the common.

'He's there!' said Max, pointing.

Alice knocked down his hand. 'Shush, or he'll see us. I knew we'd find him.'

Ahead of them, standing at the side of the common, was

56

the man they'd seen through the living-room window. He was opposite Ben's house.

'What's he doing?' said Max.

'I can't see.'

'I think he's going to steal a car.'

'Why?'

'Because he's looking in the car windows.'

'We should get Dani.'

'Why?'

'Because she's a police officer. She can arrest him.'

The man turned back to the common and stooped to the ground. He stood up again, and before either Alice or Max could move, he raised his arm and smashed a stone through the window of one of the parked cars. Alice looked at Max, her mouth open. 'That's Dr Jha's car. I know that because she came to see me before my operation at Great Ormond Street Hospital.'

'I told you he was going to steal a car.'

Alice grabbed Max's hand. Running as fast as they could, they flew up the path at the side of the common and into Ben's front garden. The pair banged on his door.

Alice was about to shout his name when the door opened.

'Ben, look!' cried Alice, pointing across the road.

'He's stealing Dr Jha's car,' said Max.

The man jumped backwards and disappeared onto the common. Seconds later, flames engulfed the car.

CHAPTER 12

I grab hold of Alice and Max and push them inside.

'Do not move!' I say, my voice thundering.

I sprint across my garden. When I look back over my shoulder, I see the pair standing static in the doorway, their eyes alight in amazement. I jump over the garden wall and head for the common but the heat from the burning car forces me back. I crouch in the road, trying desperately to see inside the vehicle, searching for any signs of life. I hurry around to the back of the car but, through the dancing flames, I can see nothing inside.

I feel the heat flowing through the tarmac to my bare feet and am forced to step back onto the grass. An exploding tyre echoes like a gunshot across the common, but I move forward again. I need to be certain there's no one trapped inside the car. As I get closer, the fierce temperature tells me any life would've long been extinguished. The intense heat causes the back doors of the car to burst open. Flames leap upwards, while black smoke and the smell of burning rubber fill the air. I cover my mouth and turn away.

I catch sight of a man standing in the middle of the common. He's watching the fire burn. When he sees me looking, he turns and starts to run towards the woods.

'Stop,' I yell. Instinctively, I chase after him. From behind me, I hear a voice cry out.

'Ben, no!' calls Dani. She's standing with Holly and Uma at the edge of the common.

'He set the fire,' I shout, gesturing towards the man, who is fast approaching the narrow entrance to the woods. Certain I can still catch him, I start to sprint across the soft grass.

'He's not worth it, Ben,' cries Dani. 'The police will pick him up.'

I look back over my shoulder. Alice and Max are running up the street towards Holly. I keep moving forward. The man pushes aside overgrown branches. I run harder. He ducks his head and squeezes through the tiny gap.

'Ben!' Behind me, Dani's voice is now a gut-wrenching cry. I stop and turn. She is crouching at the edge of the common. 'The baby,' she yells.

Two

Maggie Atkinson

'Her role in life was set,
and it was an auxiliary one.'

For Maggie Atkinson, the eleven acres of gardens at Castle Fields were her sanctuary. In the fading evening light, she sat in a small wooden arbour, her legs curled beneath her, and watched the ripples run across the reflecting pool. A small copse of trees surrounded her, their leaves now a vivid bronze. This was the only place where she could be alone.

A pair of bright green parakeets stared at their own reflections in the pool's clear water. From the corner of her eye, Maggie saw Bella, her neighbour's Siamese cat, lurking beneath a fir tree. Quick to her feet despite her age, Maggie shooed the animal away. She didn't like Bella and, if she was honest, she didn't like the Dawsons. Residents of Castle Fields for only six months, after moving from a large house in St Marnham, Graham and Carol Dawson were conspicuous with their wealth, overbearing in their opinions and a long way from the neighbours she would have chosen. Castle Fields was an estate of two hundred art deco-style apartments, built before the Second World War. Set in lush private grounds and overlooking Haddley Park, the flats were some of the most coveted in the town. Despite the ongoing challenges in her life, Maggie never forgot how lucky she and her husband, Alan, were to live in such glorious surroundings.

As a military wife, Maggie had lived her life in a supporting role. When she'd stood on the Portsmouth docks and waved frantically to Alan who, as a junior officer, set sail for the

Falklands, she'd already accepted her position. Her role in life was set, and it was an auxiliary one.

Her garden remained her refuge, even if it was rarely ten minutes before she had to be back inside. She'd learned how to make the most of the briefest respites afforded to her. For now, she'd enjoy her surroundings and her short-lived escape from captivity.

CHAPTER 13

Pamela poked her nose out of her front door and inhaled. Two hours earlier, the bus back from St Marnham to her home on Haddley Hill had felt stuffy, but now there was a freshness in the air. She pushed the door closed and reached for her summer jacket, hanging on the hook at the bottom of the stairs. It was only a ten-minute walk up the hill to Castle Fields, but she thought there might be a chill later. She popped through to the kitchen and picked up the spray of pink dahlias she'd left resting in a jug of water. Stopping in the living-room doorway, she smiled at her favourite photograph of her late husband, Thomas. He looked so handsome, with his neatly combed jet-black hair parted to one side, his dress uniform with its polished buttons and red stripe down the side of the trousers. She noticed the time approaching six on the carriage clock that stood beside the photo frame, blew him a kiss and hurried out of the front door.

As Pamela made her way up the hill, a stream of young revellers was coming down it, heading towards Haddley and its riverside bars. She couldn't remember the last time she'd gone out in Haddley on a Friday night and now even the thought of it terrified her. Often on a Saturday morning, when she walked to the St Marnham farmers' market, she'd find the river path strewn with plastic pint pots and empty beer bottles. She did wonder if people had lost all pride in their hometown.

A group of four young men, each in his early twenties, appeared out of the new housing estate. Jostling with each other and talking loudly, they walked directly towards her. Pamela's stomach fluttered. She considered crossing the road, but it was four lanes, and the Friday-night traffic was heavy. All she could do was keep walking, but as she approached the group, one of the young men stopped and stepped courteously aside.

'Keep going, you're nearly at the top,' said one of them, smiling.

She smiled back. 'Thank you,' she replied. 'This hill seems to get steeper every time I climb it.'

He laughed politely. 'Downhill on the way back.'

She walked on, hearing the four men laughing together. *We were all young once*, she reminded herself. Fifty years ago, she and Maggie would've been first to the bar on a night out in Haddley. Two pina coladas and a packet of salt and shake crisps. They only ever had to buy their own first drink. After that, the boys from the military rowing club kept them topped up all night. That was how they'd met Thomas and Alan, one summer evening. They were part of a four-man crew, along with two other junior officers from Mickelside, Larry and Simon. It had been Simon who had come over first, with a youthful bravado he never lost, but minutes later, when Thomas had offered to buy her a gin and Dubonnet, she'd been smitten from the very first moment.

She and Maggie had been friends since primary school, when they'd sat side by side at a wooden desk, writing with ink pens and blotting paper. Like sisters, after they'd met Thomas and Alan, they'd planned a double wedding. With Maggie's father away on service, sadly the dates never worked, but each had been bridesmaid to the other. When Pamela lost Thomas to an Argentine attack in the Falklands War, it was Maggie who'd helped her rebuild her life, piece by piece. Maggie and Alan had never been blessed with a family, and Pamela had shared Maggie's heartbreak over multiple miscarriages. It was even sadder now that they were all older, and life had become smaller somehow. Maggie adored her niece, Susan, but Pamela couldn't help but feel, as she puffed her way up Haddley Hill, that her friend was more alone now than she'd ever been.

CHAPTER 14

'You don't think we should call an ambulance?' I ask, sitting across from Uma in Holly's living room.

'I promise, I'm fine,' replies Dani, resting beside me on the sofa.

'All I'm saying is it might be worth getting you checked over.'

'Dr Jha's done that already! Whatever it was, it was bloody painful, but it's over now.'

Uma is standing by the window. 'There's something called lightning pain that can occur during the third trimester. It is incredibly painful, but it can also be a sign of approaching labour.'

'Exactly,' I reply. 'That's why we should be at the hospital.'

'I think Dr Jha is talking days, rather than minutes.'

I watch Dani exchange a glance with Uma. I slump back on the sofa with my arms folded. 'You know best.'

Dani leans across and kisses my cheek. 'If nothing else, I'm glad this has taught you that.'

By the time Uma and I had helped Dani back inside, a

small crowd had gathered on the common. Within minutes, the fire brigade extinguished the fire but, by then, the man who'd started it was long gone, escaping into the dark shadows of Haddley Woods.

'I've brought you an extra cushion,' says Alice, her voice an uncharacteristically tiny whisper as she creeps into the room. 'Shall I put it behind your back?'

'That's very kind of you,' replies Dani, edging forward.

Alice pushes the cushion behind Dani's back before squeezing herself onto the sofa. She nestles into Dani's side and rubs her hand on Dani's baby bump. 'I love you, baby,' she says.

In the hallway, I hear Holly's front door click open before slamming closed. 'Look out, Mummy's back,' I say. Alice tucks herself even closer to Dani.

'That's Max safely home,' says Holly, entering the room. She looks at her daughter. 'Max's mummy has told him no iPad for the next two weeks and no stories at bedtime.'

Alice looks pleadingly at her mother. 'We were only trying to help. We were the ones who found the bad man. We saw him set fire to Dr Jha's car. I'd be a good police officer, wouldn't I, Dani?'

'I think you would be, but the first thing you learn as a police officer is never tackle a criminal alone. You always need backup.'

'I did have backup. I had Max. He's my assistant.'

Dani fights a smile. 'But you should always have a grown-up as well.'

'And if you ever let yourself out of the back gate again,'

adds Holly, her tone firm, 'it's a month of no books and no colouring.'

'I'm sorry,' Alice says, quietly. 'Did the bad man get away?'

'Don't you worry about that,' replies Holly. 'It's way past your bedtime.'

'But—' Seeing her mother's face, Alice stops herself from arguing. She clambers down from the sofa. 'Night, night, baby,' she says to Dani's stomach. 'Can I still have a story?' she asks her mother.

'One only.'

Alice inhales sharply but says nothing.

'Who would you like to read it?' Holly asks.

'Ben,' Alice replies, instantly.

Holly smiles at me.

'Okay, but you go and get ready first,' I say, 'and then I'll come up.'

'Before you go,' says Uma, 'is your throat all better?'

'Mummy says I can't have ice cream any more.'

'Then I think you must be better, but for being such a good patient I've brought you a new reading book.' She reaches for the copy of *Matilda*.

'Thank you,' says Alice, politely accepting the book. 'Come on, Ben, we can start reading this upstairs.'

'You get your pyjamas on and brush your teeth first,' says Holly.

Alice rushes away and we hear her scampering up the stairs.

'What's happening outside?' I ask Holly.

'You can still smell the burned rubber. One of the fire

70

brigade said it was most likely a flare thrown into the back of the car.'

Dani's phone buzzes. 'The police will be here in fifteen minutes. We'll all probably need to give statements.'

'I'm sorry,' says Uma, 'I should have listened to you and called the police when you said.'

'It wouldn't have made any difference,' replies Dani. 'If he threw a lit flare into your car, he didn't come here to shout abuse across the common. He came with a plan.'

CHAPTER 15

DS Shawn Parker walked through the reception area at the front of Haddley police station. He raised his hand to acknowledge the desk sergeant, called a friendly farewell, but she simply ignored him. After three weeks at the station, he'd learned not to take offence. People in the south were very different to those he'd left behind in Manchester.

Outside on the high street, he darted down the building's three front steps and headed into the newly opened Chicken Joint restaurant next door to the station. Most of the other officers favoured the Mexican chain by the traffic lights, but at the Chicken Joint there were no established tables or corner cliques, with which he had little interest in engaging. The woman behind the counter greeted him with a smile that was barely a twitch of her mouth.

'Barbeque chicken sandwich, slaw, crinkle-cut chips and a diet Fanta,' she said.

He realised she wasn't even asking him a question but already keying his nightly order. Perhaps he would need to venture a little further afield, at least occasionally.

'I'll bring it over to your table,' she said, as he tapped his phone to pay.

He sat on a stool beside a high table in the back corner of the restaurant. He flicked on his phone and opened the Trainline app. If he left Haddley at six tomorrow morning, he could be back home in Manchester soon after nine. At ten, his two daughters had a Saturday-morning ballet class with Miss Gracie, and he could be there to surprise them. Miss Gracie had told Shawn and his wife, Leah, that their daughters had true balletic potential, but he struggled to imagine either girl ever appearing on stage at Manchester's Palace Theatre. Shawn appreciated Miss Gracie had enough years of experience to know how to keep her clientele fully engaged with endless years of investment in her private dance classes.

Leah would be with the girls. When he'd applied for the one-year parental leave contract with the Metropolitan Police, she'd been fully supportive. Over the past three years, he'd twice been overlooked for a step up to detective sergeant and Leah knew he'd become bored of dealing with little more than domestic disputes. In reality, although he struggled to admit it even to himself, he'd also become bored with his home life. He loved his daughters, of course he did, but he wanted more than a run-of-the-mill domestic set-up and a stalled career. His previous setbacks meant that, when he was invited to an assessment centre in London, he had little expectation of success. However, he'd quickly won the support of Haddley's most senior officer, Chief Inspector Bridget Freeman. After she'd offered him the position, he'd promised his wife he'd travel home every weekend he wasn't on duty. This was his third weekend in London, and he hadn't been home yet.

The waitress pushed his tray onto the table and Shawn clicked off his phone. He unwrapped his barbeque sandwich but paused when he saw PC Karen Cooke enter the front of the restaurant. In no time at all, she was at his table. Last Friday night she'd arranged a team night out to the Watchman cocktail bar, which overlooked the River Thames. All the officers were in high spirits after Shawn had led a successful drugs raid on a local building-supply business, Baxter's. For the first time, he'd forged a real connection with his new Met Police colleagues. Buying the first two rounds of drinks, he'd relished the repeated congratulations he received. The team had kept drinking, and after his fifth or sixth double he could barely stand. Even so, he'd insisted to PC Cooke on one more round of shots before the night ended. Instead of returning to the bar they'd stumbled out onto the riverside path and somehow made it up the high street and into the bedsit he rented above the giant clothes shop. A couple of hours later, he'd thrown up in the bathroom as it dawned on him what he'd done.

'Eat up,' said Cooke, picking up a napkin and delicately wiping barbeque sauce from the corner of his mouth. 'We're needed.'

CHAPTER 16

'You have to promise me not to come rushing back,' said Pamela to Maggie, squeezing her friend's hand as she stepped out of her apartment door.

'I shouldn't be more than an hour, an hour and a quarter at the very most. Mandy's pushed me in at the end of the day. There's always the chance she might be running late, but I doubt I'll have to wait long.'

'Don't fret,' replied Pamela, 'we'll be fine. When Mandy's finished your hair, treat yourself to a shoulder massage.'

'Thank you,' mouthed Maggie, blowing her friend a kiss before walking towards the lift.

Pamela closed and locked the door, slipping the key into her trouser pocket.

In the living room, she found the television newsreader speaking to himself. Slumped forward in his oversized armchair, Alan's eyes stared unblinking. Pamela stood in the middle of the room and looked at the kind and heroic man, who'd comforted Thomas as he drew his dying breath. She would be forever grateful to him. Both men so strong and brave. It was hard to believe it was all so long ago. At the end of his active service, Alan had transferred to a senior position at the Military Training Centre in Mickelside, southwest of London. While the final ten years of his career may have been less exhilarating for him, Pamela knew for Maggie they were by far the most tranquil.

The couple's wedding photos still hung on the wall. The bride in her lace and full train; the groom resplendent in his dress uniform. Pamela smiled. What a party they'd all enjoyed that night. She perched on the arm of Alan's chair. Gently, she placed her hand on his and slowly he lifted his head.

'Shall we put something else on? I've never liked Damien Syson,' she said, before picking up the television remote, while the man continued reading the local news. 'The way he combs his hair across his head; he must be so very vain.' She changed the channel to her favourite quiz programme. 'Do you think we'll be able to answer some of the questions?' She held Alan's hand, and he smiled.

'Where's Maggie?' he asked.

'She's gone to Mandy's for her hair doing. She wants to make herself look pretty for you. Afterwards, she's having a shoulder massage to ease the tension in her back. She won't be away long.'

Alan breathed heavily and sighed. Still holding his hand, Pamela turned her attention back to the television.

'South Dakota, Minnesota,' she said, answering a rhyming question from the television quiz. She looked at Alan, but he didn't respond.

'*101 Dalmatians*, the Temptations,' Pamela called out

another answer. 'I'm not as dim as I look.' Still Alan said nothing.

'"Day Tripper", Pippa! Three in a row,' she exclaimed, laughing. 'I think that's my record.'

Alan pulled his hand away from hers. 'Where's Maggie?' he asked.

'She's gone for her hair doing,' she said again. 'She wants to make herself look pretty for you.'

Alan nodded slowly, his face thoughtful. 'Maggie always looks pretty,' he said, and for a fleeting moment, it was as though she was speaking with the old Alan again. 'Every day, she always looks beautiful to me.'

Maggie was Alan's last remaining connection to the outside world. He lifted himself upright in his chair, briefly more alert. 'I love Maggie,' he said. 'Maggie and I have always been together.'

'You've been together for a very long time.' Pamela couldn't stop herself thinking how lucky her friends really were. She and Thomas had so little time together. 'You've had a lovely long marriage.'

Alan nodded, agreeing with her. He stared at her face. 'Who are you?'

'I'm Pamela.'

He nodded again, slowly. She could see him desperately trying to recall her name. 'You don't live here, do you?' he asked, uncertainly.

'No, I don't live here. I live down the road, only a fifteen-minute walk away.'

'Did you come on the bus?'

'No, I walked up the hill. You've been to my house lots of times. The little terrace on the main road, with the bright blue front door.'

'That must be very noisy. I wouldn't want to live on the main road.'

Pamela smiled. Sometimes Alan could be so blunt. 'It can be noisy,' she said, 'especially when the lorries rattle my living-room window.'

'I don't want to live there,' he replied, and suddenly his eyes were full of fear. 'You'll have to live here. It's quiet here. You'll like it. We've got a big garden.'

'I'm not moving in,' said Pamela. 'I'm visiting for the evening.'

For a moment they sat in silence, but Pamela could see Alan was still fighting the thoughts in his fading mind.

'Is it bedtime?' he asked. 'I don't like sleeping on my own.'

'No, we're going to have our dinner soon.'

'And then we'll go to bed?'

'Not until Maggie comes home.'

Alan furrowed his brow. 'Where's Maggie?'

'She's gone to Mandy's for her hair doing.'

'She won't like it if you're in bed with me.'

Pamela burst out laughing. 'Alan, you're a cheeky one. We won't be in bed.'

'Shall I put my pyjamas on?'

'Why don't we have dinner first?'

Alan nodded. Pamela's favourite quiz programme came to an end and something on coastal railway journeys followed.

'You'll enjoy this,' she said.

'Yes, I'll enjoy this,' he replied. 'What is it?'

'It's about trains.'

'Yes, I'll enjoy that.'

Pamela left him to it and padded into the kitchen where Maggie had left a shepherd's pie warming in the oven. All she needed to do was heat the gravy.

'Shall we sit at the table or have it on our laps?' she called. There was no reply, and she popped her head around the kitchen door. She repeated her question, but Alan still offered no response. She decided the table might be easier and hurriedly set two places.

'It's very hot,' she said, carrying the dish through from the kitchen. 'Do you want to come and sit at the table?'

Alan was slow to his feet, but his walk was steady. For his age, he looked physically strong; a lifetime of military fitness and diving, thought Pamela. Somehow that made his Alzheimer's even more heartbreaking.

'A few green beans with your pie?' she asked.

'Thank you very much,' he replied, politely, as he took his seat.

'And some gravy?'

'Most kind of you.'

He looked at the plate Pamela had placed in front of him. 'Where's Maggie?'

'She's gone to Mandy's for her hair doing; to make herself look pretty for you.'

'Maggie always looks pretty.'

Pamela served herself before sitting down next to Alan. 'This is tasty, isn't it?'

Alan half smiled, unsure. 'Who are you?'

'I'm Pamela, aren't I? Thomas's wife. You and Thomas, Larry and Simon – the four boys always in the water. Deep-sea diving, rowing in the Thames, always out causing trouble on a weekend.'

'Lots of trouble,' said Alan, laughing.

Pamela doubted he could remember.

'I married Thomas, and you married Maggie. You and Thomas served together in the Falklands.'

Alan nodded before eating a mouthful of food. Then, suddenly, he reached across and gripped Pamela's wrist.

'Thomas is back,' he said.

CHAPTER 17

DS Shawn Parker brought his police-issue Ford Focus to a stop and stared at the dead-end sign.

'I told you I should drive,' said PC Karen Cooke.

Parker crunched the gears into reverse. Accelerating backwards, the car mounted the curb. 'Or, you could have simply told me I was taking a wrong turn.'

'I thought perhaps you knew a quicker route.'

'You're twenty-six years old and you've lived in Haddley your entire life. I'm guessing you knew this was a no-through road,' he replied, snapping at the constable. He spun the wheel, jumped the car forward, only to scrape the driver's side door against a stone gatepost.

'Careful.'

'Fuck,' he replied, opening his door.

'Leave it for now. It'll only be a scratch.'

He slammed the door closed and raced the car to the end of the road.

'What's got you so stressed?' she asked, as the car stopped at the junction with the Lower Haddley Road.

'I'm not stressed.'

'You could've fooled me. Is it because you didn't get to finish your chicken sandwich?'

He pulled out into the traffic and didn't reply.

'It's the third turning on the left,' she said.

'Thank you.' He slowed the car as a fire engine leaving Haddley Common crossed the traffic.

'Do you fancy getting a drink later?' she asked.

'We've work to do here.'

'My guess is we've missed most of the action. The fire brigade are already heading home.'

'I've an early start in the morning.'

'I didn't know you were on shift?' Somehow, Cooke always had an encyclopaedic knowledge of the comings and goings of Haddley police station.

'I'm not,' he replied, 'but I should go north for a couple of days.'

'Should?' she said, twisting in her seat. 'Have you booked a train?'

'Not yet,' he said, 'but that'll only take me a minute tonight.'

'Is that when you're back in your bedsit, tucked up in your tiny single bed?'

He felt his face prickle but didn't reply.

'Even if you are travelling home tomorrow,' she continued, 'it doesn't mean we can't have a drink later. There's sure to be a few from the station in the Watchman.'

'I'm not a big drinker,' he said, turning onto the common.

'I wouldn't have said that last week.' She paused. 'If we're one and done, you just need to say.'

'It's not that it wasn't fun, but I'm married with two kids.'

'I get it. You were a long way from home, and you thought, why the hell not, she's easy.'

'No, that's not what I'm saying.'

'We're both grown-ups. I understand.'

Parker pulled up at the side of the common, opposite the burned-out vehicle. 'I doubt that will be back on the road any time soon,' he said, unbuckling his seatbelt. 'We should go and talk to the witnesses.'

'Wait one second,' said Cooke, leaning towards him. She rested her hand on his chest and straightened his tie. 'That's better,' she said. 'Don't want you making a bad first impression with DS Cash.'

CHAPTER 18

Pamela placed her hand on top of Alan's and squeezed his fingers gently to release his grip from her wrist.

'We should eat our dinner,' she said, unnerved by his comment. Part of her wanted to ask what he'd meant, but then questions might only confuse him further.

Alan kept his eyes locked on her. Uneasily, she ate another mouthful of her shepherd's pie. 'Aren't you hungry?' she asked.

He leaned back in his chair, shook his head, and pushed his plate forward.

'Maggie will be disappointed. She's made us such a lovely dinner.'

'I love Maggie,' he said, and after a moment, he picked up his fork. 'I love Maggie and Thomas loves you.'

'I'm sure he does, somewhere,' she replied, her voice quiet.

'Alan and Maggie, Thomas and Pamela,' he said, still eating his dinner. 'Alan and Maggie, Thomas and Pamela,' he repeated.

'That's right,' she said, 'but Thomas is gone now.'

He shook his head.

'Yes,' she replied, her tone resolute. 'Thomas died.'

Alan put down his fork.

'In the Falklands, you and Thomas together; a bomb attack on your ship.' She softened her voice. 'You stayed with him until the very end.' Pamela looked at Alan as tears filled his eyes. In some horrible way, was he hearing this news for the very first time? 'You were such a good friend to him. You did everything you could to help. I still miss him every single day, but it was over forty years ago.'

Alan rubbed both hands across his face and then across his shirt, before again picking up his fork. Pamela watched him as, in silence, he ate every last mouthful of his dinner.

'Would you like a little bit more?' she asked. He shook his head. 'Why don't you go and sit down in your chair, and I'll bring you some ice cream?'

Alan did as she suggested and shuffled back across the room. Clearing the dinner table, Pamela's heart broke at the thought of her friend's daily existence. How did Maggie cope, living her life in an endless circle of repeated questions and answers? She made a promise to herself to do more to help with Alan. He'd always been such a bright and caring man. Nobody's life should disintegrate in such a cruel way. She returned to the living room with two small bowls of chocolate ice cream.

'Thank you,' said Alan, picking up his spoon and taking a mouthful. Pamela sat on the sofa, reached for the television remote and changed the channel. She still enjoyed *Coronation Street* even if there was far too much violence.

'Where's Maggie?' Alan was leaning forward in his chair.

Pamela sighed. 'She's gone to Mandy's for her hair doing. She'll be back soon.'

Satisfied, Alan eased back in his chair and Pamela returned her attention to the TV. When she looked over again, his eyes had begun to droop. Carefully, she took the bowl from his hands and placed it on his side table. As he dozed, she thought how contented he seemed. Perhaps sleep was the only place left where he could find peace. Maggie kept the room warm, and with the drone of the television she felt her own eyelids begin to droop.

She woke to a knock on the door, and realised it was nearly nine o'clock. She hurried to the door and let Maggie back in.

'I'm so sorry,' said Maggie, entering the hallway.

'Don't give it a second thought,' replied Pamela, only now realising her friend had been gone well over two hours.

'Mandy was backed up with clients and when she was finished, she insisted I stay for a cup of tea. The time ran away from us. How's Alan been?'

'The perfect host.'

Pamela followed Maggie through to the living room. Alan stirred when they entered and, registering Maggie, a bright smile illuminated his face. 'Where've you been?'

'I've been at Mandy's,' she replied, taking hold of his hand. He pulled her closer and kissed her cheek. 'Did you have dinner with Pamela?'

Alan nodded, but Pamela could see him struggling to remember. Standing behind her, she looked at the back of her friend's head. She wasn't sure Mandy had done the best job. She felt Maggie needed something a little more modern. Next time, she might suggest she try her stylist, Vanessa, on the Lower Haddley Road.

Pamela picked up her jacket from the back of a dining-room chair.

'You might need that now,' said Maggie, hugging her friend goodbye. 'There's a chill in the air.'

Smelling a faint whiff of gin on Maggie's breath, Pamela smiled to herself. She was glad her friend had found time to relax, even if it was only in the back room of the local hair salon. Maggie walked her back into the hallway, but at the apartment door they turned to see Alan following them.

'Are you coming to say goodbye to Pamela?' asked Maggie.

'Yes,' he replied. 'Alan and Maggie, Thomas and Pamela.' He took hold of Pamela's hand, and again she felt the strength of his grip. 'Thomas was a good man,' he said, squeezing her fingers, 'a good, good man.'

CHAPTER 19

PC Karen Cooke wedged herself beside Dani on the sofa. 'We're all desperately waiting for baby news,' she said, excitedly.

'So am I,' replied Dani, laughing. She knew the minute her baby arrived, Karen would spread the news across the station, and probably well beyond.

'I've already got a nice collection going. You must let me know what you need.'

'That's kind of you.'

Standing awkwardly in the living-room doorway was DS Parker. 'Would you like to sit down?' asked Holly, edging past him as she carried an extra chair through from the dining room.

'Thank you,' he replied. He sat with his hands pushed beneath his legs.

'This shouldn't take long,' said Cooke, before the detective could speak. 'I'm sorry we missed all the drama, especially the firemen in action.'

Dani smiled but her eyes darted towards Parker, sitting

uncomfortably on his chair. He was covering her position for the next year, and she recognised having her as a witness was not an easy introduction. She offered him an encouraging nod.

'We will need statements from each of you,' he began, hesitantly, 'but hopefully they can be done relatively quickly.' His eyes scanned Holly's living room before landing on Dr Jha, seated in the armchair by the window. 'The man came across the common and spoke directly to you?'

'He threatened me. Told me I'd had my warning, that I hadn't listened and now I'd regret it.'

'Do you have any idea what he was referencing?'

Uma glanced at Dani. Quickly, she briefed Parker on Alaka Jha's murder, and the anniversary article published by Ben.

'Maybe we don't mention Ben's involvement to the boss,' said Cooke. 'Don't you agree, Dani?'

She smiled in response. Ben's recent success in achieving results faster than the Haddley Police had not made him a popular figure at the station. 'Perhaps one to keep to ourselves for now.'

'Prior to this evening, have you received any other threats?' asked Parker.

Uma passed him the scribbled note from her windscreen. 'This afternoon there was an incident at the surgery, but I'm sure it was nothing.'

'Go on.'

'There's a woman I've tried to help, an addict; not officially as a patient, but someone I've seen in the village. She came looking for a prescription.'

89

'Is that something you'd normally give her?'

'No, it is not,' she replied, sharply. 'I've encouraged her to attend a drug recovery programme.'

Parker nodded.

'She became embroiled in an argument with our receptionist. A small amount of damage occurred but we cancelled the call to the police.'

'Do you know the woman's name?'

'Cheryl. Cheryl Henry.'

Dani clasped her hands together. 'I knew I recognised him,' she exclaimed. 'The man on the common was Liam Kane. He and Cheryl have hung around together for the last couple of years.'

'He deals drugs out of the abandoned Peacock boathouse, on the river path between Haddley and St Marnham,' added Cooke.

'That's the one,' said Dani. 'He works for the Baxter family, but only at the very bottom of the food chain.'

Parker turned to Dani. 'Any idea where we'll find them?'

'Last I heard they were renting a room above Baxter's yard.'

Parker returned to questioning Dr Jha. 'Could you think of any reason why either Liam Kane or Cheryl Henry would want to threaten you?'

'None whatsoever,' she replied.

'Could either be linked in any way to your mother's death?'

'Neither of them would've been alive,' said Dani.

'PC Cooke,' said Parker, 'could you take brief statements?

90

I'd like to look outside at the area of the common from where Kane approached.'

'Let me go with you,' replied Dani, pushing herself up.

'Dani, you stay there,' said Holly, but she was already on her feet.

'I need to stretch my back.' Alongside Parker, she left the room and stepped out of the front of the house.

'The reach of the Baxter family goes far and wide,' he said, standing with his fellow officer in Holly's front garden.

For over forty years, generations of the Baxter family had used their building-supplies business as a front for a drug-running operation across Haddley and into southwest London.

'Despite decades of work, Haddley Police have failed to make any charges stick on senior members of the family. You did a great job with the raid last week.'

'Thank you,' he replied, 'but you did all the groundwork.'

'Nothing worse than some new guy coming in and stealing all the glory. Is that what you mean?'

'I'm sorry,' he said, hesitantly.

'I'm joking,' she replied. 'I couldn't be more delighted. My only wish was we'd landed further up the chain. My fear is all it will do is slow them down for a few weeks and then it'll be business as usual.'

'They're smart. It was a decent haul, but Baxter's solicitor comfortably laid everything at the door of a junior shift manager, employed in the yard.'

'Can you make the charge stick?'

'Yes, but their legal guy is top-notch, and I doubt the shift manager will serve more than a couple of years.'

'And then be royally looked after on his release.'

'Where does Liam Kane sit in the Baxters' priorities?' he asked, as the pair walked along the edge of the common.

'I doubt the family even know his name. He's a street dealer. He means nothing to them.'

'The family couldn't be involved here in some way?'

'It seems unlikely to me.'

'How long have they been active in Haddley?'

'Since before Alaka Jha's murder, if that's what you mean,' Dani replied, thinking of her own father's pursuit of the family when he was the senior officer in Haddley.

'So, not impossible?'

'No, but if it was them, why put their trust in a street dealer who's off his head most days? I don't see it.'

Parker shrugged and the pair walk towards the burned-out car. 'Kane came to deliver a warning,' he said thoughtfully, looking at the ravaged vehicle. Dani could sense where his thoughts were going.

'But from whom?' she replied, quietly.

CHAPTER 20

I walk down the stairs after reading Alice's bedtime story just as Dani is coming back into the house. She introduces me to DS Shawn Parker. He asks me about the fire.

'By the time I'd dragged the two kids back towards my house, flames had engulfed the car. When I was certain there was nobody trapped inside, I ran after him.'

'Could you identify him?'

'His face was half covered, but probably, yes.'

'Good. We'll be in touch once we've brought him in.'

'Anything else I can help you with?'

'Your ... Dani ... DS Cash has already been very helpful.'

'You know where to find us,' I reply.

'Hi, Ben,' says PC Karen Cooke, appearing in the living-room doorway.

'PC Cooke, always at the centre of the action.'

She smiles. 'New arrival any day now.'

'That's what we're hoping.'

DS Parker steps back into the living room. I follow him,

but behind me I hear Dani ask PC Cooke how's she's finding working with the new detective sergeant.

'He's cute,' replies Cooke.

'Karen, you know that's not what I meant.' Dani's voice is quiet. 'You've always told me you want senior officers to take you more seriously.'

'I'm my own worst enemy, I know.'

'Don't sell yourself short.'

'I'll try not to. Feel free to call me if Ben needs any help on his latest assignment!'

Dani laughs. 'I just might.'

'Do you need a lift, Uma?' I ask. 'I'm happy to run you home?'

'If you're sure,' she replies.

'Absolutely.'

Parker rests his hands on the back of a dining-room chair. 'I'd anticipate us picking up Liam Kane within the next twenty-four hours. Once we've interviewed him, in all likelihood we will need to speak with you again.' Uma nods in response. 'Dr Jha, I take the threats made against you very seriously. Until we pick up Kane, I would urge caution.'

'I'm expecting my husband home this evening, and I'm not due back in surgery until Monday.'

Parker turns to me. 'If any information does come to light, in response to your article, I urge you to contact us before taking any other action.'

Dani leads her two colleagues back into the hallway and I hear them discussing the location of the flat shared by Kane and Henry.

'Alice is waiting for you to say goodnight,' I say to Holly.

'I fear she may be awake for a while yet. A little bit too much detecting excitement,' she replies, before leaving Uma and me alone in the room.

'How are you holding up?' I ask.

'I'm fine.'

'Still not nice.'

'Ben, it's only a car.'

'No regrets?'

Uma shakes her head. 'I need to do this. It's already been thirty years, this could be my last chance to uncover the truth. This tells me we're getting close. Somebody's scared.'

'I never wanted to put you in danger.'

'You didn't. I made all my own decisions. What's next?'

'We should avoid jumping to any conclusions. Let's wait until the police talk to Kane, see what he tells them.'

I remember my own determination to uncover the truth behind my mum's death, ten years after my brother's. Until I was able to understand who stole away her life, it was impossible for me to move on with my own. I want to help Uma in the same way.

'If you hear anything significant, I want to know.'

Dani returns to sit beside me.

'No more pain?' asks Uma.

'Nothing.'

'I'll call by tomorrow, just to check on how you're doing,' she says, getting to her feet.

'Thank you,' replies Dani.

In the hallway, I stop. 'Dani's definitely okay?' I ask Uma.

'I promise you, she's fine.'

'That's a relief,' I reply, slowly exhaling.

'And you? Big moment becoming a father for the first time.'

'I can't wait.'

Uma turns her head. 'The stairs in this house are the opposite way around to yours?' she says, a puzzled look on her face.

'Holly had them turned when she did some renovations. Gives her a little more space for all of Alice's clutter.'

'That'll be you soon.' Uma stops in the doorway. 'What a beautiful stained-glass window,' she says, looking up at the glass above Holly's front door. 'The poppies are such a bright red, they're almost real.' Captivated by the colours, Uma stands for a moment before following me outside. 'Ben, you more than anyone understand my desire for the truth.'

'I do.'

'I need to know for me, but also for my mum. She's entitled to more than outpourings of sympathy. Does that make sense?'

'It does. I felt exactly the same way with my own mum.' We stop and stand beneath a streetlamp. 'But what I also learned very quickly is what you uncover might not be what you expect. You have to be ready for anything and, in my case, it came very close to home.'

Beneath the bright light, Uma holds my eye. 'I want to uncover the truth, whatever it might be.'

'I get that, but DS Parker is right. After Kane's threat, you need to be careful.'

'I will be,' she replies. 'Threats didn't deter my mum, and I won't easily be put off either.'

I think of Alaka's bravery and her refusal to let threats to her safety intimidate her. In the face of such danger, I can't stop myself wondering how she remained so resolute.

Three

George Lennon

'Every time he saw his grandmother now, she told him the only thing that kept her alive was the hope that one day she'd see him married with a family of his own. But how could he ever be responsible for another human being? He didn't even like himself.'

With his head throbbing, he stood outside the front door of the tiny, terraced cottage and took a deep breath. He waited until the door closed silently behind him. He'd left the woman sleeping in her bed. He didn't remember her name.

His surroundings felt vaguely familiar, and five minutes later he found his way onto the main road into Oreton. Through an early morning mist, ahead of him he could see the Catholic primary school he'd attended as a child. He stopped and looked through the gates. The school buildings had expanded considerably in the two decades since he'd left. New classrooms and a small sports hall covered much of the open space he remembered.

However hard he tried, he couldn't stop his mind from wandering. From the age of six, at the end of each day, he'd run to the back of the school, clambered over a wooden gate and emerged onto the road of his childhood home. Outside the back door of his house, which he'd shared with his mum, was the milk-bottle holder where the milkman left two fresh pints each morning. Beneath the empty bottles was the door key. One warm summer's day, he'd arrived home eager to tell his mum how he'd scored six correct spellings out of ten in his class test. Never had he written so many right answers, and he never would again. His teacher told him it was luck. In adulthood, he'd developed doctors' handwriting to disguise his dyslexia. Eager to share his news, he'd unlocked the back door, run through the kitchen and into the small living room at the front of the house. Lying on the sofa, the summer sun warming her face, he found his mother, Helen, sleeping. He kissed her cheek, and talking quickly he'd told her of his triumph. His voice had slowed, and he'd bent to kiss her again. Even in the warm sun, her face was cold. Five minutes later, he'd realised she was dead.

Now he turned away from the school gates, and continued walking up the hill before cutting across the corner of the golf course and on towards his home. Later today, he would go to the gym. And tomorrow, he'd run in Richmond Park. He'd not drink for the next two weeks either. Feeling in his pockets for his latch key, he found a small plastic bag with the last remnants of the cocaine he'd inhaled last night. At the traffic lights at the end of his road, he stopped and dropped the bag down the drain. He wouldn't buy that again – not for at least two weeks. That was his rule, two weeks between binges, and not once had he cracked. His grandmother said he inherited his self-discipline from his father. She had no idea about the binges. Every time he saw his grandmother now, she told him the only thing that kept her alive was the hope that one day she'd see him married with a family of his own. But how could he ever be responsible for another human being? He didn't even like himself.

SATURDAY

CHAPTER 21

An early morning sun peered through a break in the clouds when DS Shawn Parker rattled the padlocked gates at the front of Baxter's Builder's Merchants. Three generations of the Baxter family had run the building firm, and it had occupied the East Haddley site for over forty years. Bertie Baxter, the latest scion to operate the business, was both ruthless and rash. His ruthlessness, he inherited from his mother, Betty. His rashness, perhaps from his father. Parker understood Betty Baxter to be a shrewd woman, unwilling to allow the enterprise she had built to descend into little more than barbaric violence. She kept a tight rein on her truculent son. The raid by Haddley Police the previous week must have done little to enhance her confidence in him.

Karen Cooke touched Parker on the arm. 'Follow me,' said the police constable, before leading him along a narrow alley, which ran down the side of the yard. A brick wall covered in graffiti separated the builder's yard from the neighbouring second-hand car lot. 'Wait here,' she said, disappearing briefly to the back of the lot. Seconds later, she returned, dragging an industrial bin behind her. 'Jump up on this and you can drop down on the other side of the wall.'

Parker raised his eyebrows, unconsciously running his hands over his slim-fit suit. 'We don't have a warrant.'

'No, but we want results. And we have DS Dani Cash as a police witness to Liam Kane torching a local GP's vehicle.'

'Not quite a direct witness.'

Cooke rolled her eyes. 'What more do you need? Just now, when we were at the front gates, I saw a light flicker in the upstairs room where we have reason to believe Kane resides.' Cooke grinned. 'Do you want me to give you a bunk up?'

Parker climbed up onto the bin and leaped over the wall. Cooke was quick to follow.

'What do you fancy doing tonight?' she said, brushing her hands across her trousers as they stood together inside the yard.

'What?'

'Tonight?' she replied. 'There's a new Indian opened on the Lower Haddley Road. I thought we might try it.'

At the bottom of a short, metal staircase, leading to a small first-floor area, he stopped. 'We're not dating.'

'You have to eat, especially now you're here for the whole weekend.'

He moved a step closer to her. 'We had too much to drink and both of us know it was a mistake.'

'Last week, yes, but what about last night?'

'We shouldn't have gone to the pub.'

'But we did.'

'And drank too much again.'

106

'Is that your excuse? You only sleep with me when you're drunk? I don't think you were drunk this morning.'

'I'm married.'

'I won't tell anybody.'

He climbed the first two steps of the staircase and stopped. 'We have to work together, Constable, and that's where I want your focus.'

Cooke followed him up the first two steps. 'After you, sir,' she replied, her mouth taut.

He raced up the staircase. The first-floor building appeared to be little more than a portacabin, dropped onto a flat roof below. A rusty iron grille covered the single window; behind the window thin, pink curtains failed to meet in the middle. Parker looked through the gap.

'I can't see anyone inside,' he said.

Cooke didn't reply.

He looked over his shoulder. 'Are you sure you saw a light flicker when we first arrived?'

'Certain.'

He banged on the door. There was no reply. He took a step back, raised his boot and kicked the door open.

'Like breaking into a cupboard,' said Cooke.

Parker moved inside and found the room deserted. A heavy smell of stale skunk hung in the damp air. 'Leave the door open,' he said.

A torn leather sofa, covered in cigarette burns, filled one corner of the room. Parker tossed aside the cushions, kicked through a pile of unwashed clothes. Cooke flipped over a mattress, which lay directly on the floor.

'Ugh,' she said, putting her hand to her mouth when she saw the stain-covered reverse.

The kitchen was nothing more than a microwave, small fridge and kettle. Unwashed plates, covered in dry ketchup, filled the sink. Parker pulled open the single drawer. Inside, he found spoons, foil, a lighter and straws.

'I doubt this lot is for cooking up the latest Jamie Oliver,' he said, looking at the drug paraphernalia.

Cooke crossed the room. She pulled back a concertinaed plastic door to reveal a soiled toilet and grimy shower. Again, covering her mouth, she turned away before suddenly catching sight of a figure standing in the doorway.

'Shawn!' she yelled, as the man ran forward, swinging a metal pipe.

CHAPTER 22

'Why didn't you call me?' asks Sam, excitedly, as soon as I answer my phone.

'What?' I reply, pushing my AirPods into my ears. I creep out of my bedroom and stand at the top of the stairs.

'Last night, the fire, you should've called me. I could have come over and taken some photos for the paper.'

'Strange as it may seem, at that moment, I had one or two other things on my mind,' I say, keeping my voice low.

'Speak up, I can't hear you.'

'Hang on, Dani's still dozing.' I hurry downstairs and into the kitchen.

'There are pictures all over the Neighbourhood app,' Sam tells me. 'I'll probably end up using some of those. I think it's best if the follow-up article comes from you, but if you want me to draft something I can get it over to you this morning.'

'Let's not get ahead of ourselves,' I say, clicking on my coffee machine and searching for a fresh carton of milk.

'Or I can write the article, but you still put it on your site.

We can share the byline if that makes it easier. Ben, are you still there?'

'Still here,' I reply, taking two coffee pods from the jar.

'You can reach a much bigger audience. We've got some momentum now. I told you the note was relevant. They really are running scared. The sooner we have something up, the better.'

'Hang on, Sam. I wrote the original story for the anniversary of Alaka's death. It's been on site less than twenty-four hours.'

'But now, this is really news,' he replies.

'Burned-out cars happen every night of the week. I'm sorry, but for us that's not news.'

'Why are you stalling? This isn't about a burned-out car. This is about a direct threat made against Uma that must link to Alaka.'

'Sam, the answer is no.'

For a moment he is silent. 'Madeline thinks . . . '

'Don't you dare,' I reply, my voice rising.

'I'm sorry,' he says, 'but I'm desperate to seize this chance.'

'So am I, but I don't want to put Uma in further danger. When she left here last night both Dani and DS Parker stressed the need for caution, at the very least until they pick up Liam Kane.'

I hear Sam tut. 'Not like you to run scared of the Haddley Police. Somebody's threatening her, Ben, and they're doing it for a reason.'

'Liam Kane is a lowlife drug dealer. His girlfriend is an addict. Perhaps she was simply pissed off at not getting the prescription she wanted.'

'You don't believe that. His girlfriend couldn't get a few painkillers, so Kane torched Uma's car?'

'For an opioid addict, it's a lot more than a few painkillers.'

'I know, I watch Netflix documentaries as well. Kane made a threat, but the burned-out car took it to a whole other level. If we don't run the story, somebody else will.'

'Not in the next forty-eight hours,' I reply. 'Putting the pieces together won't be easy. Uma wants to talk to her husband. She's as committed as you are, but it's her story and her life.'

Dani wanders into the kitchen, a long sweater covering her pyjamas. She kisses me on the cheek before running the cold tap and reaching for a glass.

'Uma and Edward will be at the farmers' market this morning,' I tell Sam. 'You should speak to them then.' I drink my coffee.

'Will you come with me?' he asks. 'People always listen to you.'

'I'm not even sure I agree with you! And anyway, I need to be here with Dani.'

'You go,' she whispers in my ear. 'I'm meeting Holly for a walk on the common, and then I'll be back resting up on the sofa.'

'Are you sure?' I mouth to her.

'If anything happens, you can be home in fifteen minutes.'

She stands beside me, and I run my hand across her back. 'Okay, Sam,' I say, 'I'll meet you there.'

'Excellent,' he replies.

'Sam,' I say, 'in the days before Alaka's murder, when the threats were made against her, what exactly did they say?'

'Bullshit stuff about stirring up trouble where it didn't exist. A woman's place being in the home, that kind of crap.'

'And the final threat that came to the *Richmond Times*?'

I wait for Sam to reply.

'You didn't listen and now you'll regret it.'

I repeat the phrase to Dani.

'Exactly the words used by Liam Kane,' she replies.

CHAPTER 23

Parker spun around and raised his arm in front of his face.

'Police!' he yelled.

The man swung the metal pipe, stopping within a hair's breadth of the detective's head. 'Whoever you are, you're trespassing.' The man lurched forward.

The police officer took two quick sideways steps. 'Drop the pipe,' he said, trying desperately to keep his voice calm.

The man's fleshy fist gripped tighter around the metal bar.

'I said drop the pipe.' He recognised the man as one of the Baxters' heavies who hung around the building site, supposedly working security. Slowly, the man turned and tossed the bar through the open door; a metal clank echoing as it rolled to the foot of the stairs.

'Where's Liam Kane?' said Parker.

'Who?'

'Lowlife dealer who resides in this delightful penthouse apartment?'

The man sneered. 'Nobody living here by that name.'

PC Cooke moved forward. 'We understood he was living here with his girlfriend, Cheryl Henry.'

'That skanky bitch.'

'You are acquainted with her?'

The man curled his lip. 'Couldn't pay their rent. Moved out last week.'

'You charge money for this place?'

'Luxury studio flat with ensuite facilities.' When the man laughed, he sucked air through the gap in his front teeth.

'Why couldn't they pay?' asked Cooke.

'Change in circumstances, from what I understand. Haven't you heard, there's a cost-of-living crisis.'

'Meaning?'

'He lost his fucking job. It always pays to put something away for a rainy day, don't you think?'

Parker realised the Baxters would have ditched Kane the moment drug supplies ran dry after the raid. 'He had no other use?'

'Do you think we're going to have him fitting fucking bathrooms?'

'We're keen to speak to Mr Kane in connection with an arson attack on Haddley Common last night.'

The man shrugged. 'He didn't leave a forwarding address.'

'Why don't you remind me exactly what it is you do here?'

The man thought for a second. 'Shall we say head of security?'

'Well, Mr Head of Security, we're going to need your name and contact details.'

'I'm not the one trespassing.'

Parker pointed towards the drug paraphernalia in the kitchen drawer. 'There's evidence of significant illegal drug use at this property.'

'Drug users are scum.'

'I think it's the dealers who are the problem.' Parker smiled. 'I'll be stationing a forensic team on site today. I'm afraid they could be here for some considerable time. You might want to think about closing the business for the day. I am sorry.'

'Fuck you.'

'Name, please.'

'Donald Trump.'

Shawn stared at him, but the man's expression was inscrutable, and Shawn concluded he wasn't joking. 'Well, Mr Trump, we'll have somebody here in the next hour.' Parker pushed past the man and out of the door. 'Have a great day,' he called. At the foot of the stairs, he stopped and blew out his cheeks.

'Got yourself firmly on the Baxters' radar now,' said Cooke, standing beside him in the yard.

'Good,' he replied, 'but listening to *Donald Trump*, I'd say the family have cut Kane loose.'

'Either he's got his own grudge against Dr Jha, or last night somebody else paid him for his handywork.'

Parker nodded. 'We need to find Liam Kane before he's paid to do something far worse.'

CHAPTER 24

At the flower stall Pamela slowed and waved to the florist who had served her the previous afternoon. Then she crossed towards the large car park outside the doctor's surgery where she could see stallholders busily setting up for the Saturday-morning farmers' market.

She was early, and in the mild weather found herself an empty bench at the side of the duck pond. She always tried to be one of the first to arrive at the market, as it gave her time to browse the stalls before wealthy locals overran the space. Her punctuality also ensured she had the pick of the baked goods, with her favourite raisin-and-walnut loaf always the first to sell out.

Today she was particularly early. She hadn't slept well. Last week she'd changed from her summer duvet to her thicker one for winter, but even with her bedroom window wide open it was far too warm in this mild weather. Hot and restless, she'd felt her arms and legs tingle throughout the night. Every time she had started to drift off to sleep, she'd found Thomas at the front of her mind. So often, even after so many years, she dreamed about him, but last night she was worried. She couldn't shake what Alan had said. Of course, he was confused, but why had he seemed so certain? What now had made Thomas alive again in his jumbled-up mind? She wished she understood.

Twisting on the bench, she looked across the road towards the stallholders putting the final touches to their displays. At the far end of the surgery car park, Dr Jha's husband, Edward, was unboxing his jars of jam. He owned a small business, Cotswold Preserves, producing jams, chutneys and mustards. His thick-cut, vintage orange marmalade was among her favourites, and she bought a jar every two weeks, even if it did seem rather expensive. It was twice the price of Tesco's, but she did have to admit it was ten times tastier. In the past, Dr Jha had been on hand to help her husband every Saturday morning, and Pamela had enjoyed the opportunity of a brief chat with her. However, recently, she'd become only an occasional assistant on the stand. Pamela was unsure as to why, although of course, she recognised Dr Jha had a very busy schedule. She hoped she might be here this morning as she'd read on the Neighbourhood app about last night's fire, and she wanted to reassure herself all was well.

On the opposite side of the pond, in the far corner of the village green, stood the small village hall. Pamela knew the clock above the door always ran five minutes fast. It was currently telling the uninformed there were only five minutes until nine o'clock. Behind her, the first two market patrons were forming a queue outside the car-park gates. Pamela picked up her bag, crossed quickly and joined the line, saying a brief *good morning* to the couple standing in front of her. At the head of the queue, standing sentry at the gate, stood Linda, the surgery receptionist and, at the weekend, organiser of the farmers' market. Pamela never understood why she didn't simply let shoppers into the market once the queue started to form, but rain or shine, Linda stuck rigidly to her 9 a.m. rule. Not once had she been seen to allow a customer to cross the threshold of the car park early. An occasional outsider, perhaps visiting from Richmond or Oreton, would wave in the direction of the village hall clock and demand entry. Linda, however, was not somebody who would ever be deceived by a fast-running clock.

With a couple of minutes to wait, Pamela pulled her purse out of her backpack (by far the easiest way to carry her goods home) and slipped her bank card into her pocket. She glanced over her shoulder and saw the line had grown to over thirty people. Across the pond, the sun was beginning to break through the clouds and she saw a nice crowd gathering outside the florist's stall. Nothing was ever too much trouble for the lady owner, and Pamela liked the way she always had two minutes for a chat. She hoped the florist was set for a busy day. Pamela peered closer at the people gathered around the florist's stall. Was that Maggie at the back, waiting to be served? Yes, it was. Pamela called a cheery *yoo-hoo*, but immediately realised her voice would never carry. She began to wave, only to see Maggie drift away from the back of the crowd. Alone, Maggie walked slowly towards the small rose garden at the side of the village hall. Pamela waved again but, with her head down, Maggie was never going to see her. From the front of the line, she heard Linda speaking with the couple who'd been first to arrive. The gates were about to open. With one last half-hearted wave in Maggie's direction, she stepped forward. She gave Linda an especially warm smile, given what the receptionist had endured at the surgery the previous afternoon, and then entered the market. First, she hurried towards the bakery stall to make her choices; to her walnut-and-raisin loaf she added four cherry Bakewells and two chocolate buns. Next was the butcher's for honey-mustard sausages plus two pork chops, which she'd roast on Sunday night. As the butcher wrapped her meat, Pamela's eyes wandered towards the far end of the car park, and she saw Dr Jha standing at the preserves stand with her husband. Pamela would pop over in a minute for some marmalade and a chat, but first she wanted to see if she could catch sight of Maggie.

For the first hour of the market, to control the early rush of shoppers, Linda operated a strict one-way system. Pamela hurried to the side gate that led out onto a narrow street of terrace houses. She found the road deserted and quickly made her way up onto the main road. Back facing the village pond, she came to an abrupt stop.

'Maggie!' she exclaimed, almost bumping into her dearest friend, who was standing at the entrance to a narrow ginnel, which led into the maze of St Marnham's Victorian alleyways. 'What are you doing here?'

'Just catching my breath, avoiding the opening rush.'

'I didn't expect to see you here today.' In the past Maggie

119

had walked with Pamela to the farmers' market on an occasional Saturday morning, but it would have been eighteen months since she had joined her along the river path.

'I needed a few bits, so I thought I'd take advantage of the warm weather and wander over.'

'Why didn't you say? We could have walked together.'

'It was very much a last-minute decision,' she replied. 'Susan called last night, almost as soon as you left, and asked if she could come over to see her uncle this morning. Very kindly she said she was happy to sit with him for a couple of hours, although,' she paused to look at her watch, 'I shouldn't be away for too long.'

'The market's busy today,' replied Pamela. 'You don't want to be hanging around out here for too long, or you'll miss all the best goods. They're like gannets around the bakery stall.'

Maggie looked tired, even when she tried to smile. 'Actually, I thought I might walk down onto the high street and avoid the crowds. M&S will have most of what I need.'

'Are you sure?' replied Pamela, failing to understand why her friend had walked over from Haddley. 'You won't find homemade blueberry jam on the high street.' She linked her arm with Maggie's. 'Come and browse with me.'

'No, really, I shouldn't. I don't like to leave Alan for too long and Susan will wonder where I am.' She squeezed Pamela's arm. 'Thanks again for last night.'

'You only have to ask. You do know that? Whatever you need, Maggie, I'm here for you, even if it's nothing more than a ten-minute break.'

Maggie's eyes grew glassy and she fiercely brushed away

a tear, but before Pamela could say anything more, her friend was hurrying away. She didn't even have her shopping basket with her. It was so unlike Maggie; Pamela didn't know anybody so well organised. Pamela called after her. Maggie could have the spare carrier bag she always kept in her rucksack. But Maggie didn't respond, clearly already lost in her own thoughts.

Pamela walked back in front of the surgery. She looked towards the florist's stand and the village hall beyond, then did a double take. Rather than heading towards the high street, Maggie had circled around and was once again standing outside the small rose garden. Beside her was a man wearing a bright red-and-white diamond-patterned sweater. He rested his hand in the small of Maggie's back before bending to kiss her softly on the cheek.

Pamela took a step back and tried to steady herself against the surgery wall. She felt as if she was about to faint.

CHAPTER 25

'Pamela!' I call, as I follow the path around the village pond. I cross the road in front of the doctor's surgery. 'Pamela!' She is sitting on the white-washed wall that runs along the practice car park. 'Hello,' I say, quietly, before gently touching her arm.

She lifts her head. Her face is pale.

'Are you okay?' I ask. 'You look like you've seen a ghost.'

'Ben, what a lovely surprise,' she replies, regaining her composure. 'The crowds seem to get bigger here every week. I was just taking two minutes to catch my breath.' Her eyes dart over my shoulder, and she moves her head to one side. 'I thought I saw an old friend outside the village hall, but I think it was my age catching up with me. Now, tell me how Dani's doing. I'm guessing still no news?'

'Nothing yet.' I perch on the wall beside her. 'We're both getting a little anxious but excited at the same time.'

'Of course you are,' she replies. 'I remember with my Jeannie, I was on my own by then and slightly terrified, but the first few years were still the most wonderful time of my life.' Following the death of her husband, Pamela raised her only child alone. During Jeannie's childhood years, mother and daughter lived next door to Dani and her late father, Jack. For a time, Pamela and Jack became close; Pamela almost like a mother to Dani. When the relationship between Pamela and Jack ended, the pair lost touch. Over the last year, Dani and Pamela have slowly begun to rekindle their friendship. 'I was three days in labour with Jeannie. I thought it would never end, but it was worth it in the end.'

'Three days!'

'Perhaps don't mention that to Dani right now,' she says, holding my arm.

'Were you on your own that whole time?' I ask.

'In my day, they still took you into hospital at the start of labour. Everyone was very kind; most knew I was a widow. My friend, Maggie, came with me and stayed the whole time.' Pamela turns to face me, and her eyes are as caring and comforting as ever. 'Cherish every moment,' she tells me. 'You and Dani will be the most wonderful parents. Your child will bring you so much joy. However exhausted you might feel, don't waste a second. They grow up far too quickly.'

Pamela's daughter succumbed to an aggressive cancer late last year. While circumstances forced mother and daughter apart for many years, I know, even now, Jeannie is in Pamela's thoughts almost every single day. She made unimaginable sacrifices for her daughter, and I only hope I can cherish my own child in the same way.

'Now,' she says, straightening her back, 'what on earth happened on the common last night?'

123

I can't help but smile. Pamela is faster to the news than my own site. 'You heard about the fire?'

'I saw the pictures on the Neighbourhood app. Who would do such a thing to Dr Jha?'

I tell her about Liam Kane and the exchange with his girlfriend, Cheryl, at the surgery earlier in the afternoon.

'I was there,' says Pamela, eagerly.

'Why doesn't that surprise me?'

'My knees were playing up,' she tells me, 'but Cheryl was after something.'

'A prescription of some sort?'

Pamela presses her lips together. 'I know that's what Linda told Dr Jha, but Linda sees the world through only one perspective – her own. Yes, the girl was confused, probably on some kind of drugs, but there was only one thing she wanted.'

'What was that?'

'To speak to Dr Jha, of course.'

'Why?' I ask, but at that moment I hear Sam calling my name as he hurries down the road from the station.

'No Vlad?' I ask, as he comes and stands beside us.

'I gave him the weekend off. I'm still happy to travel with the ordinary folk on the train.' Sam laughs. 'I never knew so many people were up at this time on a Saturday morning,' he says, looking towards the crowded farmers' market. His eyes fall upon Uma and her husband. 'Have you spoken to her?'

'No, I thought that's why you were here.'

'If we can get her to agree to a follow-up, you will run the story on your site?'

124

'Let's talk to Uma first.'

'Do you think last night's attack on Dr Jha is linked to your article?' Pamela asks me.

'Absolutely,' replies Sam, before I have a chance to answer. He sits on the wall, squeezing himself between Pamela and me. 'The burned-out car is a threat. Somebody's read the article and is warning us off.'

Pamela ponders Sam's response.

'We don't know anything right now,' I say, getting to my feet and walking towards the market entrance. Sam and Pamela follow. I can still hear them talking.

'Somebody's kept this secret for more than thirty years and now they're worried.'

'Do you think it's the killer?' asks Pamela, the gossiping pair reminding me of Alice and Max.

'Whoever arranged for Kane to set the fire wanted to scare us off. Even if they're not Alaka's killer, they must be linked in some way.'

Inside the market the crowd is thick, and we find ourselves edging forward in single file. We move slowly towards Uma's stand but the bustle in front of the bakery stall slows us further.

Suddenly from behind, a swell of people sweeps us to one side. I turn quickly and raise my hands above my head.

'Hold on,' I shout, as other voices are raised in anger. 'Can everybody take a step back?' I see a woman forcing her way through the crowd. 'Wait!' I cry, but panic in the crowd pushes me to one side. I feel Pamela grab hold of my arm.

'That's her,' she tells me. 'Cheryl Henry.'

The crowd parts and Henry staggers forward. People push backwards and Sam stumbles to the floor. I'm worried the crowd will trample him underfoot.

'Everybody stand still,' I shout.

Cheryl Henry looks as if she's in a trance. Her eyes wide and wild, she stumbles forward. Only when she stands directly across from me do I understand the reason for people's panic. Held tight in her hand is a blood-soaked, metal claw hammer.

CHAPTER 26

I dive across the startled crowd and reach for Henry's arm. Seeing me coming, she swerves to one side and moves directly towards the Cotswold Preserves stand.

'Uma!' I yell. She is wrapping a jar of jam for a young girl in a bright blue dress.

Edward is first to react, taking three quick steps to the side and pushing his wife backwards. Uma grabs hold of the girl's hand and pulls her down beside her.

Henry staggers forward, the hammer still clutched in her hand. 'Dr Jha!' she screams.

I throw myself forward and seize hold of Henry's blood-covered hand. She twists and swings the hammer. Instinctively, I turn away while forcing her arm down towards the ground. Uma's husband runs forward, but before he can reach us Henry kicks out at me. I stumble backwards. She runs towards the open side gate, hurling the hammer onto Uma's stand as she goes and the sound of breaking glass fills the air. Henry disappears into the neighbouring street. I follow, skirting around alarmed pedestrians and parked cars.

But I leave the car park just in time to watch her mount an electric scooter, and before I can stop her she is disappearing up Station Road.

I go back inside the farmers' market, still catching my breath. Pamela is helping Sam to his feet, leading him towards a chair at the back of the pottery stall. Already, people have congregated in small groups, speaking in hushed voices. Despite the crowd, an eerie calm now hangs over the space. Shoppers begin to drift away, moving out towards the duck pond, to find seats at the water's edge. Linda is on her phone, speaking to the police. Uma is talking to the young girl she shielded as the girl's parents hurry towards them. The mother scoops her daughter into her arms while the father shakes Uma's hand. Edward is picking up the larger shards of glass with his hands when another stallholder appears with a broom.

In front of the preserves stand, the hammer lies on the ground. Dry blood runs from the face, across the head and down the rusty claw. Along the cracks in the black wooden handle, I can see further red smudges. Pamela appears at my side.

'You did a brave thing,' she says, holding my arm. She bends to look at the hammer.

'Don't touch it,' I say, as she reaches down.

She turns and raises her eyebrows. 'I do watch *Vera*.'

I can't stop myself from smiling.

'Somebody's been on the receiving end of a fair wallop,' she says. 'I wouldn't fancy anyone's chances against a hammer that size.'

Holding a mug of tea, Sam comes to join us. I put my arm around his shoulders.

'Are you okay?'

'Assailed in the pursuit of truth and justice,' he replies. 'All in a day's work.' He stares down at the hammer. 'Cheryl cracked one victim over the head and then came here searching for Uma,' he says.

Pamela looks puzzled. 'Do you really think she planned to attack Dr Jha?'

'We all saw her. If Ben hadn't acted when he did, she was next on her hit list.'

We walk towards the preserves stand. The little girl in the blue dress hugs Uma, before her parents steer her away. We walk towards the mangled stand.

'Thank you, Ben,' says Uma.

'I was in the right place at the right time. Anyone else would have done the same.'

'Or the wrong place at the wrong time,' adds Sam. He stretches his back. 'Uma, I might need you to refer me for some massage therapy. At my age you can't be too careful.'

Edward joins us. I am about to tell him I'm sorry about his stand when he speaks to his wife.

'This has to stop.' His voice is sharp. 'I said this morning for you not to come to the market, but you didn't listen to me.'

'And I said I had no intention of hiding away.'

'For Christ's sake, Uma, the woman might have killed you.'

'Edward, you're overreacting.'

Ignoring his wife, he rounds on me. 'However well

129

intentioned, this campaign ends now.' He turns back to Uma. 'Whatever you do won't bring your mother back. What happened to her will live with us forever, but your safety is my only concern.'

I see Sam take an awkward backwards step, but Uma reaches for her husband's hand. 'I love how much you care, but I need to do this. I'm not stopping now.'

Edward shakes his hand free. 'Uma, you're playing a dangerous game, and I don't want any part of it.'

CHAPTER 27

Linda follows PC Cooke's instructions to the letter, informing each of the stallholders that she is closing this weekend's
market. With a considerable amount of goods left unsold,
several traders depart slightly disgruntled, mumbling about
an overreaction.

Sam gives a brief statement to the police, while Pamela
busies herself by helping to clear the bakery stand.

'You'll have to forgive Edward, he means well,' says Uma,
as we sit on the wall at the front of the surgery car park.

'I can understand his concern,' I reply.

'He'll never love London and is convinced it's full of
crime, but he moved his whole life here to support me.'

'He misses Leamington?'

Uma nods, and glances in her husband's direction. He is
dismantling his broken stand. Next to him is a half-empty
crate of the jars he managed to salvage from the wreckage.
'I was only there for four years, but for Edward it's home.
Following my father's diagnosis, I said I wanted to come
back to London. He didn't hesitate. I didn't know then I was

returning as much for my mum as I was for my dad.' She shifts on the wall to face me. 'I know there's a risk, but I'd like you or Sam to write about everything that's happened in the last twenty-four hours.'

'Are you sure?'

'I don't believe Cheryl would have hurt me. Somebody wants to scare me, but I'm not that easily deterred.'

'Can you think of anything to connect Kane and Henry to your mother's murder?'

She shakes her head.

'You've not met Kane before?'

'Never.'

'They strike me as a couple who'll do pretty much anything if there's enough money in it for them.' I pause. 'Edward is right. They both still pose a very real threat.'

Uma's smile is gentle. 'Ben, did you ever stop when you needed the truth?'

I say nothing in reply. Uma touches my arm before crossing the car park to help her husband. When DS Parker invites me to sit with him at the side of the dismantled cheese stall, the statement I give to him is brief.

'You saw Henry leave in the direction of the railway station?'

'Yes,' I reply. 'From there, she might have jumped on a train, or if she crossed the footbridge, it brings you straight out onto the Oreton Road.'

He nods slowly in response, clearly still unfamiliar with the area.

'It's not much more than a twenty-minute walk from St Marnham station, up the hill into Oreton.'

'Thank you,' he replies. 'Uniform will follow up on any sightings of her, or Kane, throughout the day.'

Back outside the car-park gates, I look across the village pond and see Sam and Pamela walking along the water's edge. Catching my eye, Pamela waves and they hurry back in my direction.

'Mind the bus!' I call, as they dash across the road.

'By the time you've reached our age,' Sam tells me, 'you know bus drivers will always slow for pensioners.'

'Not sure I'd put that theory to the test too often, if I were you,' I reply. 'Where have you been?'

'I needed to visit the little boy's room, so we popped to the village hall.'

Pamela nudges me in the ribs. 'I think the excitement was too much for him.'

Sam laughs.

'Coffee?' I ask.

'That would be lovely,' replies Pamela.

'As long as you're buying,' says Sam.

We walk onto the high street, and I tell Sam that Uma wants us to go ahead with a follow-up article.

'Excellent work,' he replies, patting me on the back. 'I'll write a draft this afternoon.'

'Our number-one priority remains Uma's safety.'

'Yes, yes, absolutely,' he says, but I can see his mind already racing away.

Outside the coffee shop, Sam and Pamela position themselves at a sunlit table.

'Two cappuccinos, please, Ben,' he says to me.

Five minutes later, I return with our drinks and sit opposite Sam. 'We still need something concrete that will lead us to Alaka's killer.'

'I agree.' Sam downs half his coffee and leans across the table.

'I've read all the comments beneath your original article.'

'All of them? The last time I looked there were over three thousand.'

'Three thousand, four hundred and seventy-two when I left home this morning. I was up early.'

'Did you learn anything?' asks Pamela, holding her cup tightly.

'I did,' he replies.

'I'm sure you're going to share,' I say.

'Only if you're interested.'

'Yes, absolutely,' says Pamela.

'One name was mentioned one hundred and fourteen times.'

'The same name?' asks Pamela.

'The same name.'

I finish my coffee. 'Let me guess,' I say. 'Eileen Blenkhorn.'

'Spoilsport,' replies Sam, rolling his eyes, 'but that doesn't mean she's not important.'

'No, but she's refused to speak to anyone for the past thirty years and I don't see that changing now.'

'Who's Eileen Blenkhorn?'

I explain to Pamela how at the time of her death Alaka was writing a series of articles on abuse within the home. 'Eileen Blenkhorn was one of the women she interviewed.'

'Except at the time,' adds Sam, 'Alaka conducted all the interviews in the strictest confidence. Not even I knew who she was speaking to. Then, after her murder, somebody leaked Eileen's name to the press.'

'Was it you who did the leaking, Sam?' asks Pamela.

'No, it was not me who did the leaking,' he replies, indignantly.

'A tabloid newspaper uncovered Eileen's name and ran a splash story,' I say. 'What secrets had she told Alaka, that kind of thing.'

'The story put her and her husband, Dennis, into the national spotlight.'

'That must have been incredibly hard for her,' replies Pamela.

'Horrendous,' says Sam. 'The paper filled page after page with speculation on the suffering Eileen endured during her marriage. After one interview with the police, she refused to speak to anyone again.'

'Her husband died no more than a year ago,' I say, 'but even after that, she's said nothing more. There's no reason to think she'll act differently now. Eileen Blenkhorn wasn't just one of the women Alaka interviewed. She was the final one.'

Pamela frowns. 'What does that mean?'

'It means she remains the last known person to have seen Alaka alive.'

CHAPTER 28

My phone buzzes. I fumble in my pocket and flick on the screen. When I see it is a message from Dani, my heart jumps.

I shouldn't let you out of my sight

I respond with a smiley face before typing, I take it you've heard?

Karen Cooke is here. You sure you're okay?

I'm fine. You?

Exactly as you left me.

What does Karen want?

My advice.

On cheryl henry?

And her boyfriend. Where she might find them.

Any suggestions?

I've often seen them on the bus to oreton.

Going where?

They deal out of the beer garden at the back of the
Rose and Crown.

Big student pub

How long until you're back?

Heading home now xx

'Any news?' asks Pamela, eagerly.

'Still nothing.'

'Who'd like another coffee?' says Sam, already on his feet.

'I hate to say no, especially when you're offering, but I've
told Dani I'm on my way home.'

Sam sighs.

'Don't you have an article to draft?' I add. 'I'll call you
later.'

Pamela and I part from Sam and begin to make our way
back along the river path to Haddley. At first, we walk in

silence, passing runners, cyclists and dog walkers as we make our way along the water's edge. When we come to the bend in the river and turn towards Haddley, Pamela touches my arm.

'Eileen Blenkhorn,' she says.

'What are you thinking?'

'Fear of her husband stopped her saying anything?'

'I'd imagine so. All her conversations with Alaka were in confidence and suddenly there she was on the front page of a national newspaper.'

'Grandmother who shared her secrets with tragic Alaka.'

'Something like that,' I reply.

'And now?'

'She'll be getting on. She was close to sixty at the time of Alaka's murder.'

'Nearly ninety now. She's even got a few years on me,' says Pamela, smiling. 'She's lived in Haddley all her life?'

'I'm not sure,' I reply. 'The last I heard she was living in the giant block of flats on Beyton Road.' I look at Pamela. 'What are you thinking?'

'Only what a difficult life she must have lived.'

We walk on, before slowing when a group of secondary-school children emerge from the Cygnet boathouse. Precariously, the group carry an eight-person rowing boat down to the river.

'Before you know it, that'll be your little one,' says Pamela, as we stand and watch the group of eleven- and twelve-year-olds stagger under the weight of the boat. 'Boy or a girl? What are you hoping for?'

138

'I honestly don't mind. For the first time since I was three years old, I'm going to be part of a real family. That's all I want. Dani and me and our child.'

'Three years old? Was that when your father left?'

I nod. 'From that moment, my family never felt whole.' I turn to Pamela and a broad smile covers my face. 'I can't wait.'

'I can tell,' she replies.

'I've spent so much of my life alone. Now, I have the chance of my own family, and all I want to do is keep them safe and happy.'

'You'll be a wonderful dad,' she tells me.

The path becomes stonier. To steady herself, Pamela slips her arm inside mine. The breeze picks up off the river, and as we approach the abandoned Peacock boathouse I see its rotten door swinging loose on its rusty hinge.

'That's so sad to see,' says Pamela, looking towards the derelict shed. 'I can remember when a Peacock crew won the Head of the River race,' she says. 'That's how old I am!' she adds, laughing. 'Look at the place now. It needs tearing down. The door will fly off its hinge if you don't close it.'

I run up the decaying ramp at the front of the building and try to push the swinging door shut. When I press against the door, it refuses to budge. Flicking on the torch on my phone, I step into the dark interior to find what's jamming the door. I glance over my shoulder and see Pamela following me up the ramp.

'Careful,' I say, 'it's slippery.' I wait in the doorway and hold out my hand. At the top of the ramp, she grabs hold of it. We walk inside and I point my torch behind the door.

Pamela gasps and clamps a hand over her mouth. I aim my light onto the concrete floor, where a trail of blood runs from the shattered skull of Liam Kane.

CHAPTER 29

'He's dead,' I say, crouching beside the body.

Her hand still covering her mouth, Pamela bends forward. 'You wouldn't wish that on your worst enemy.'

Kane's face is badly beaten. His right eye has been ripped from its socket. Frenzied blows must have rained down upon him, until a final blow obliterated the side of his skull.

Pamela takes hold of my arm, and we walk back down the ramp at the front of the boathouse. 'Killed by his own girlfriend?'

I think of Cheryl Henry and the hammer's blood-soaked wooden handle. 'Those injuries must have been inflicted by a pretty heavy weapon.'

'Perhaps Sam was right. She murdered Liam and came to the farmers' market to kill Dr Jha?' says Pamela. 'But why?'

We stand together at the bottom of the ramp. 'I should call the police,' I say, pulling my phone from my pocket. As I report the incident, we walk slowly towards a wooden bench, nestled in the riverside shrubbery. Finishing the call, I watch Pamela read the dedication engraved on the back of the seat: *In memory of Cyril Jones, a loving father and grandfather.*

'Did you know him?' I ask.

Pamela shakes her head. 'At my age you just notice these things a little bit more. You can't help wondering what kind of life he led, who he left behind.' She pauses and runs her fingers over the inscription. 'And who'll be left to remember me.'

'If you want a bench, Dani and I will make sure it happens.'

'That might be nice, but not for a while yet.'

Within minutes, we hear police sirens approaching from Haddley, forcing their way along the pedestrian river path. Dog walkers pull their animals to heel in order to let them pass. A police vehicle stops outside the front of the boathouse and two uniformed officers climb out. By the time I reach them, they're already unrolling police tape to secure the area. I tell them I'm the one who made the call, and what I saw inside the boathouse. Almost immediately, a second police vehicle appears and Shawn Parker and Karen Cooke get out. DS Parker steps inside the boathouse. Two minutes later, he comes back outside, ducks beneath the police tape and crosses towards us.

'Busy morning,' I say, as he approaches.

'Are you both okay?' he asks.

'All good,' I reply.

'Mrs Cuthbert?'

She smiles. 'A little shocked, but I'm sure I'll live.'

'We'll have to wait for a formal identification, but do you

believe the victim you saw inside the boathouse is the same man you pursued yesterday evening on Haddley Common?' the detective asks me.

'Yes,' I reply. 'I didn't know him then but my partner seemed certain his name is Liam Kane.' I explain to him how Pamela and I discovered the body.

'Have you seen him since he ran onto the common yesterday?'

'No,' I reply, 'not until we went inside the boathouse.'

'Any sign of Cheryl?' asks Pamela.

'Not yet, but we expect to bring her in later today.'

Pamela pauses. 'She was very frightened.'

'I'm sorry?' he replies.

'At the farmers' market, I think she was afraid.'

'We'll see what she has to say when we bring her in for questioning.'

A motorbike weaves its way down the riverside path, slowing as it approaches the small crowd now gathered outside the boathouse entrance. When the rider stops the bike at the side of the building, I briefly raise my hand to acknowledge him. George Lennon nods in response before dipping below the police tape. He speaks briefly with PC Karen Cooke before the pair disappear inside.

'The medical examiner,' I say, as Parker turns his head.

'I should go,' he replies.

'DS Parker,' says Pamela, her voice soft. 'If Cheryl Henry didn't kill her boyfriend, could her life now also be in danger?'

The officer stands and stares at Pamela but says nothing in reply.

143

With the sun now shining directly on us, I lean back on the bench. 'Is that what you think?'

'Ben, what would I know? But in some ways Cheryl is so very childlike. When little Mabel Green lived three doors down from me, one afternoon she ran up the back alley and burst through my garden gate. Cupped in her hand was her pet hamster, Milly, sadly assailed by Mitz, the long-haired cat belonging to Jason Munton, who lived a further two doors away.'

'The hamster was dead?' I ask.

'Oh, yes, very dead. Mitz had somehow snuck into the cage, and Mabel returned from school to discover the butchery.'

'Had she had the hamster a long time?' I ask, struggling to follow Pamela's train of thought.

'Not long at all,' she replies. 'But you see, Ben, Mabel was so horrified at what she'd found, she brought the evidence with her to show me.'

I frown. 'You mean Cheryl merely . . . '

But before I can say anything more, George Lennon emerges from the boathouse. I catch his eye, and he walks towards us. I stand and we briefly hug.

'You after a story?' he asks.

'Always,' I reply, before explaining how Pamela and I discovered the body. 'If you're around in the morning, come over for coffee. Dani would love to see you.' At sixth-form college, George was the year ahead of me. An incredibly intelligent extrovert, George often held court in the common room, telling tall tales of his latest exploits. Somehow, we formed a much quieter friendship, sharing the family grief we'd both experienced. George's father was one of two men who drowned in a training accident at the Military Training Centre in Mickelside, south of Haddley. At the time, George was only two years old. As if that wasn't enough to contend with, his mother died whilst he was still in primary school. We understood each other. Our losses brought us together and created a friendship which endured, even though, at times, I struggle to understand the complexities of his character.

'Count me in,' he replies.

'What happened here?' I ask.

'It was a savage attack, but he put up a fight.'

'I saw that on his hands,' says Pamela.

I look at her questioningly.

'His hands were badly cut,' she explains.

'Defensive wounds,' continues George. 'Whoever attacked him did so with significant force. He fought them off, my guess is until his eye was ripped from its socket.'

I wince. 'A hammer claw?'

'I can't say right now, but quite possibly. Somebody launched a frenzied attack.'

'Full of rage?' I ask.

George nods.

'But one with some considerable strength,' adds Pamela.

Four

Eileen Blenkhorn

'Her husband had preferred it to be just the two of them. For Eileen, life became simpler without friends.'

Every Saturday afternoon, whenever the weather allowed, she ventured out onto the busy high street. She was shaky on her legs, so she only ever went to the same three shops — the card shop, the German supermarket, and the hardware store.

She rarely bought anything in the card shop — who would she send a card to? She'd had no close friends in years, not since she'd married. When she'd briefly had a job working in a kitchen, she'd found a friend in a woman named Fiona but they'd soon lost touch. Her husband had preferred it to be just the two of them. For Eileen, life became simpler without friends.

Arriving next at the German supermarket, she found her coupon for four almond croissants for only two pounds.

'Sold out, my love,' the woman beside the bakery told her. 'When they're gone, they're gone. Why don't you come back tomorrow.'

Leaving the supermarket, her legs ached, but she imagined Dennis telling her to stop complaining. She put her head down and pushed on to the hardware store. She needed a new light-bulb for the lamp she left on overnight to light her tiny hallway. Inside the shop, she found the lightbulbs offered only in packs of three. She'd never use three and a pack was nearly seven pounds. She took a pack of batteries that were on sale instead. For the radio, her only companion these days.

Dennis had taken charge of their money and made all the big decisions. When he passed, a little over a year ago, she realised there was very little money left. His pension ended with his life and left her with no other choice but to ask her son, Andrew, to help pay her rent. He'd immediately moved her out of her East Haddley home and into a damp, one-bedroom flat. She'd barely seen him since. But then, he always was more his father's son.

CHAPTER 30

Pamela stepped inside the lift and, smelling the stench, held her nose. Eileen Blenkhorn's surname was unique in the Haddley telephone directory, so her address had been easy to find. When the doors opened on the fourth floor, she hurried out. Flat 42 neighboured the lift and she knocked on the door. While she waited, she heard her phone ping in her pocket. She looked at her screen and carefully typed in her code.

Such a nice afternoon, I thought we'd have drinks by the pond.

It was a message from Maggie. Another followed.

Would you like to join us?

That would be lovely she typed in reply.

Around five?

She slipped her phone back in her pocket and knocked again. Still no answer, but the door to the neighbouring flat opened.

'You looking for the old girl?' asked a man wearing only a vest and shorts. Pamela found herself wondering why middle-aged men didn't realise they'd long since reached a stage in life where it was far wiser to cover up, but she said nothing and smiled. 'She goes out all on her own most Saturday afternoons,' he told her. 'My missus always says she doesn't know how she makes it back alive, but off she shuffles up the high street with her shopping trolley.'

'I'll pop back later,' replied Pamela.

If it wasn't for the state of her own knees, she'd have taken the steps down and avoided the smell inside the lift. Instead, she held her breath and waited for the slow descent. Outside, the gardens surrounding the flat were little more than a concrete flowerbed and a few trees. Pamela was soon glad to be back out on Beyton Road. She followed the footpath towards the high street but began to linger when she saw an elderly woman standing with her hand pressed against the side window of Snappy Snaps.

'Are you okay there?' she asked, approaching slowly.

'Just catching my breath,' replied the woman, timidly dropping her head.

'I know exactly how you feel,' replied Pamela, resting beside her.

The woman lifted her eyes and offered a self-conscious smile.

'The high street gets so busy these days. You're braver than me heading out on a Saturday afternoon,' Pamela added.

'I just needed a few bits.'

'Are you heading home now?'

'Yes, I can't wait to put my feet up with a cup of tea and a slice of cake, even if it is inside the concrete monstrosity. That's what I call it,' said the woman, pointing towards the giant block of flats.

'Why don't you take my arm, and I can help you home?' said Pamela. The woman hesitated, but Pamela held out her arm.

'People are so kind,' she replied, looping her arm through Pamela's. 'I'm Eileen,' said the woman, not telling Pamela anything she didn't already suspect. Inside the lift the woman looked embarrassed. 'I'm sorry about the smell,' she said, as they rode up to the fourth floor, 'but I can promise you it isn't me.'

Pamela laughed. 'You'd think people would be able to hold on until they made it home,' she said, and for the first time she saw Eileen relax.

'Men drinking too many pints at the pub,' she replied. 'I dread to think where my Dennis relieved himself over the years.'

'He liked a tipple?'

Eileen didn't reply. As the lift doors opened, she took hold of Pamela's arm and allowed herself to be steered out to the corridor.

'This is me,' she said, feeling in her pocket for her key as they stood outside number 42. 'Thank you for your help.'

'I bet you're ready for that cup of tea,' replied Pamela, not stepping away.

'I'll be putting the kettle on right away.' Eileen unlocked her door. She stopped and looked at Pamela. 'I suppose I could invite you in for a cup?' she asked, hesitantly.

'Only if you have a spare ten minutes,' Pamela replied, realising how uncomfortable Eileen was inviting anyone inside her home. 'Don't feel obliged, especially if you're busy.'

'It's not that, although I do have my shopping to unpack.'

'Then I should leave you be,' replied Pamela, beginning to slowly turn away.

'No, wait, please do come in,' said Eileen, edging inside her home. 'It's just I'm afraid it's not very much.'

'It's a cup of tea we want, not a tour of Buckingham Palace.' Pamela took her opportunity to follow the woman inside. 'This is lovely,' she said, entering a neatly kept living room. A small two-seater sofa sat opposite a tartan wingback chair. Still holding her trolley, Eileen moved from one piece of furniture to the next as she made her way through to the little kitchen at the back of the flat.

'Can I help you with anything?' asked Pamela.

'No, no, everything's under control. Apologies if it seems a bit dark in the hallway. I meant to buy a new lightbulb today but ran out of time. I don't know when I'll next get back out onto the high street.'

'You manage incredibly well.'

'I'm ninety next month. My grandson helps me when he can, but he's always so busy.'

'That's the way with the young. I'm sure we were probably

154

the same.' Pamela stood in the kitchen doorway as Eileen filled her kettle and slowly unloaded the few bits of shopping from her trolley. There were so many questions she wanted to ask, but she told herself to be patient.

'Have you lived in Haddley all your life?'

'No, but I've been here over fifty years,' replied Eileen. 'When I first met Dennis, he was running a pub in Scarborough, by the seafront.'

'Oh, what fun,' replied Pamela.

'Yes, it was. I helped out in the kitchen, made all of the puddings.' Pamela briefly heard the joy in Eileen's voice before it quickly faded away. 'But Dennis always wanted something more. Not long after we were married, out of the blue, he gave up the pub and said we were moving to London. It was a big change.' Eileen loaded two cups and saucers on a tray. She filled her teapot and took a home-baked cake from a tin.

'Let me carry that,' said Pamela, and after a moment of resistance Eileen agreed. 'Did you have another pub here in London?'

'For a year, yes, in Haddley,' replied Eileen. 'A lovely old place, with speciality beers. After twelve months, Dennis said he was done with serving on. He told me he'd had enough of drunks and that he was better than all of them. I'm sure he was right, although I did miss it. Dennis found a job in insurance.' Dropping into the high-back chair, she shrugged. 'But that was never enough for him either.'

Pamela poured the tea and waited to see if Eileen would say anything further.

'He did stick with insurance, but like the pub, he always believed he was better than those around him. Throughout his life, he was disappointed not to be given a chance to progress further. He felt undervalued, became bored and ended up drinking too much.'

'I'm sorry,' said Pamela. She wondered if Dennis's drinking was at the root of Eileen's suffering.

'It is a treat for me to have someone to chat with. My legs are bad, and I don't get out much these days.'

'I'm much slower on my feet. Everything seems to take me so much longer. I bet you had to be fleet of foot behind the bar.'

Eileen sipped on her tea. 'I was happiest when we had the pub. It's a funny thing to say, but when we were living there Dennis hardly touched a drop. I knew it was a mistake the moment we left.' Eileen pulled a tissue from her sleeve and wiped her nose. 'Enough about me. You don't want to hear about all my memories.'

'At our age, that's what we have left.' Pamela smiled. 'I still talk to my Thomas every day, even though he's been gone more than forty years.'

'I wouldn't dream of talking to Dennis, he'd be sure to shout back at me.' She drank again from her cup. 'Forty years, that's a long time.'

Pamela ran her fingers across the embroidered cushion, nestled beside her on the sofa. 'He was a military man, killed in service.'

'How sad.' Eileen sat upright in her chair. 'From here in Haddley?'

156

Pamela heard a tension in her voice. 'We lived in Haddley, but he was a lieutenant commander in the navy.'

'Unusual place for him to be based.'

'Not really,' replied Pamela. 'There's a training station, MTC Mickelside, forty minutes south of here. All the boys loved to spend time out on the river. We met on a night out at the military rowing club. I bet you had a few of the boys drinking in your pub. They never said no to a good pint after a day on the river.'

Eileen shook her head. 'Not in East Haddley, no. I think it was probably too far for them to travel. We never saw the military in our pub.'

CHAPTER 31

DS Parker manoeuvred around the packed car park at the rear of Haddley police station, looking for a free space.

'There's a spot in the far corner, against the wall,' said PC Cooke.

'Thanks.'

'I can back it in for you if you like.'

He ignored her, focusing instead on his mirrors as he reversed into the space. Shutting off the engine, he climbed quickly out of the car and, without waiting for Cooke, strode across the car park. At the station's rear entrance, he slammed his hand against the entry button before scanning his pass on the sliding doors that led directly into the CID offices.

As he stood beside his desk, he clicked on his phone. He opened a message from his wife. A photograph of his two daughters, dancing at Miss Gracie's, filled his screen.

'Cute,' said Cooke, suddenly at his side.

He felt her run her hand across the base of his spine and slip her fingers inside his belt. He jerked away.

'What the fuck are you doing?'

'Nothing,' she said, with an innocent smile he realised was anything but. 'What's your problem?' she asked. 'Nobody can see us. We're at the back of the room.'

'Karen, no,' he replied, but that didn't stop her hand slipping back inside his belt. He stumbled backwards against the ancient radiator, burning hot even in the mild weather. 'What's wrong with you?'

'You weren't so worried this morning.'

'I am now.'

'What's got you so stressed?'

He made no attempt to hide his astonishment. 'The guy who threatened Dr Jha, who we were meant to be bringing in, just got his brains smashed in, while we were messing about at Baxter's yard. Did you miss all of that?'

She traced her fingers up the back of his thigh. 'You can't blame yourself for any of that,' she said, smiling.

The door at the top of the room opened. Parker moved out from the corner. With half a dozen quick steps, Chief Inspector Bridget Freeman crossed the room. 'My office. Now,' she said.

'Yes, boss,' he replied, but she'd already moved away.

'Me as well?' said Cooke.

Freeman ignored her.

'I think that means no,' said Parker, edging past the constable. He followed Freeman out of the room and when he reached her office she was already seated back behind her sleek white desk.

'Close the door,' she said.

159

'Yes, boss.'

'I didn't work twenty years and reach a *relatively* senior position within the Metropolitan Police for you to come in here with a chummy nickname as if we're in some cosy Sunday-night TV drama.'

'No, ma'am.'

'You entered Baxter's building yard this morning. I hope with due cause.'

'PC Cooke believed she saw a light flickering in the home of Liam Kane.' Parker bit his lip.

'While you were turning over his lodgings, somebody else was bashing in his skull with a claw hammer.'

'I can explain, ma'am.'

Freeman laced her fingers together. 'I'm waiting.'

'The discovery of considerable drug paraphernalia at Kane's former home gave us cause for a fuller inspection of the Baxters' property.' Parker paused and dropped his voice. 'Ma'am, at that moment, following the successful raid on the yard last week, I felt it was too good an opportunity for us to pass up.'

The chief inspector raised her eyebrows. 'And what did you find?'

'Nothing, ma'am.'

'Exactly,' replied Freeman, getting to her feet and moving to the front of her desk. She perched opposite Parker. 'With a family like the Baxters, you move only when you have something concrete. Last week, we knew exactly what we'd find, and we did. It was great work, a real warning shot. But, up against the Baxters, you never go in blind.'

'Yes, ma'am. No, ma'am, I mean.'

'You were pissing in the wind. And now Kane is dead.' The chief inspector walked back around her desk and returned to her white leather chair. 'Where are you on that?'

'His girlfriend, Cheryl Henry, appeared at St Marnham farmers' market with what I think we can presume was the murder weapon.'

'A claw hammer.'

'We're running forensics now, but the medical examiner seemed pretty certain.'

'Where's the girlfriend?'

'We don't know, ma'am.'

'You don't know much.'

'Uniform have a full description. In the past, she's dealt out of the Rose and Crown pub in Oreton. We'll have a presence there this afternoon and evening.'

'You believe she killed Kane?'

'She's our main person of interest, although it's not impossible our search of Baxter's yard provoked the family into taking action.'

'The Baxter family?' replied Freeman, suddenly back on her feet and pacing the room. 'Are you out of your mind? Liam Kane was an end-of-the-chain two-bit dealer. I doubt Bertie Baxter even knows his name.'

'No, ma'am.'

Freeman pulled a chair across the room and sat beside the detective. 'Shawn, in this role you need to think. That might be something new for you, but you need to start now.'

'Yes, ma'am.'

'Liam Kane was drug-dealing scum. Forget the Baxters.

Why would they sully themselves with him? It's the girl-friend we need. Get out there and do your job.'

Parker understood he was dismissed and crossed the room.

'Shawn,' said Freeman, as he gripped the office door handle.

'Yes, ma'am,' he replied.

'I took a chance on you. I know how tough it can be when for years you deliver good results only to be overlooked by the powers that be. I want us to work well together. Don't let me down.'

CHAPTER 32

'The boys I remember,' said Pamela, 'would have travelled across London for a strong pint of beer.'

Her head down, Eileen nibbled on a small slice of cake. 'I spent so very little time serving behind the bar, I wouldn't know,' she replied. 'Whenever I tried to pull a pint, I ended up with a glass half-filled with foam. Dennis did his best to teach me, but from the start he could see I'd never do it right. All I did was get in the way.'

'But you enjoyed your life in the pub?'

'Dennis thought I was best in the kitchen, and if I'm honest, that's where I was happiest.'

Pamela smiled. She didn't quite believe Eileen, but she wasn't sure why. 'I've never been much of a cook,' she said. 'I've not got the patience.'

'I only ever did the basics, nothing fancy.'

'That, I don't believe,' replied Pamela. 'I can't remember tasting a lighter cake. You should have a stall at the farmers' market!' Pamela watched Eileen flush from the merest praise. 'I mean it.'

'Would you like another slice?' she asked, hesitantly, a note of pride in her voice.

'I don't want to appear greedy, but yes please.'

Eileen cut a fresh slice and dropped it onto Pamela's plate. Breaking off a corner, Pamela declared it, 'Delicious! Next thing you'll tell me is you're cordon bleu trained.'

Eileen giggled. 'Oh, no, no. My mother wanted me to go to secretarial school in York. I had no interest, but she was quite insistent. That was until my father came home one night and told me he'd registered me at a cookery school in Leeds. I travelled by bus each day for six months. After that, I found a job at a tearoom in York. It was mostly serving tables, but twice weekly the owner allowed me to work with the men in the bakery. I loved it.'

Pamela took another bite of cake. 'It was time very well spent,' she said. 'When you let go of the pub in East Haddley, did you keep working?'

'Dennis felt it was best if I didn't work. He said the reason he was selling the pub was so I didn't have to keep working in the kitchen. He was doing it for me.'

'But you loved cooking?'

'You know what men are like. They get ideas into their heads and don't really listen. Other than for a few months when Dennis was approaching retirement and we needed a bigger pot of savings, I didn't work again.'

'You must have missed it?' asked Pamela.

'I still baked at home.' Eileen paused. 'And I had a secret that Dennis never knew.' She spoke so quietly, it was as if she feared he might actually overhear.

'Really?' said Pamela. 'I promise not to tell anyone.'

'Years after we sold the pub and our son had grown up and left home, I entered a baking competition I saw advertised in the local newspaper. And I won!'

'How wonderful,' replied Pamela, clapping her hands. 'Just like *The Great British Bake Off*.'

'After I'd won, you'll never believe what happened. The newspaper contacted me and asked if I'd like to write a weekly baking column. Of course, I didn't use my real name. I called it "Mrs Cooper's Cookery Course". Cooper, that was my maiden name. I'd bake a cake each week, and a journalist came to take photographs. From what she said, the series was quite popular.'

'I bet everyone at the paper loved you.'

'Oh, no, they only ever knew me as Mrs Cooper. Dennis would have hated it if he'd found out. I couldn't risk anyone else knowing it was me. Only the one journalist knew who I really was. All my contact was through her. She was so lovely and spent almost half an hour with me every week.'

That's how you knew Alaka Jha, thought Pamela.

Eileen pushed herself up in her chair. 'I should get these cleared away.'

'Let me help,' replied Pamela.

'No, no, I can manage,' insisted Eileen.

Pamela could see Eileen felt she'd already said too much. She watched her shuffle into the kitchen, her tray precariously balanced in her hands. When she heard Eileen run the sink tap, she got to her feet.

'Are you sure I can't help?' said Pamela.

'No, I'm fine.'

'Eileen,' said Pamela, 'can I ask you a question?'

'What would that be?' she replied, opening her cake tin.

'The journalist who helped with the Mrs Cooper series. Was that Alaka Jha?'

Eileen turned off the hot tap, leaving the cups to soak. She reached for a towel and dried her hands.

Pamela took a step forward and touched her arm. 'Dennis is gone. He can't hurt you now.'

Eileen turned to face her. Her expression was suddenly different. 'If that's why you came, then I think you'd better go.'

CHAPTER 33

'I wish we had a bigger garden,' I say to Dani.

We're sitting in two garden chairs on the small, square patch of grass at the back of our house. Dani is resting her feet on the narrow stone wall I built with my mum more than fifteen years ago. The wall surrounds a small flowerbed that thanks to Dani's arrival has seen more colourful blooms this year than at any time in the past decade.

'How much more space do you need? This is the biggest garden I've ever had.'

'I'm thinking in a year or two, when the little one is wanting to play football. There won't be much room.'

'You mean when *you* want to play football,' she says, smiling. 'Isn't that the point of living by the common? I don't want you destroying my flowers.'

'But when we've two or three . . . '

Dani's bright blue eyes widen. 'Is that what you imagine?'

'Definitely two.'

'I could live with that.'

'Maybe three,' I add, quietly.

'Let's get one out of the way first,' she replies, shifting in her chair.

'I'd hate for the little one to be lonely.'

'So would I,' she replies, 'but let's see how we go over the next couple of years.'

In the warm sun, I rest my head and let my eyes drop closed.

'Have you messaged your dad yet?' she asks.

I hesitate. 'I still don't know if I will.'

I can feel Dani turning to face me. 'Doesn't he deserve to know he's about to become a grandfather?'

I don't reply.

'Ben, open your eyes.'

'I'm asleep.'

Dani slaps me on the arm. 'I mean it.'

'I've nothing to say to him.' When I first met Dani, I confided in her that on the day of my brother's murder my father had arranged to meet with him. My dad never showed up and instead of spending time with him, Nick ended up following the two girls who would ultimately kill him. 'Throughout my life, my dad's been nothing more than an unreliable chancer. He cheated on my mum, and after he left Haddley I can count on one hand the number of times he's been in touch. On the few occasions I have seen him, he was after something. I barely know him.'

'Exactly. You don't know him, and you never really have. He left your home when you were three years old,' says Dani. 'Nick was his son. Don't you think he's lived with the consequence of what he did ever since?'

168

'I will never forgive him.'

'I'm not asking you to, but perhaps our child offers you both a chance to heal.'

When I close my eyes, I feel Dani reach across and link her fingers with mine. 'After the baby's born, I'll send him a picture,' I say.

The gate at the back of the garden is suddenly thrown open. I jerk myself upright.

'Keeping me out of the loop again!' says Sam, bursting in, his face flushed bright red. 'Why didn't you call me?'

'Come in, why don't you?' I say, as he hastily enters the garden. He drags a chair from beside the open kitchen door.

'Liam Kane is dead,' he tells us, still catching his breath.

'I know,' I reply.

'You discovered the body?'

'I did.'

'Killed by his girlfriend with the hammer she brought to the farmers' market.'

'Possibly.'

He doesn't hear my response. 'The hammer that she threatened to kill Uma with.'

'Sam,' says Dani, 'can I get you a glass of water?'

'No, no, I'm fine. I ran across the common, so I'm a bit sweaty.' He turns his attention back to me. 'Liam threatens Uma. Cheryl kills Liam. Why?'

'I don't know,' I reply, 'and until the police bring in Cheryl, we're unlikely to find out.'

'I've written a new article.' He reaches into his back pocket and passes me a crumpled sheet of paper.

'*Chief suspect in thirty-year-old murder case found slaugh-tered*,' I read aloud. 'That's stretching it a bit?'

'I thought that's what you and Madeline did all the time?'

I don't reply.

'Okay, maybe you don't,' he continues, 'but the facts are all there.' He wipes the sweat off his forehead and turns to Dani. 'A cup of coffee might be nice.'

'Sam!' I say, sitting up.

Dani laughs. 'Don't worry, I could do with stretching my legs.' She eases her feet onto the grass and heads inside.

'Will you post the article?'

'If I do, I'm changing the headline.'

'Whatever.'

'You've got all the facts,' I say, skim reading Sam's story, 'but what do we want this next article to say?'

'What do you mean?'

'Look at it this way. We all want to tell a good story, but if somebody has reacted to the first article this is our chance to speak directly to them. What do we want to say?'

'Give yourself up.'

I laugh. 'Not sure that'll work.'

'That we're on to them?'

'Yes, possibly, but they know we can't talk to Liam Kane so why make him the main focus of the story?'

'Because he's the only possible link between what's happened in the past twenty-four hours and what happened to Alaka, thirty years ago.'

'What about Cheryl?' I remember what Pamela said to me when we sat together outside the Peacock boathouse. 'In

170

the past Uma's tried to help Cheryl. There's a bond between them.'

'Go on,' says Sam, before standing to take a mug of coffee from Dani.

'What if yesterday afternoon Cheryl went to the surgery not to threaten Uma but to help a woman who'd helped her in the past. Then this morning, she came to the farmers' market desperate and distraught. She needed Uma to understand the danger she was facing.'

Sam sips on his drink. 'But the way Cheryl acted. Ben, I was pushed to the ground.'

'I'm sure you were very brave, Sam,' says Dani, 'but was it Cheryl who pushed you?'

'No, but she was the one waving the hammer about. I'm sure she was off her head.'

'Waving the hammer about may be a bit of a stretch,' I say.

'The crowd reacted to what they saw, or thought they saw?' Dani continues.

'Possibly,' replies Sam, 'but she was still rampaging around with a murder weapon.'

'Haddley Police expect to pick up Cheryl later today,' says Dani.

'Can I quote you?'

She smiles. 'An unnamed police source, if you must.'

'If the police get hold of Cheryl the game is up,' replies Sam. 'That's the message we want to send. *Police urgently seek witness with link to thirty-year-old murder.*'

'That's your headline,' I say. 'Once the police have Cheryl, whoever recruited her and Kane is on their own.'

171

CHAPTER 34

'What can I get you?' asked the woman serving behind the bar of the Rose and Crown in Oreton.

Shawn Parker introduced himself before opening his phone. He showed her an image of Cheryl Henry, captured the previous day inside the St Marnham doctor's surgery. 'Do you know this woman?'

'We're kind of busy this afternoon,' replied the bartender, pointing in the direction of the packed beer garden.

'She's a regular here.'

'I wouldn't know.'

'I need you to take a look.'

The woman passed two pints across the bar before stopping to view the image.

'If I'm not mistaken, thanks to her and her boyfriend,' Parker continued, 'your burger shack trades in a lot more than Big Macs.'

'A few smokes? College kids are going to buy their stuff somewhere.'

'So, might as well be here? Is that what you're saying? Do you take a cut?'

'Don't be stupid. We run a good pub. We're not on the make.'

'You just help provide a service by looking the other way and ignoring any trouble.'

'Any trouble's more likely to come from the university professors, not the kids.'

Parker held up his phone and the woman glanced at the image of Cheryl Henry as she pulled a pint of Guinness.

'I'm not interested in her petty dealing,' he said, 'but somebody's taken a claw hammer to her boyfriend's head.'

The woman stopped.

'He'll not be bothering you again,' added the detective.

The bartender hesitated a moment longer, then nodded in the direction of the garden. 'Behind the burger shack, there's an overgrown path and a gate that leads out onto the street. Whenever they're here, that's where they deal.'

'Thank you,' said Parker, tapping his hand on the bar.

The exposed brick walls kept the inside of the pub cool. Walking outside, into the packed beer garden, the heat hit Parker. A stench of spilt beer mixed with adolescent sweat filled the air. Under the bright mid-afternoon sun, he weaved his way between crowded tables towards the burger shack. Two men, no more than students themselves, were flipping burgers and melting cheese.

'I paid for three burgers, not two,' called a loud and leary voice.

'And we want extra pickles,' added a plummy voice from behind.

'This is what you paid for,' replied the man inside the shack. He pushed a tray forward. 'Take it or leave it.'

Parker edged behind the shack. He sidestepped an over-flowing green wheelie bin just as two students appeared from the back of an overgrown bush. Both were smoking freshly lit spliffs.

'She's by the gate,' one of them said, inviting Parker to follow the path.

He pushed his way past the bush and found a small clearing, where he discovered Cheryl Henry standing in front of a painted wooden gate. She was busy making another trade with a lanky man whom Parker guessed to be in his late teens.

'I can do you twenty quid's worth, but that's all I've got.'

Cheryl's eyes locked onto Parker and, instantly, they widened in recognition. Before Parker could say anything, she stuffed her bundle of cash in her pocket, snatched her bag and slammed her hand against the latch.

The gate flew open. Parker shoved past the teen as Henry jumped down two steps and onto the pavement outside. That was when Parker saw the blade glistening in her hand.

'Knife!' he yelled to Karen Cooke, whom he'd positioned outside the gate before entering the pub.

But Cooke had already launched herself forward, landing a rugby tackle on Henry. When Parker jumped down the two steps, he saw the blood oozing through the constable's shirt.

'Officer down,' he screamed, as Henry sprinted away towards the university.

CHAPTER 35

Pamela slipped off her jacket and hung it on the small brass hook beside her front door. She sat on the second step of her stairs to unlace her shoes and heard the faint ping of her phone. She dragged her bag towards her, and rummaged inside it, but couldn't find her phone. It pinged again. 'Damn,' she muttered, and pulled herself up on the banister. She found her phone zipped inside her coat pocket.

A message from Maggie. Using her index finger, she carefully typed her passcode.

Still on for five?

She looked at the clock; not yet four. She had time for a quick nap before walking up the hill.

I'll be with you around 5.15 she replied.

Maggie's response was instant.

Pamela closed her phone and clasped it to her chest. She thought of the man she'd seen Maggie with earlier in the day. Could the surprise have something to do with him?

In her living room, she stood in front of her small set of bookshelves. There were more photographs than books, with her favourite picture of Thomas taking pride of place. She straightened the frame and pulled it slightly forward on the shelf.

'I'm worried,' she said, softly.

Thomas would tell her not to fret, but there was something in the way the man had rested his hand on Maggie's back, something so familiar about his stance. Had she seen him before? She sank down into her favourite armchair, and with the late afternoon sun still lingering through the window, enjoyed the warmth on her face. But when she closed her eyes, her mind was racing, and she knew she wouldn't sleep. What was Maggie doing?

By a quarter to five she was ready to leave. She'd changed into a dress. She hardly every wore dresses these days, but it felt right to make the effort. She paired it with her best cardigan, but stepping out of the door she reached for her jacket as well. It might be cooler by the pond.

For so many years, she'd treated Maggie's flat as a second home, popping in and out of each other's homes on an almost daily basis. This evening, passing through Castle Fields's imposing wrought-iron gates, she felt her stomach flutter. She approached the garden with a slight sense of

176

trepidation. It was a feeling she'd never had before when visiting Maggie.

Across the lawn, at the side of the pond, Pamela saw an older couple relaxing on the cushioned garden chairs, and she crossed the neatly manicured grass towards them. It was only once she'd navigated the three steps at the side of the pond that she realised it wasn't Maggie and Alan seated beside the water. Seeing her approach, the man was quick to his feet. With her fading eyesight and without her glasses, he was almost upon her, engulfing her in a bear hug, before she even recognised him.

'Simon?' she said, pulling back as he planted a kiss on her cheek.

'You look wonderful!' he exclaimed. She wasn't sure she did, but she was glad she'd decided to wear her best cardigan. He wrapped his arm around her shoulders. 'It can't have been ten years, can it?'

Like so many youthful friendships, where unbreakable bonds were bound to last forever, life had overtaken the group who were at one time inseparable. While never losing touch, time spent together had become rare. For Pamela, that meant over the last decade, it was only Maggie and Alan she'd seen.

'What are you doing here?' she asked, as her husband's former military colleague ushered her across the lawn.

'Louise is here as well. Come and say hello.'

Simon's wife of forty years took hold of her hand. At times slightly aloof, Louise smiled a thin smile. She told Pamela how wonderful it was to see her.

'You as well,' she replied. Only then did she notice Susan,

Maggie's niece, seated on the neighbouring garden bench. 'I wasn't expecting such a party.'

Susan came to greet her, hugging Pamela close. Pamela had always held Susan in warm affection. Like her, she'd lost her husband, Mark, at a young age. After he drowned in an accident at the Mickelside Military Training Centre, Susan had lived her life alone for more than thirty years.

'Maggie told me you were here this morning,' said Pamela.

'Only for a couple of hours. Uncle Alan slept most of the time.'

'Come and sit beside me,' said Louise to Pamela, patting a neighbouring cushion. Susan squeezed Pamela's hand and quietly retreated to the bench.

'If I'd said it once, I'd said it a million times,' began Louise. 'We must visit the old gang in Haddley. Simon, you have to admit I've said that many times.'

'So many, I've lost count.'

'But at the last minute, something always seemed to come up.' Louise leaned in closer. Pamela wasn't quite sure why as, other than the four of them, there was only the fish to hear. 'I said it again this morning, and then suddenly, all spur of the moment, Simon brought the car around. Fifty minutes down the road and here we are.' She touched Pamela's arm. 'We'd heard Alan's deteriorating and decided we had to make the effort while it was still worth it. We both felt it would be sweet to bring the old gang back together.'

Not quite all the old gang, Pamela thought, but she didn't say anything.

'Called Maggie this morning, told her we were on our

way and that we wouldn't take no for an answer.' Simon's strong voice filled the grounds. His career in the forces had extended long after the others and he had progressed far higher. Pamela smiled and recalled how Simon, the youngest of the four friends, somehow became their unofficial leader. His strength of character and natural authority ensured loyalty from all those around him.

'Let me pour you a drink,' he said, lifting a fruit-filled jug of Pimm's.

'Lovely,' Pamela replied. 'We're lucky to catch you both here, and not off in some far-flung corner of the world.' Every year, tucked inside her Christmas card from the couple, came a round-robin letter telling all their friends of the incredible places they'd visited that year. Pamela thought of it as showing off.

'We're travelling to Vermont at the end of the month for the fall foliage,' said Louise.

A move into the security services, after twenty years in the military, had afforded Simon Carmichael an OBE and two handsome pensions. That, combined with his wife's family money, allowed the couple to enjoy comforts of which Pamela could only dream.

'I'm sure the colours in Vermont will be wonderful, just like the ones in Richmond Park.'

Simon handed Pamela her glass. 'Before she comes down, why don't you tell us how Maggie's coping?'

'Susan's probably far better placed to do that than me,' she replied. 'I don't know how Maggie would manage with-out her.'

'I wouldn't say that,' replied Susan, modestly. 'She does amazingly well. I help when I can. I only wish I could do more.'

'I've no doubt you're invaluable to them both,' said Louise.

Dropping her eyes, Susan sipped from her glass.

'Alan's still strong in himself,' said Pamela, breaking the brief silence, 'and very occasionally he can suddenly be the Alan we all love and remember.'

'He can be lucid?' asked Louise.

'Only briefly, very briefly.'

'So sad, and so unfair,' said Simon. 'He was always strong as an ox.'

'Getting old isn't fair,' said Pamela.

Simon looked across the lawn towards Maggie and Alan's apartment. 'Here they come,' he said, as three figures emerged from the building.

'Is that Larry with them?' Pamela asked.

'Yes,' Louise replied. 'Like I said, all the old gang back together. When I called Maggie and said we were on our way, she said why didn't she phone Larry.'

Pamela took a gulp of her drink, which raced straight to her head. Her mind spinning, only now did she realise she was seeing Larry for the second time that day. He was the man she'd seen Maggie with at the farmers' market.

'I told you I had a surprise for you,' said Maggie, as she greeted her friend with a hug and a kiss.

'You certainly did,' replied Pamela. 'Larry, so good to see you.' She hugged him briefly, noticing how thin he'd become.

180

'Are you here on a visit?'

'No,' he replied, 'I moved back home for good at the start of the year.'

Over twenty years ago, upon his leaving the forces, Larry and his wife, Rosie, had sold their home in Tunbridge Wells and bought a bed and breakfast on the Portuguese Atlantic coast, where Larry ran a small diving school. Pamela had visited once, but that would have been fifteen years ago.

'Thank you for your kind letter,' said Larry, quietly.

After Rosie's passing last autumn, Pamela wrote to Larry recalling all their most joyous youthful memories.

'Without Rosie, I knew I wouldn't be able to keep running the place on my own, not at my age, so I sold up. It was time for me to come home.'

Pamela wondered how long Larry and Maggie had been back in touch.

'We missed you at Rosie's funeral,' said Louise to Pamela.

Pamela caught Maggie's eye. Last autumn, at the time of the funeral, Pamela had served her short period on remand at Silvermeadow prison because she'd refused to implicate her daughter, Jeannie, in a killing from decades earlier. Louise knew very well where she had been. They all did.

'I missed all of you as well,' Pamela replied. 'I think I only had Maggie on my visitors list.'

'Anyway,' said Simon, hastily, raising his glass, 'I'd like to raise a toast. To the four single boys and the wonderful women who tied them down.'

Maggie sat on a small, two-seater garden sofa, her husband silent beside her. Louise leaned forward in her seat to speak to Alan. 'Isn't this lovely?' she said, her voice loud and slowly enunciated. 'All of us together again.'

He's not deaf, thought Pamela, but she told herself not to be so harsh.

'Who'd have thought it, over forty years later,' added Simon, pouring more drinks. 'Us boys still going strong.' Alan flinched when Simon squeezed him on the shoulder.

'Not quite all,' said Pamela.

'No,' Simon replied, his voice dropping. 'Let's take a moment to remember our two dearest fallen friends. I served with Mark in the Gulf, and Thomas in the Falklands.' He moved along the edge of the pond and placed his hand on Susan's shoulder. 'Neither could have made me more proud.'

Everyone raised a glass, while Alan reached his hand across to Pamela, taking hold of hers.

'Look out,' said Larry, 'I think Alan always had his eye on you.'

Everyone laughed, but when the group fell silent Pamela turned to Larry.

'And I'll always have my eye out for him.'

CHAPTER 36

'I think you upset Sam,' says Dani, taking hold of my hand as we walk around the edge of the common.

'No, I didn't!'

'He was your first ever boss, and now you're telling him how to rewrite his article.'

'Sam's got a thick skin. He's happy the story's up online.' In the early evening sun, Dani and I turn at the end of our small terrace row and follow the narrow path that runs along the south side of the common.

'Now you've drawn a direct line between Cheryl Henry and Alaka's murder, you'll have the TikTok detectives out in force.'

Dani's right, but fear of madcap conspiracy theories can't deter us from reporting what is true. 'Perhaps that's the price we must pay, but something links Liam and Cheryl to Alaka's killing. We need to understand what.'

'Or who.'

Dani and I walk slowly on until a football trundles off

the edge of the common. I hurry forward, stop the ball and kick it back towards Ted Grace.

'Thanks, Ben,' calls eleven-year-old Ted, who lives in one of the Victorian villas overlooking the common.

I slip my hand back inside Dani's.

'You can go and play if you like,' she says, looking towards Ted and Max.

'I'd rather be walking with you.'

'Of course, you would,' she replies, laughing.

We pass in front of the home of Sarah Wright. She and Holly are sitting at the top of the flight of stone steps, which lead up to the front door of Sarah's Victorian villa, sharing a bottle of wine.

'Still no news?' calls Sarah, while keeping one eye on her young son, Max, as he fires shots at Ted.

'The wait goes on,' replies Dani, as we stop at the end of Sarah's driveway.

'Enjoy the peace while you can,' says Holly. 'Can we tempt you to a glass?' she asks, lifting a bottle of rosé.

'I'm good thanks,' I reply.

'I'd love a glass!' calls Dani.

'Come and join us,' says Sarah. 'One won't hurt.'

'Don't tempt me! I've been good for so long. I haven't touched a single drop, although with eagle-eyes here I don't think I'd be allowed.'

'I said you should have a glass if you fancy it,' I reply, my voice rising.

'Of course, you did.' Dani, kissing my cheek. 'But I love you anyway.'

184

We wave and walk on into the middle of the common. When we pass the two boys, I kick a stray shot back to Max. We stop by the bench where Alice is busy with her colouring pens and stickers.

'Aren't you playing football today?' asks Dani, sitting beside her.

Alice puts down her red pen. 'Dani, sometimes it's good for us girls to do our own thing and let the boys play their sweaty games.'

Dani bites her lip. 'You are so right.'

'I can play football whenever I want,' Alice continues, 'but at the moment I'm busy with my colouring.'

I step away from the bench and look towards my own home as a small white van parks in front of my garden. Painted on the side are the words *Cotswold Preserves*. When Uma climbs out, I walk to greet her.

'I called the insurance company this afternoon,' she tells me, pointing towards her burnt-out car, 'but whoever was on the other end of the phone line told me she could do nothing without photographic evidence. According to her, the assessors need to decide what is salvageable.'

I shake my head. 'Sadly, I don't think there's much left to save.'

'She said the insurance company won't even pay for a rental car until they've concluded their initial assessment. I asked her to look on the Neighbourhood app for images, but she didn't seem impressed.'

I reach for my phone and show Uma Sam's new article on the search for Cheryl Henry, now live on our site.

'Edward wants me to take a few days off work. I don't see why I should. We argued again. Ben, you understand why I need to do this?'

'I do,' I reply. Only when I discovered the truth behind the deaths of my own mum and brother could I lay their memories to rest. Until then, I found it impossible to live my own life. Without knowing the truth, I would never have let myself love Dani the way I do now. 'I absolutely understand.'

'I suggested to Edward he go back to Leamington.'

I raise my eyebrows.

'Only for a couple of days,' she reassures me. 'We both need some space. He planned to go tonight but then I told him I was using his van.' She smiles. 'I think he'll go in the morning,' she continues. 'I can't bear arguing with him. He has my best interests at heart, but I've lived with this for so long. I have to keep going.'

When she sees Uma, Alice jumps off the bench and comes running towards us.

'Dr Jha,' she calls, 'I'm making you a present. I've not quite finished but you can have it now if you like.'

Uma bends to greet Alice as she thrusts a sheet of paper into her hand.

'Those are the poppies from above my front door,' Alice tells Uma. 'I have them on the walls of my bedroom as well.'

'They're beautiful,' replies Uma. 'Such a bright red colour.'

'I drew them with my best colouring pens.' Alice takes back hold of the paper. 'These are my favourite stickers,' she says, pointing at the page. 'Red and pink flowers.'

'They're lovely. Thank you so much. I'm going to put your drawing up on my surgery wall.'

Alice smiles proudly, before giving the picture to Uma and running back towards the bench. Uma's phone buzzes and she pulls it out of her pocket, glancing at her screen.

'My youngest cousin's already read about the farmers' market.'

'Good of him to check you're okay.'

She slips her phone back into her pocket. 'Of all my family, he's the one who actually cares. All okay with Dani?' she asks, waving in her direction.

'Still waiting; perhaps a tad less patiently.'

'It won't be long, I promise.' Uma's phone buzzes again and she reaches into her jacket. 'I have to fly,' she says. 'Duty calls.'

She turns back in the direction of her husband's van, but before she does, she looks down at Alice's drawing, and slowly traces her fingers across the bright red flowers.

CHAPTER 37

With the sun dropping slowly in the sky and a chill in the air, Pamela slipped on her jacket. She looked at Alan, dressed only in a sweater and trousers, and saw him shiver.

'What a wonderful surprise this has been,' she said, 'but it's time for me to be thinking about home.' She turned to her dearest friend. 'Would you like me to walk upstairs with Alan?'

Maggie sipped on her glass of Pimm's, which Pamela had counted to be her third. 'If you're sure?' she replied.

'You stay here and see everyone off.' Pamela reached for Alan's hand and, smiling, she said, 'Shall we go inside and get warm?'

'And Maggie?' he replied.

'I'll follow on in two minutes,' said his wife, 'once I've tidied the garden.'

Alan looked at her but remained quiet. For a moment there was silence, until Simon quickly drank down his glass and got to his feet. 'I think it's time we were making tracks as well,' he said.

Louise followed his lead. 'Yes, we've quite a drive home.' She turned to Pamela. 'Can we drop you? Your little house isn't far from here, is it?'

'That's right, not far, so I'll be fine to walk.' She stood and, still holding Alan's hand, encouraged him to follow.

The group crossed the lawn, steadily making their way towards the small car park at the rear of Maggie's home. Parked on the gravel driveway, in front of the building, was an ambulance.

'I do hope nothing's wrong,' said Maggie.

'One of your neighbours, perhaps?' asked Louise.

'We're none of us getting any younger.'

The group walked on into the car park. 'What a smashing little sports car,' said Pamela. 'You'd love to drive that, wouldn't you, Alan?' She smiled at Simon.

'Sadly, nothing quite so glamorous for us,' Simon replied, pointing towards a Volvo SUV. 'Ferrying three grandchildren from after-school clubs to rugby practice forces the Carmichael family into something far more practical. The Porsche is Larry's.'

Pamela glanced over her shoulder. 'Really?'

'You only live once,' he said, a touch sheepishly. 'It is a little expensive to run, but after Rosie passed, I cashed in some pensions and thought why not.'

'It must be great fun to drive.'

'I'm always very careful, but when the road is clear it feels nice to be able to put your foot down.'

Old men could be so stupid, thought Pamela. She had to bite her lip to stop herself from giggling. She couldn't help but think God must have blessed Larry with a very small penis.

Alan shivered again, and Pamela took that as her cue for a series of quick goodbyes.

'Larry and I will clear the garden. We'll be no more than five minutes,' called Maggie, as Pamela and Alan walked inside.

Riding up in the lift, Alan was silent, his eyes fixed on his shoes. When the doors opened on the third floor, Pamela reached for his hand.

'Here we are,' she said.

Alan didn't move.

'Come on, let's get back inside your lovely warm flat.'

Like a tired and cranky child, he shook his head.

'We won't get warm in here.' The lift doors began to close, and Pamela reached out her arm to hold them open. Outside in the corridor she heard voices. 'Come on,' she said, her own tone betraying a hint of irritation. 'Somebody else needs the lift.'

When she took a step forward, Alan pushed himself back into the corner. Other than Maggie, he hated anyone touching him. He folded his arms across his chest. Pamela took a deep breath. She felt nothing but sympathy for her dear friend. How painful it must be for her to see her husband like this, every minute of every day. Every conversation a Herculean effort.

'When we're back inside your flat, why don't we make you a cup of hot chocolate?' she said, remembering Alan's sweet tooth.

He grinned. 'And Maggie?'

'Yes, and one for Maggie.'

'Where's Maggie?' he asked.

'She's tidying up the garden, isn't she? She won't be long.'

He nodded and edged forward. Pamela held out her hand. 'That's it,' she said, feeling in her pocket for the apartment key.

'Maggie's in the garden,' he said, as they walked slowly down the hallway.

'Yes, Maggie's in the garden.'

Suddenly, he squeezed her hand tight.

'Alan!' she exclaimed, fearing he might crush her fingers.

He let go of her hand and took a step backwards. Tears filled his eyes. 'Maggie's in the garden with—'

He stopped, betrayed by his fading mind. He closed his eyes and pressed his fingers against the bridge of his nose. 'Maggie's in the garden with Thomas,' he said.

'Alan, no,' she said, softly. 'Maggie's in the garden with Larry.' She slipped the key into the apartment door, turning sideways as she did. The door to the neighbouring apartment stood open. Pamela looked for any sign of life, and taking a step forward peered inside. When two paramedics appeared, wheeling an ambulance chair, she moved swiftly backwards. She'd briefly met Maggie's neighbour, Graham Dawson, in the past. Seeing him now, he did not look well.

'Let's make room,' she said to Alan, smiling at the two paramedics as they passed. At the end of the corridor, she heard the lift doors open, and then a gasp from Maggie as she saw her neighbour being taken away.

'Come on,' said Pamela to Alan, 'let's get you inside.' She pushed the door open, but he refused to move. 'You've heard Maggie coming, haven't you?' she said.

'Maggie's coming now,' he replied.

Seconds later, Maggie and Larry appeared down the hallway, while from the neighbouring flat Graham's wife, Carol, emerged, accompanied by Dr Jha.

'I do hope Graham's not too unwell,' said Maggie, approaching her neighbour, while Larry lingered awkwardly behind her. 'Please do let me know if there's anything you need.'

Behind her, Pamela felt Alan pull away from the small group assembled in the corridor. When she turned, he began violently to shake his head. He stared at the group with an expression of terror.

'Alan, what is it?' Pamela asked.

'I didn't change the time!' He pointed at Larry. 'He made me do it!'

Five

Gordon Harper

'His youngest child had never forgiven Gordon for his elder brother's death. What Ben didn't understand was that he'd never forgiven himself.'

Lying in his bed, he reached for his phone and the time flashed upon the screen. Ten minutes after two, fifty minutes since he'd last looked. He rarely enjoyed more than an hour of unbroken sleep. He pushed himself up on his pillow and clicked onto the BBC News app. The new government had issued proposals to cut underage smoking. Surely a good thing. He scanned the story of an ultra-runner completing a marathon a day for six months. He switched to X, found the runner's charity feed and sponsored him twenty-six pounds. The weather for tomorrow was changing, more overcast although still warm. He'd wear his shorts again. He put the phone back on his night table, but his mind never stopped racing.

Reaching across the bed, he felt the empty space next to him. For six years, Sylvie had filled that side of the bed and filled his life. He'd loved Sylvie and she'd been good for him but, in the end, he was too unreliable for her. Somehow, he always found a way to justify his cheating. For Sylvie, this time had been once too often. He picked up his phone again and clicked on another news site. He read about an incident close to his hometown. Police were hunting for a woman with a claw hammer, who'd now stabbed a police officer. He'd read the article over and over the previous evening. His son had been involved with the hammer attack.

He climbed out of bed and decided not to shower. He'd

hardly been in bed, so he didn't feel the need. He glanced at his phone. A little over two hours since he'd brushed his teeth. No point in wasting time cleaning them again. Around eleven the previous evening, he'd drunk two glasses of red wine. That was four hours ago. He'd be fine to drive now. Empty roads led him out of Bristol and onto the motorway. With the road to himself, he sat his car in the middle lane. He thought again of his estranged son. His youngest child had never forgiven Gordon for his elder brother's death. What Ben didn't understand was that he'd never forgiven himself.

SUNDAY

CHAPTER 38

'Ben,' says Dani, her voice quiet.

Immediately I sit up in bed. 'Is it the baby?'

'There's somebody knocking at the door.'

We sit in silence, our bedroom still swathed in darkness. I hear a tapping on the front door.

'There,' says Dani.

I switch on a bedside lamp and reach for my phone. It's five-thirty. Whoever is outside rattles our letterbox. I climb out of bed, wrestling a T-shirt over my head, and crack open the window blinds. In the darkness, I can just about make out a figure standing by the front door.

'Be careful,' says Dani, as I open our bedroom door.

In the hallway, I turn on the outside light. Through a pane in the door, I can see a figure pacing up and down the narrow garden path. He walks to the gate before turning and walking back towards me. The light illuminates his face. Even through mottled glass, I recognise the shape of his features and unlock the door.

'Ben!' says my father. 'You're awake.'

'I am now.'

'I didn't want to wake you, thought I'd knock on the off chance you were up.'

'What are you doing here?'

'I wanted to see you.'

'It's five o'clock in the morning.'

He doesn't say anything.

I shake my head. 'You'd better come in.'

'Only if it's convenient.'

'Dad, I'm guessing you've driven at least a couple of hours to get here. Why didn't you call first?'

We stand awkwardly in my small hallway.

'It's good to see you,' he says.

I run my hand across my unshaven face and look at the man who is my only living relative. I hate myself for being unable to tell him I'm pleased to see him too. 'Can I make you a coffee?' is all I say in reply.

In the kitchen he sits beside the island. He's distracted, looking at his phone.

'How's Sylvie?' I ask, taking milk from the fridge.

'In Bolton.'

'Visiting her family?'

'No, that's where she lives now.'

'I didn't realise. Is it over with you two?'

'She'd had enough of me. They always do in the end.'

'I'm sorry.'

I brew the drinks before pulling out a chair to sit opposite him.

'I've a Google alert on your name,' he tells me. 'It sends me a message whenever you write a new article.'

My heart sinks. This is how my father keeps in touch with my life.

'I should send you a link whenever I publish anything.'

'The alert also tells me whenever somebody else mentions your name. Yesterday, I received an alert about the farmers' market. The woman had a hammer.'

'It wasn't very pleasant,' I reply.

'Why do you think she had a hammer?'

'Somebody'd been killed.'

'Was she making threats?'

'Kind of, but it was fine. Don't worry about it. I'm sure you didn't come all this way in the middle of the night to talk about St Marnham farmers' market.'

He lifts his coffee and drinks half the cup. 'I do still worry about you.'

'You really don't need to.'

'I'm your father, I can't help it.' He pauses. 'When Sylvie left, I wanted to call you.'

'You should have,' I reply, but I know why he didn't. We both know – I'd never have answered the phone. 'What happened with her?'

'I became distracted, failed to realise she and I had a good thing.'

'You cheated on her?'

My dad picks at the skin at the corner of his thumb, drawing blood. 'It's what I always do. Whenever I'm happy, I self-destruct.'

201

I know he's about to tell me about him and my mum. I don't need to hear it again.

'It's exactly what I did with your mother.'

I hold up my hand. 'Dad—'

'I should have been more honest with her. We never were a match. Your mum gave me too much freedom.'

'Let's not do this,' I reply.

'No, you're right.' He looks down at his coffee. 'Sylvie kept me on track, made me focus. I miss her.'

'Are you still in touch?'

He shakes his head. 'She couldn't forgive me, not this time.'

He tells me about his break-up, Sylvie moving out after the husband of the woman he was seeing broke into their house in the middle of the night. A confrontation followed and my father ended up with a broken nose.

'Only took three weeks for it to heal. I was surprised.' He turns his head sideways. 'Can you see the bump?'

'It's hardly noticeable,' I reply.

'That's what I thought. Amazing thing, the human body. A nose can heal in three weeks, but a thigh bone could take five months.'

'How about some breakfast?' I ask, telling myself not to become exasperated by my father's stream of consciousness.

Immediately he's on his feet with his head in my fridge. 'I've got the recipe for the perfect bacon sandwich,' he tells me. 'Frying pan?' he asks, as he grabs a packet of bacon from the fridge and a tub of butter. 'Bacon must be fried, not grilled, for the ideal level of crispy. Thick bread, Ben, to absorb all the sauce and juices. Very, very, lightly toasted.'

I sit and watch him cook, hurriedly moving from frying pan to toaster, while our conversation drifts along. 'I still remember how much you love ketchup,' he tells me. He talks of taking me to nursery when I was only three, but it is such a distant memory it is impossible for me to share. He recalls us playing cricket on the common before telling me about his local cricket team in Bristol. I smile when he talks of the over-sixties team he's joined, where the guy who opened the batting lost his glasses and couldn't see the ball. He tells me how good his own eyesight has been since his cataract operation. Did I get my eyes checked regularly? He had glasses before he was forty so I might find I need the same. His barber told him he'd still have all his own hair when he was eighty, so that was good news for me as well. When he puts my sandwich down in front of me, he tells me it will be the best I've ever tasted.

'It's very good,' I reply, my mouth half full.

'The best ever, Ben. Don't tell me it's not the best ever.'

'It's really good.'

He sits opposite and bites into his own breakfast. I look at the clock on my cooker. I've been with my father for almost an hour and he's yet to ask me anything about my life.

CHAPTER 39

George Lennon sat on his kitchen floor and pulled on his running shoes. Yesterday evening he'd eaten poached salmon with green beans and broccoli. After that, ten hours of restorative sleep had left him feeling fully refreshed. This morning he'd run for at least an hour and had set himself a 15 km target.

With music pulsing through his AirPods, he ran through Oreton's narrow streets, away from his house and towards Richmond Park. The open space was vast and the undulations challenging, but each time his running app spoke to him he increased his pace. After his run he'd take a quick shower, Greek yogurt with blueberries for his breakfast and a cup of decaf coffee. Then, a visit with friends before working in the morgue this afternoon. Liam Kane had no living relatives. When he'd examined the man's body in the boathouse, he was almost certain it was multiple blows to the head that had killed him, but he needed the body on the table to be sure. Only then could he closely view the defensive wounds Kane sustained as he fought for his life.

His digital running coach told him his pace was slowing. He replied by shouting, 'Look at how steep this hill is!' The app didn't respond but he pushed on, and when the hill plateaued the voice congratulated him for increasing his speed. He continued out of the park, through the village of Ham and into the woods neighbouring Teddington Lock. The uneven surface forced him to step carefully. He jumped over exposed roots, and as the undergrowth became denser, he wished he'd followed the river path. He emerged into a clearing where a sudden movement in a small copse of trees caught his eye. He ran to the side, fearful of disturbing a fox's den, but slowed when he saw a figure scrambling out of the bushes.

A woman stood directly in front of him. He recognised her immediately.

'Hey,' he said, edging sideways.

Cheryl Henry said nothing. She moved towards him. In her hand she was clutching a rusty knife.

He held up his hands. 'I'm not here to hurt you. I'm out for a run, that's all.'

'Liam's dead,' she said.

'I know, I've seen his body,' he replied. 'Hiding here won't help you. You need to talk to the police.'

'No,' she said, still moving forwards, 'but you could help me.'

He took two steps back.

'You always bought the good stuff. *None of the crap for Dr Lennon*, that's what Liam always said. You were happy to pay for the premium.'

'The best thing you can do right now is talk to the police.'

'Why would they listen to me? I'm a dealer, they'll be looking for any excuse to do me. But lucky for me, I'm *your* dealer. I need money to get away.'

'That's not going to happen.'

'I haven't hurt anyone!' she screamed.

'Cheryl, I understand that,' he replied, trying to keep his voice calm, 'but that's why it's best for you to speak to the police.'

She moved nearer. He knew he could outrun her if he needed to. 'If you turn yourself in, I can help you.'

'Dr Lennon, I didn't do anything wrong. Liam threatened Dr Jha after talking to some Indian at the pub.'

'Give yourself up and let me help.'

'Do you think I'm stupid?' She lifted the knife and charged towards him.

'Wait!' he shouted, but she kept running.

He turned to run, but his foot tangled on a tree root hidden beneath the fallen leaves. He stumbled. When he fell forward, Cheryl swung the knife.

CHAPTER 40

DS Parker hurried down the back stairs of his building, happy to leave behind his drab bedsit for another day. Sunday morning on the high street was quiet. He grabbed a cup of coffee, and with another hour until he was due on shift walked quickly up the hill. At the junction with the Upper Haddley Road, he turned towards East Haddley and the newly built apartment block, which neighboured the Underground station. A young couple were leaving the building, heading out for a weekend run, and he thanked the woman for holding the door. Inside, the windows gleamed, and the plush carpets maintained a smell of newness. Standing in front of the polished elevator mirror, he found himself checking his hair before the doors opened on the seventh floor.

Outside the apartment was a digital bell, but instead he tapped gently on the door.

'You brought me coffee, how sweet,' said Karen, greeting him.

'Sorry, I didn't think,' he replied.

She walked away. He stepped inside, silently pushing the door closed behind him.

'I wanted to check how you were doing?'

'I'm fine,' she replied, 'no thanks to you.'

'That's a bit harsh,' he said, following her into an open-plan living space, sleekly decorated with white furniture and glass fittings.

'You can sit down as long as you leave your coffee cup on the kitchen counter.'

He did as instructed. When Karen bent to sit on one of the white sofas, she twisted her arm, and he saw her wince. He took a seat opposite her.

'How's your cut?' he asked.

'Sore.' The blade of Cheryl Henry's knife had sliced into her upper arm. 'Four stitches.'

'I did try to warn you.'

Karen sighed. 'Don't worry, I'm not blaming you. Don't want to get you in trouble with the boss.'

He smiled nervously. 'Sorry you stumbled.'

She stared at him. 'What do you mean?'

'Cheryl didn't stab you. It was more a case of you falling forward onto the blade.'

'I was attempting to apprehend her, and she had a knife. Simple as that.'

He nodded. 'I'm good with that, if that's what you're saying.'

'It's what happened!'

'Absolutely, yes. She had a knife.' He felt the need to change the subject. 'This is a great place you've got.'

'I'm waiting for a new dining suite, but I'm pleased with it.'

'I bet the rent's not cheap?'

'I don't pay rent,' she replied. 'The flat's mine.'

'Really?' He failed to disguise the surprise in his voice. He struggled to pay the mortgage on his own two-bedroom terrace in Manchester, and the outrageous rent he paid for his dingy bedsit. Karen must be paying a fortune. 'You'll be hoping interest rates don't go up any time soon.'

'Are you here to quiz me on my household finances?'

'Sorry, no, I don't mean to pry. This is a lovely flat.'

'Thanks.' Karen curled her legs up on the sofa. 'The boss has signed me off for a week. I'm bored already. Hopefully I can find some way of filling my time.'

'I can keep you in the loop, on cases, if you like.'

'Why don't you pop around this evening? I'm sure I can rustle up some dinner.'

'Only if you're sure?'

'It's no trouble and it'll be a nice change for you. I promise it won't be barbeque chicken burgers.'

Parker leaned forward. 'It should only be dinner.'

'That's all I'm offering.'

'I've a wife and two kids.'

'And a kitchen with no proper food. Nobody would want you to go hungry.'

Parker felt his phone buzz. 'Shit,' he said.

CHAPTER 41

DS Parker bumped his car onto the pavement and stopped behind a London ambulance. Hurrying along the river path, ahead of him in the woods he could hear dogs barking. Police handlers were now assisting in the pursuit of Cheryl Henry. He approached a park bench and waited briefly as a paramedic treated George Lennon. The medical examiner inhaled sharply before biting his lip.

'Brave boy,' said the paramedic, who was old enough to be his mother. 'Are you up to date with your tetanus shots?' she asked.

He looked over his shoulder. 'What do you think?'

'You should get a booster course. Pop upstairs at the hospital and we'll sort you out.' She ripped a strip of fabric tape from a roll. 'This will be sore for a few days,' she said, applying the tape, 'but you were lucky. It's only a graze.'

'Thanks,' he said, pulling his torn running shirt back over his head.

The paramedic smiled at Parker as she packed her bag. 'He's all yours,' she said, getting to her feet. 'Good luck,' she said to Lennon, giving him a quick wink before she walked away.

DS Parker sat beside him on the bench. 'All patched up?' he asked.

'Not much more than a scratch.'

'Tell me what happened?'

Lennon explained how he'd run through Richmond Park, before cutting down towards the river and into the woods. 'I backed away from her, told her that her best option was to give herself up to the police.'

'You spoke to her?'

'Briefly.'

'How did you know who she was?' asked Parker.

'She had a knife in her hand. It didn't take a genius.'

'What happened next?'

Lennon paused. 'She asked me for my help.'

'In what way?'

When he shrugged, he flinched and pressed his hand against his shoulder. 'Money to get away, I guess. I don't know.'

'Had you met her before?'

Lennon held his arm and sighed. 'Let's say I've seen her around. That's probably as far as it goes.'

'At the Rose and Crown?'

The medical examiner pinched his lips. 'None of us are perfect, detective. I might like an occasional treat on a special night out.' He raised his eyes to Parker. 'Very occasional, of course.'

Parker scratched the back of his neck. 'Let's say she

recognised you, perhaps from the beer garden at the Rose and Crown. She thought you might help her leave the area. You rejected that suggestion by turning your back on her and she assaulted you with the knife?'

'Exactly,' replied Lennon, relieved at the detective's understanding.

'I'll need a written statement once you've been home and cleaned yourself up. Anything else?'

'She kept insisting she'd done nothing wrong.'

Parker smiled. 'Mr Lennon, everybody thinks they've done nothing wrong until they get caught.'

Lennon said nothing in reply and a uniformed officer appeared out of the trees.

'Sarge!' yelled PC Fidler.

Parker ran towards her. 'Have you found her?'

'The handlers have her cornered.'

He followed Fidler into the woods, scrambling through the undergrowth until they reached a small picnic area, which backed onto the riverbank. Two handlers, each with their animals straining, stood opposite Cheryl Henry. In her hand, she still clutched the knife.

'Keep those dogs away from me,' she screamed, frantically waving the knife. Parker could see she was aggravating the dogs.

'Cheryl, I want you to put the knife down on the ground in front of you,' said Parker.

'Not until you call the dogs off,' she replied, her terror-stricken eyes locked on the snarling animals.

He gestured to the dog handlers, and they pulled their animals away. 'There,' he said.

'Further!'

Taking a step towards her, he shook his head. 'Now, you drop the knife.'

She hesitated and looked quickly over her shoulder.

'Don't even think about running,' said Parker. 'The dogs would be on your back before you even reached the trees.' He gestured again for the handlers to retreat. 'You've nowhere else to go.'

Henry exhaled and her shoulders fell.

'Drop the knife,' said Parker.

She did as instructed. Parker ran forward and seized hold of her arms. Pushing her face down onto a wooden picnic table, he pulled her hands behind her back, locking her wrists in handcuffs.

'Cheryl Henry, I'm arresting you on suspicion of the murder of Liam Kane.'

CHAPTER 42

Pamela sat by the window in the living room, her cup of tea on the table beside her, and her breakfast plate in her hand. Two slices of her favourite walnut-and-raisin loaf, toasted and generously covered with thick-cut marmalade. Dr Jha would tell her she was eating too much sugar, but it was her Sunday treat and, besides, Pamela needed it today more than ever. Last night, Alan's fearful reaction had startled her. She'd left immediately after, Maggie knowing best how to calm her husband. Still, now she struggled to understand what triggered Alan's reaction. *I didn't change the time.* What could he possibly mean? What deep-seated memory had seeing Larry suddenly unearthed, and why now? Perhaps it was the sight of him standing beside the wife he so cherished. She wondered if Larry had visited the flat before. She understood what a heartbreaking task it was for Maggie to care for Alan. But she worried Larry appearing back in Alan's life, spending time with the wife he so patently adored and relied upon, would only make him more upset and confused.

After breakfast, she tidied her pots and popped them into the kitchen sink. A walk would help clear her head.

On the high street she called into the hardware store before following the turning onto Beyton Road. The ride up in the lift was no better than yesterday. Pamela was relieved to step out onto the fourth-floor landing and knocked on the door of flat 42. While she waited for Eileen to come to the door, she reached inside the hardware-store carrier bag.

'Peace offering,' she said, when the door opened, holding up a new lightbulb.

Eileen stared at her for a moment, and Pamela pointed to the darkened bulb in the hallway light. Eileen relaxed. 'You shouldn't have. Coming all this way, you really are too kind. You must be exhausted.'

'I enjoy a good walk,' replied Pamela, 'although it would be nice to rest my feet for a few minutes.'

Removing her steadying hand from the door, Eileen stepped slowly aside.

'I'm sorry if I upset you, yesterday,' said Pamela, entering the flat. 'That was the very last thing I wanted to do.'

'Oh no, you must think me very odd.' Eileen edged her way across the room.

'Not at all.'

'I shouldn't have sent you away like that. I enjoyed talking to you.'

Pamela smiled. 'I only mentioned the journalist as I'd read about her recently in the local paper.'

Eileen sat in her high-backed armchair and held her hands in her lap. 'It's thirty years since she died.'

'How awful,' replied Pamela. 'Such a terribly sad story. You knew her through the baking competition at the *Richmond Times*?'

'Yes, at the start of her career Alaka had to be willing to turn her hand to anything. Lucky for me, she had quite a sweet tooth. It was her who telephoned me to tell me I'd won. Soon after, she asked if I'd be interested in writing a weekly column and did I have enough recipes? I told her I'd make sure I did. For my first column I baked a Black Forest gateau with fresh cherries. Alaka took the photographs, and when she'd finished, we sliced into the cake over a cup of tea. I baked every Wednesday morning for six years, and, in the afternoon, she'd come and take pictures for the paper; just the cakes, never me. I'd write out the recipe along with a few baking tips – "Mrs Cooper's Cookery Course".'

'You really were years ahead of *The Great British Bake Off*.'

Eileen giggled. 'I suppose I was.'

'You and Alaka became friends?'

'In as much as she visited each week. Often it was for little more than twenty minutes, but we'd talk about what was happening in our lives. Dennis would come home on a Wednesday evening, and I'd serve him a slice of cake for his dessert. Not once did he say thank you or tell me how much he'd enjoyed it.'

Eileen glanced down, and Pamela's heart went out to her.

'You never told him you were writing the column?'

'He never would've allowed it.'

'How very sad,' replied Pamela.

'He'd have hated me receiving any attention.'

216

'And that's what happened when Alaka died?' Pamela watched Eileen squeeze her hands together, turning her fingers bright red. 'Suddenly you received lots of attention.'

'She was writing a series of articles for the paper and planned on writing one more.' Eileen closed her eyes.

'Alaka wanted to write about you?' asked Pamela, softly. She leaned over and touched Eileen's hand.

'I don't think Dennis ever realised what he was doing.'

Pamela wanted to tell Eileen not to apologise for her husband, but she knew that wasn't what Eileen needed to hear, so she simply said, 'He's not here any more.'

Eileen sighed. 'Somehow a Sunday newspaper found out my name. I told the police I knew nothing, but my secret was a secret no more. Dennis wasn't happy.'

Pamela hated to think what that meant.

'He despised our names appearing in the paper. I could understand why,' Eileen continued, her voice quiet. 'Much of what they wrote was untrue, or simply wasn't about us, but they didn't care. He told me not to go outside and not to speak to anyone again.'

'And you never spoke about Alaka again?'

Eileen shook her head. 'Not only did I never speak about Alaka again, other than Dennis, our son and his family, I never spoke to *anyone* again. Not until Dennis was dead, twenty-nine years later.'

217

CHAPTER 43

'He seems very sweet, if slightly chaotic,' says Dani, sitting on the threadbare sofa at the back of our kitchen. She's drinking a mug of tea. Her meeting with my dad hadn't been a long one, and he'd done little to hide his obvious shock at his imminent grandfather status. He'd disappeared upstairs for a shower soon afterwards.

'He can't stay here,' I say. 'Not with the baby due any minute.'

'It's not ideal, I agree, but it feels harsh to kick him out. He's come to see you and he's brought a bag.'

'He hasn't even said why he's here,' I reply. I cross the kitchen to make myself a fresh cup of coffee. '

'Whatever the reason,' says Dani, 'he's driven two hours through the night. We can't simply send him away.'

'He can stay for lunch.'

'How about we let him stay for one night? He can sleep in the loft room.'

'Nick's room?' I reply. The bedroom at the top of the house belonged to my brother. In the decade that followed his death, my mum left it almost untouched. In the years since, while I've gradually redecorated the rest of the house, I've also left Nick's room largely unchanged.

'Maybe it's time,' says Dani. 'Your dad being the first person to use it might be the right thing.'

I feel my old anger rising within me. It isn't directed at Dani but towards my father. Even so, I have to fight hard not to tell her she's wrong, and that she doesn't understand. I put the milk back in the fridge door and sit beside Dani.

'I know you're trying to do a nice thing, but having him here, as well as the baby, would be way too much for us both.'

'If you don't want him upstairs, why don't we offer him the sofa for tonight and go from there? Who knows, by tomorrow morning he might have decided to move on.'

'One night?'

Dani nods.

'Okay, agreed,' I say. When I hear him coming down the stairs, my skin bristles. Dani holds my hand.

'Feeling refreshed, Gordon?' she asks, when he enters the kitchen.

'You need a new shower head, Ben. I could fit one for you, if you like.'

'We're fine.'

'I used two towels out of the cupboard. They weren't very wet, so I folded them up and put them back where I found them.'

'I'll sort them out later,' replies Dani, smiling.

My dad reaches for his shoes before pulling out a chair from beside the island.

'Going out?' I ask him.

'With it being so mild, I think I might take a walk across the common, perhaps on to St Marnham.'

'That sounds nice,' replies Dani. 'Will you be back for lunch?'

'I thought we'd all go to the pub. My treat.'

'Dani's not going to sit in a pub all afternoon,' I say, snapping at my father.

'That's a kind thought, Gordon,' she adds, stretching her back, 'but I'm happier here right now.'

'What about you and me, Ben?'

'No!' I reply, my voice rising until Dani kicks me with her heel. 'Why don't I cook us something here?'

He climbs down from the chair.

'Would you like another drink, before you head out?' asks Dani.

'I had a glass of water in the bathroom.'

I glance towards Dani, but she refuses to catch my eye.

'Perhaps another hot drink?'

'I don't like too much caffeine. It keeps me awake all night.'

'You must have drunk a lot yesterday,' I say, my tone sharp, 'because you spent most of the night driving here.'

'Best time for driving,' he replies. 'You wouldn't believe how little traffic there is at four in the morning.'

I shake my head. Dani puts her hand on my arm, but it's too late. I can't take this any longer. 'Dad, you drove half the night. What the hell are you doing here?'

He stares at me blankly. 'To see you. After yesterday, I wanted to reassure myself you hadn't been hurt by the mad woman at the market.'

'You could've called.' I'm certain he's lying. My father only ever thinks about himself. There is a knock on our front door. 'Wait there,' I say to him, jumping to my feet.

I race out of the room and slide down the hallway tiles. 'George!' I say, opening the front door. With my father's arrival, I'd forgotten inviting him over for coffee.

'Not a good time?' he asks.

'Totally fine,' I reply. 'You'll get the chance to meet my father.'

He raises his eyebrows, and I lead him towards the kitchen. 'Dad,' I call, as we enter, 'This is an old friend of mine from sixth-form college.'

Dani is leaning against the island. The back door swings open and my father has already disappeared.

CHAPTER 44

DS Parker stood in the narrow corridor outside the Haddley police station interview rooms. Waiting for Chief Inspector Bridget Freeman to join him, he began to pace the airless space. The frenetic buzz of a bluebottle fly, trapped inside an ancient strip light, filled the hallway. Under the fluorescent glare, Parker felt increasingly claustrophobic.

Following the arrest of Cheryl Henry, Freeman had informed him of her intention to personally lead the interview process, and he'd tried to conceal his disappointment. He'd hoped to lead it himself. But, new to his role, and already indebted to the station's senior officer, he had no other option than to reluctantly accept her decision.

The door at the far end of the corridor clicked open.

'All set,' asked Freeman, approaching with a brisk step.

'Yes, ma'am,' he replied, instantly alert.

'We can't afford any further missteps, not where the Baxter family are concerned.'

He was hesitant in his response. 'Do you now believe the family was somehow involved with the Liam Kane murder?'

'As I said to you before, highly unlikely, but we need to see if Henry can offer us any other names further up the chain.'

'Yes, ma'am.'

'Which room?' she asked, looking at the four closed doors.

'Interview Room 2, ma'am.'

'Duty solicitor?'

'She's not someone I've met before, but yes, I think so,' he replied.

'Good, she'll be of little use to her.'

Freeman opened the door to the interview room, quickly introducing herself and her junior officer. Across the table, slumped in the corner, sat Cheryl Henry; the hood of her anorak pulled over her head. Alongside her, her young solicitor looked anxious as she leafed through her notes. After informing Henry her interview would be conducted under caution, Freeman edged her chair forward and smiled softly.

'All I want to do is understand what's happened,' she said.

'I didn't mean to hurt anyone.'

'But you did. One of my officers went to hospital for four stitches in her arm.'

'She ran towards me. I didn't stab her. It was her own stupid fault.'

'But you had a knife.'

Henry dropped her head.

'Why don't you and I see if we can work out exactly what did happen? Does that sound like a plan?' Henry didn't respond, but Freeman kept talking as if she was coaxing the truth from a child. 'Now, it's quite warm in here, so why don't you start by taking your hood down and slipping off your coat?'

After a brief pause, Henry did as Freeman asked her.

'You've got a glass of water for now,' continued the chief inspector, 'but after we've spoken why don't we get you a cup of tea?'

Henry gave a small nod. She really did seem like a child, Parker thought.

'Can you start by telling me where you live?'

Parker watched the suspect squirm uncomfortably in her chair. He could tell she was embarrassed to answer.

'Do you have a home, Cheryl?' asked Freeman.

'We've been living in the old Peacock boathouse.'

'By we, you mean you and Liam Kane?'

Henry sniffed. 'Yes. There's a little room upstairs, only tiny, but we called it our bedroom. Downstairs, at the back of all the racking, we made a table out of an upturned boat. That was our living room.'

'How long did you live at the boathouse?'

'Only for a week,' replied Henry. 'We were looking for another room, and Liam had some cash but—' She stopped herself.

'But what?'

Henry shook her head. 'But we could never afford a deposit or anything like that.'

'I see,' said Freeman. 'Before the boathouse, where did you live?'

Henry pulled on her lower lip before whispering to her solicitor. The woman nodded in response.

'We had a flat, with a kitchen and a bathroom, above Baxter's building supplies.'

'That sounds nice. Why did you leave?'

'They didn't need us any more. The flat kind of came with the job.' Henry's eyes darted towards Parker. 'His handy-work put paid to that.'

'You and Liam were employed in the distribution of street drugs in Haddley, St Marnham and Oreton?'

Henry sat upright in her chair. 'I'm not stupid,' she said. 'I know what you want me to say.' She tipped her head backwards. 'Liam and I did odd jobs in the yard, nothing more than that.'

Freeman responded with an exaggerated sigh. 'Come on, Cheryl. I thought you and I were working together. Let's not pretend DS Parker didn't see you dealing in the Rose and Crown yesterday afternoon.' Freeman leaned forward. 'Who was your contact?'

Henry hesitated. 'Don,' she said, after a moment. 'He runs the yard.'

Freeman looked at Parker. 'Do you mean Donald Trump?' he asked, remembering the heavy who threatened him with the metal pole.

'Is that his name?' replied Henry, oblivious to any other Donald Trump ever existing in the world. 'We only ever knew him as Don.'

Freeman glanced again towards her fellow officer, biting her lip to conceal a smile.

'Donald Trump was the only person working for the Baxter's you ever dealt with?'

Henry nodded, and Parker quickly realised they were travelling down the Baxter family chain of command, not up.

'Cheryl, you do understand you are in serious trouble?' asked Freeman.

'I didn't mean to hurt anyone,' she repeated.

'I know that's what you say, but if you are able to tell us about more senior figures within the Baxters' operation, or even have evidence against members of the family, this is the moment to say.'

Shaking her head, Henry turned to her solicitor. After a whispered exchange, Cheryl turned back to them.

'I honestly don't know anybody. I promise.'

Freeman leaned back in her chair and exhaled. Parker could see she was satisfied with Henry's response. 'Why don't you have a sip of your water and then tell me what happened after you moved out of the builder's yard? You found yourselves homeless. That must have been tough for you both?'

'Not much we could do about it,' replied Henry, putting her glass back on the table.

'I bet you were annoyed with Liam, for losing your lovely flat?'

'Wasn't his fault,' she replied, looking again at Parker.

'Moving into the boathouse can't have been easy?'

'We managed.' Henry pulled on a sore beneath her bottom lip.

'Cold and damp, no nice kitchen or bathroom. If I was you, I'd have felt fed up.'

'It wasn't great,' admitted Henry.

'I bet it wasn't. I imagine you were exhausted.'

'I hardly slept. We didn't have a proper bed.'

'Liam had got you into a right mess.'

'A bit.'

'Tired and angry, you argued. Of course you did, it was impossible not to. I understand that.'

Cheryl said nothing.

'By yesterday morning, you'd had enough, and you snapped. Another argument, but this time you couldn't stop yourself. You picked up the hammer and hit Liam. Hit him over and over until he was dead.'

'No!' Parker could hear the anger in Henry's voice. She turned to her solicitor. 'That's not what happened.'

Before the solicitor could respond, Freeman rested her hands on the table. 'Cheryl, regardless of what happened with Liam, you're facing some very serious charges. Assault on Dr Lennon, causing grievous bodily harm to a police officer, threatening Dr Jha with an offensive weapon. Now is the time to tell us exactly what did happen.'

CHAPTER 45

'We did argue, me and Liam.'

Cheryl Henry glanced nervously at her solicitor, but Freeman pressed on before she could clam up again.

'Yesterday morning?'

'No,' replied Henry, shaking her head vigorously, 'the day before. Late on Friday morning.'

'Why did you argue?'

Henry sucked on her fingers and bit on an already gnawed nail. 'I don't think either of us had really slept and we were hungry. We knew the food store in St Marnham village has those self-checkouts. Whenever there's a truck making a delivery, the staff are all distracted. We planned on nicking some sandwiches. We waited most of the morning. Once we'd got our food, Liam suggested we sit on a bench by the river.'

'That's when you argued?'

'We were looking at the flats on the opposite side of the river road. Liam pointed at a window on the fifth floor and told me that was where Dr Jha lived.'

'How did he know?'

'That's what I asked him. He said something stupid like a little bird told him. I realised we were sitting there for a reason. He showed me a note he was going to put on her car window. I snatched at it, but he ran over the road and disappeared up a side street. The note was a threat against Dr Jha.'

'What did you do?'

'Waited on the bench. I didn't want anything to do with it. Dr Jha's been good to me. She helped me with some meds and tried to get me onto a programme.' Henry laughed at herself. 'She did get me onto a programme, but surprise *surbloody-prise* I didn't go. I told him Dr Jha was a good person and to leave her alone. When he came back, I hit him.'

'On Friday afternoon at the surgery, you tried to warn her?' said Parker, picking up the questioning.

'That bitch behind reception wouldn't let me see her. I only wanted to tell her to keep away from Liam.'

'He followed her to Haddley Common on Friday night?'

Henry nodded. 'When he arrived back at the boathouse, I could smell the fumes from the burned-out car. I screamed at him. He told me to keep my bloody nose out. I said he was fucking stupid and that's when he flashed five hundred quid in cash. I told him I didn't want his money and left. That was the first night I slept in the woods.'

'Who paid Liam the five hundred pounds?' asked Parker.

Henry leaned back in her chair and folded her arms. 'I don't know.'

'I don't believe you,' he replied.

229

Henry flicked him her middle finger.

Parker slammed his hands on the table. Freeman reached across and held his arm. 'Cheryl,' she said, 'after you left the boathouse on Friday night, you slept in the woods, but I think you went back the following morning. Am I right?'

'Yes,' said Henry. She dropped her head and covered her eyes with her hands. The sharp pant of her breathing told Parker she was trying not to cry.

'What happened when you arrived back at the Peacock boathouse on Saturday morning?'

'I found Liam, with his head smashed in. There was blood everywhere.' Henry's breath caught in her throat.

'What did you do?' asked Freeman.

Henry lowered her hands from her face, looking again at her solicitor. The woman indicated she should keep talking. 'I picked up the hammer from beside his body. Then, I felt in his pocket for the five hundred quid, but the money was gone.'

CHAPTER 46

'Take it!' I say, throwing an old sweater across the kitchen to George. 'You've got a blood-stained rip in the back of your shirt!'

He pulls the top over his head. 'Thanks,' he replies. 'It was good of her to attack me when I was close enough to yours.'

'I can drop you back when you're ready.'

'Don't worry, I can jog back.'

Dani laughs out loud. 'A woman has just attacked you with a knife.'

'Not much more than a graze.'

'Let's see how you feel in the morning,' she replies, emptying a bag of carrots into the sink. 'I bet you'll be barely able to move.'

'I promise you, Dani, it's a superficial cut.'

'When we were at college, George sliced open the back of his thumb while opening a tin of tuna. Somehow, he still made a sandwich.'

'And I've got the scar to prove it,' he says, holding up his thumb. 'A high pain threshold.'

'You're mad,' laughs Dani.

George finishes his coffee. 'I should get going,' he says, opening the dishwasher and putting his cup on the top shelf.

'You're welcome to stay for a late Sunday lunch,' replies Dani, scraping carrots in the sink, 'although until Ben's dad shows his face, we've no idea what time we'll be eating.'

'I'm putting the roast in now. If he's not back in time, he'll go hungry. I've invited Sam over. At least he'll be grateful.'

'Thanks for the offer,' says George, smiling at Dani, 'but I need to go into the hospital this afternoon. I promised DS Parker I'd take a look at Liam Kane. After this morning, I want to keep on Parker's good side.'

'Or you could simply not buy drugs at the Rose and Crown,' she replies.

'Do you know a better place?'

'You know that's not what I meant.'

'It's only ever tiny amounts.'

'A tiny amount is too much.'

'Yes, Sarge,' replies George.

'Don't expect me to help you out when you get arrested.'

'The police wouldn't arrest me for that, would they?'

'I wouldn't be too sure,' says Dani. 'Don't plan on popping around to visit the baby if you're introducing such bad behaviour.'

'I promise I'll do my best to be good.' He kisses Dani on the cheek.

'Are you expecting to learn anything from the Kane post-mortem?' I ask.

'Doubt it,' he replies. 'What's your theory?'

'I'm a journalist. I don't have theories, I report the truth.'

'Bollocks,' he replies. 'You always have a theory.'

'On that, George, I think we can agree,' adds Dani.

I hold my hands up guiltily. 'When Cheryl spoke to you, she insisted she hadn't hurt anyone?'

George nods. 'Yes, and I believed her.'

'Why?'

'No point in her lying to me, not then.'

'True. So, she must have come back to the boathouse, found Kane and picked up the hammer?'

'Which she took to the farmers' market to warn Dr Jha,' adds Dani.

'In the woods, right before she hit me,' says George, 'Cheryl said Liam threatened Dr Jha *after talking to some Indian in the pub.*'

I reach for my phone. 'Which pub?'

'The Rose and Crown.'

I click on Uma's contact details and wait for her to pick up.

'Ben?' she says, answering her phone.

'Uma, the only reason Liam Kane set light to your car was because somebody paid him to do it. In the days before he threatened you, he met with someone of Indian heritage at the Rose and Crown pub in Oreton.'

There's silence on the line.

'Uma?'

'My father drinks in that pub.'

Six

Manish Jha

'Spending more time alone in his house, haunted by reminders of the life he might have led. It was his unfulfilled dreams he feared the most.'

He eased himself down into his favourite chair. He'd sat in the same concealed corner of the same pub and drunk the same beer for over thirty years. Throughout that time, he'd lived in the same house and made the same fifteen-minute walk to work each day. He'd bought his home with his wife; a place to raise a family together, but instead he'd spent thirty years alone. With his sixty-eighth birthday approaching at the end of the month, he knew the university would again ask him about his retirement plans. Perhaps he would like to take the opportunity to reduce his working hours? He struggled to think of anything worse. Spending more time alone in his house, haunted by reminders of the life he might have led. It was his unfulfilled dreams he feared the most.

From an ice-cold bottle, he poured a Kingfisher beer into a small glass; a bead of liquid ran slowly down the side. When he took his first sip, he didn't notice a tattered beermat stuck to the bottom of the glass. He stared at his phone and read an email he'd received the previous evening from a second-year student. She'd sent him a link to a newly published article on his wife's murder. Alongside the link, she'd asked him a direct question. 'Were any witnesses, from thirty years ago, available to corroborate his alibi at the time of the killing?' He'd chosen not to dignify her question with a response.

He took another drink from his glass. The same student had

237

now sent him a second email. His failure to respond to her initial enquiry had proved 'unsatisfactory', leaving her with 'nascent concerns around the domestic dynamic between him and his late wife'. He felt enraged but typed only a short reply. He told her leaving the course was her prerogative before wishing her well with her future endeavours. He'd had no knowledge of his daughter Uma's intention to support the publication of the article. Part of him wished she'd come to him first but he recognised he had no right to expect that. The gulf between them during her childhood years had established the foundation of their distant adult relationship. He thought back to Uma as a young child, before Alaka's death. She'd been so bright and quick-witted. Her mother's daughter in every respect. That was part of the problem. She reminded him of Alaka, and those memories overwhelmed him.

CHAPTER 47

Even early on a Sunday afternoon, the traffic on the main road into Oreton is heavy. At the junction with the university hospital, I sit and watch the same red light change for a second time. Beside me, Uma stares out of the window as two students cut across the congestion, bump their bicycles onto the pavement and race onto the college campus. Lost in her own thoughts, I'm not sure Uma even notices them.

Ahead of us on the left is the Rose and Crown pub. Uma's eyes drift towards its walled beer garden, surely once again packed with lunchtime revellers. 'It's the next right,' she tells me, bringing her attention back to the road.

We turn onto an unremarkable 1970s side street, where red brick, terrace homes fill each side of the road. Some of the houses are neatly kept, their gardens filled with brightly coloured flowers and meticulously maintained squares of lawn. Others are more run-down, paint peeling from wooden garage doors and grass left to grow almost to the height of front windows.

'My father hated it when buy-to-let investors started

purchasing houses on his street. Suddenly, the students he taught during the day were also his neighbours in the evening,' Uma tells me. She points to the left side of the street. 'His house is right at the very end.'

I stop my car outside her father's house, where a brightly coloured row of tulips stands sentry beside the gate.

'He and my mother bought this house because of its garden. The space in the back is twice the size of most others. As a child, I can remember him toiling silently for hours, tending to his flowerbeds while I sat in the shade and read.'

'Are you sure you want me to go in with you?'

'I asked you to come as I need to find a way to make him understand. This is his opportunity to speak to us, before he's faced with the police. I don't believe it was him, Ben. But I also know that there's a lot he isn't telling me.'

At the door to her childhood home, Uma stops. She looks through the front window, where four wooden slat-back chairs are tucked neatly beneath a cloth-covered dining table. 'From the age of seven, every night I'd sit with my father and eat dinner at that table, almost always in silence. Once we'd cleared our plates, he'd retreat to his study to grade papers, and I would hurry upstairs to my room. Every night was the same.'

Uma knocks on the glass front door. When her father appears in the hallway, he looks at her and stops. For a moment, I wonder if he will open the door, but eventually he steps forward and turns the latch.

'I wasn't expecting you until later,' he says, greeting his daughter.

'It's not our usual Sunday time, but I need to speak with you,' she replies.

He keeps his hand resting on the door latch and looks directly at me.

'Your husband isn't with you?' he asks.

'Edward's in Leamington. He sends you his best.'

'Professor Jha,' I say, 'I'm Ben Harper.'

'Ben's a friend of mine,' adds Uma. 'He works as—'

'A journalist.' Manish Jha's expression is stern.

'Please, Dad, I want you to hear what he has to say.'

Professor Jha steps aside. Clasping his hands behind his back and holding his shoulders upright, he leads us into his living room. With a polished floor, light-coloured walls and dark wooden furniture, the room is carefully maintained. Outside is a small patio area, where a bright umbrella stands above a wrought-iron table.

'I was working in the garden,' he tells us, gesturing towards a stack of papers sitting beneath a large glass jug. He takes a step down onto the patio.

'Dad, be careful,' says Uma, as her father steadies himself, resting his hand on the back of a chair.

'Please,' he says, offering us a seat. 'May I pour you a drink of lime water?'

'Let me get some glasses,' says Uma.

'I am not so decrepit,' he replies, reaching for the door handle to pull himself up and back inside. His tall, narrow frame appears frail; his once thick hair now thin.

Sitting next to me, Uma leans across. 'He refuses to admit how much the chemo slows him down.'

241

'How's he doing?'

She tilts her head to one side. 'Pretty well, but he's stubborn and won't cut down on his schedule, which is madness.'

Professor Jha returns to the table and serves us both a drink.

'You're eating properly? You know that's important.'

'Always. If I don't feel like cooking, I go to the pub.'

'I hope not to drink too much.'

'This is lovely,' I say, drinking from my glass and interrupting the conversation.

'Uma's mother's recipe.' Professor Jha takes the seat opposite me. 'What is it you've come to tell me, Mr Harper?'

'Dad, Ben wrote an article last week, on Mum's thirtieth anniversary.'

'A student sent me a link. I was able to read it for myself. I'm sorry you didn't feel able to speak to your father before you spoke to a journalist.'

'Dad, let's not do this now. I didn't want to pass up the opportunity of the anniversary.'

Professor Jha lifts his hands. 'As you can see, I have work to do. If you have something to tell me, please go ahead.'

'I want you to listen,' says Uma.

Her father looks at me and waits. I explain to him our aim in publishing the anniversary article was to seek out potential new witnesses. The subsequent threats against Uma were an unexpected and not very pleasant consequence.

'But you tell me the man is now dead?' he asks. 'The man who threatened Uma.'

'Yes,' I reply.

'Good.'

'But Dad, the police are now questioning his girlfriend. If somebody paid him to make the threats against me, she might be able to identify who that was. Do you understand? Whoever that was, the police will arrest.'

'The girlfriend is no concern of mine.'

'Dad! You're not listening,' exclaims Uma, her frustration with her father showing. She pushes back her chair, the metal grating against the patio tiles. 'Cheryl Henry claims an Indian man at the Rose and Crown paid Liam Kane to threaten me.'

Professor Jha stares at his daughter.

'So, you come to me? My own daughter, making accusations. How dare you?' He flings his arms forward, sending the glass jug crashing onto the stone patio.

CHAPTER 48

I jump quickly to my feet. 'Let me get something to clear this up.'

'In the cupboard beneath the stairs, there is a brush,' Professor Jha instructs me. I step into the living room, but immediately hear him turn to Uma.

'You are still my daughter! You bring this man here and you start accusing me?'

'No, Dad, I'm just trying to understand. I'm not accusing you, but you've never told me anything about the time before Mum's death.'

'You are too young to remember the threats made against your mother. I begged her, but still she refused to stop her campaigning.'

'When the threats worsened, why didn't she stop?'

'I do not know.' For a moment there is silence, until he continues. 'It felt as if she was determined to put herself in danger.'

'Do you really believe that? Mum's work gave women a voice.'

'Uma, this must stop now. I will not go through it again.'

'Dad, it's too late. I won't stop until I know the truth, and neither will the police.'

In a hallway cupboard crammed full of boxes, I find a plastic sweeping brush and pan. When I walk back into the living room, Uma has resumed her seat next to her father.

'Whatever I'm asking, the police will ask you far worse.'

'I did not pay a man to terrorise you. Is that what you want me to say? Uma, how little do you think of me?'

'You're my father. I never believed that.'

'Yet you still ask me the question.'

'Because you've not been honest with me. If her life was in danger, why was my mother so determined to continue?'

When I step back outside the pair are silent.

'Let me do that.' Uma takes the brush from me. She bends beneath the table to sweep the glass. 'Ben, will you tell him the police will want to speak to him?'

I sit on the edge of my chair. 'Professor Jha, I'm sorry for invading your home, but Uma asked me for help. What seems certain is somebody paid Liam Kane to threaten Uma in the same way as somebody threatened your wife thirty years ago.'

'I was not that man.'

Sitting across from Professor Jha, I have no reason to disbelieve him. Like Uma, he has endured sadness throughout much of his life. To cope, he has withdrawn into his own small space, keeping away from the outside world.

'Cheryl Henry has suggested an Indian man, at the Rose

and Crown, paid Liam Kane. Do you have any idea who that might be?'

Uma puts down the brush and sits beside me. 'Dad?' Her voice is soft. 'We're here to help.'

Professor Jha shakes his head. 'This girl says an Indian man paid her boyfriend. There are almost two million British Indians. To that, we can add at least one and a half million of Pakistani origin as I assume this girl fails to differentiate ethnic heritage.'

'Dad, that's not the point. It was in the Rose and Crown!'

'We are a diverse group in Oreton.'

Uma leans back in her chair and, folding her arms, twists away from her father. 'You're impossible. You don't want help.'

We sit in silence until I turn to Uma. 'I think I should go. I'll leave the two of you to talk.'

She touches my hand. 'Thank you for coming. I'm sorry my father wasn't more receptive.'

'Come over to the house this evening, if you can,' I say.

'I will.'

I offer my hand to Professor Jha, and he dismisses me with a cursory handshake. Inside, and with the sun shining on the living room, for the first time I notice a fine layer of dust covering the polished floor, scuffs on the light-coloured walls and scratches on the dark wooden furniture. Behind me, I hear Professor Jha speak to his daughter.

'I could have been a better father to you, but without your mother, perhaps I didn't know how. I did everything possible to protect her, but she was steadfast in her determination to continue. Despite constant pressure from our family, I never failed to support her.'

I stand in the hallway. By the front door hangs a faded photograph of the Jhas' wedding day. Inside the tight family group, I can't help but wonder what secrets still remain.

CHAPTER 49

'I want you to take my arm,' said Pamela, as she stood beside the table in her favourite Haddley coffee shop.

Eileen didn't need a second invitation, pulling herself up from a deep-seated chair. 'I've never had such a tasty cup of coffee,' she said to her new friend, 'but I can't get over the price. Nearly four pounds a cup. Are you sure I can't give you something?'

'No, I told you this was my treat,' replied Pamela, as arm in arm the two elderly women walked out of the shop. On her way out, Pamela waved to the woman behind the counter, who was never too busy to stop for a chat whenever she called in.

'Next time, I must treat you,' said Eileen, as they walked slowly down the high street.

'Don't be silly,' she replied. 'You've already spoiled me with your delicious homemade cakes.'

'You are such a kind person.'

Hearing of the desperately lonely life Eileen had led,

Pamela's immediate response had been to take her out of the four walls of her home to enjoy the simplest of pleasures. When they ordered their drinks in the artisan coffee shop, Pamela watched Eileen's confusion at the different array of refreshments on offer, and realised that not once had she even been out for a cup of coffee.

'I don't know how you can call that progress!' said Eileen, pointing to a line of six empty double-decker buses edging their way up Haddley High Street. Over coffee, Eileen had complained to Pamela how Haddley had changed over the years, but Pamela had told her it was impossible to stand in the way of progress.

'I didn't say everything was perfect,' she replied, laughing, as they turned back onto Beyton Road. 'There are a lot of things I miss, but none of us can live in the past.'

Eileen was silent. Given a chance to live her life over, Pamela felt certain Eileen would embrace the opportunity. Or would she? Had Dennis so destroyed all remnants of her self-esteem, it was impossible for her to imagine any other existence? Pamela resolved, in whatever time Eileen might have left, to help her enjoy life's smallest pleasures.

'Why don't you come to my house for supper tomorrow night?' she said. 'Nothing fancy, I can't cook like you, but it would be lovely for me to have a little company other than the television.'

'Oh no, I couldn't do that. I would never dream of going out in an evening, not in the dark.'

'How about lunch? You've entertained me royally at your home and it's only right that I reciprocate.'

'Only if you're sure,' Eileen said, uncertainly. 'But how will I even get to yours?'

'I've a dear friend who I'm sure will collect you, but if for some reason he can't I will send you an Uber.'

'An Uber?' asked Eileen.

Pamela shook her head. This really was going to be a long education. 'A taxi, but these days everyone calls them Ubers.'

They stood on the footpath in front of the concrete monstrosity. 'If you can walk with me to the lift, I'll be fine from there,' said Eileen.

'Of course.' Throughout the morning, Pamela had fought with a question bouncing around in her mind. Approaching the lift, she slowed. 'Eileen,' she said, 'on the afternoon of her murder, Alaka came to see you.'

Eileen stopped. 'I want to trust you, Pamela,' she said, looking at her friend.

'You can.'

'Then, ask your question.'

'Can you remember what you talked about?'

'We'd spoken a lot in the past about me and Dennis and our life together. She was very understanding, but I'd nothing more to tell her. I'd always enjoyed talking about the times when I'd worked and how different my life had been.'

'Back when you had the pubs?'

'Yes, but we'd also spoken about the job I had when I was older. Do you remember? I told you Dennis said we needed more money before he could retire?'

'Yes, I remember,' replied Pamela, although she wasn't sure she did.

250

'For eight months, I got up at three o'clock in the morning, six days a week, to work in the kitchens at the Mickelside Military Training Centre. That's what Alaka asked about that Friday afternoon.'

CHAPTER 50

'I'm hungry,' says Alice, spinning on a chair beside our kitchen island, her legs flying out in front of her.

'Come on, let's eat,' I say to Dani and Holly, sitting together on the sofa at the back of our kitchen, deep in conversation. 'I'm not waiting for him any longer. If he re-appears, he can eat the leftovers.'

I carry a roast chicken from the oven and onto the island. There's still no sign of my father.

'I need three Yorkshire puddings,' Alice immediately tells me.

'Me too,' adds Sam.

'If you eat three, Sam, you'll get fat.'

'Alice!' says her mum. 'Don't be so rude.'

'I'm not being rude.'

'I thought you were having three?' says Sam.

'I run around all the time. I need them for energy.'

He laughs.

'I think you'll find,' says Dani, 'that Sam runs around all the time chasing stories.'

'Are you a journalist, like Ben?'

'I write in a newspaper.'

'That's quite old-fashioned,' replies Alice. 'I'm going to be a detective, like Dani. I won't need any help from you.'

'Is that what you think journalists do, help the police?' I ask my goddaughter, as I carve our very late Sunday lunch.

'You're always helping Dani,' she replies.

'Ben's sometimes more of a hindrance than a help,' says Dani.

'Two Yorkshires for everybody to start,' I say, 'and when everyone's eaten up, we can see who's still hungry.'

'The baby will eat one for Dani,' Alice replies. She leans across and rests her head on Dani's stomach. 'You're so lucky to have Ben as your daddy,' she says. 'He makes delicious lunches, reads stories and is good at football. And he plays games.'

Dani smiles. 'I play games as well.'

'Yes,' replies Alice, thinking, 'you do. And you're quite good at them but I do win nearly every time.'

'Can you manage to cut your chicken?' asks Holly to her daughter.

'Yes,' she replies instantly.

'Get cracking, then.'

'I am,' replies Alice, biting into a Yorkshire pudding.

'Who does your father still know in Haddley?' asks Sam.

'Nobody that I know of,' I reply. 'He's not the keeping-in-touch type.'

'When did you last see him? Before he turned up here this morning, I mean.'

'The night I was arrested and questioned by Dani,' I reply, remembering a time soon after we met, when I investigated my mum's death.

'We had to explore every avenue,' she says, smiling.

'Were you in prison, Ben?' asks Alice, her eyes wide and her ears always listening.

'No, he wasn't in prison,' says Dani. 'We just had to ask him some questions.'

'Had he been naughty?'

Dani laughs. 'A little bit, I think, yes.'

'Don't you believe her, Alice, I'm never naughty.'

Alice studies my face. 'You are sometimes,' she tells me. 'You let Max score a goal when you could have stopped him. I know you did!'

'He was too speedy for me,' I reply.

Alice keeps her bear-like stare fixed upon me as she eats another Yorkshire pudding.

'When you weren't arrested,' says Holly, 'what made your dad appear?'

'Read about me online. That's how we keep in touch, apparently.'

Dani touches my arm. 'He's never going to win dad of the year, but Ben's not in the running for son of the year either.'

'I said he could stay tonight,' I reply to Dani.

'He's a bit lost and doesn't quite know how to express himself. Deep down I think he's a kind man.'

'It's good to be kind, Ben,' says Alice. 'Mrs Foster says we should always be kind. Can I have another Yorkshire?'

I pop another pudding on her plate.

'And one for me!' adds Sam.

I drop one on his plate. Alice leans across, rubs his tummy and smiles.

'Why's he here now?' asks Holly.

I shrug. 'He turned up unannounced a little after five this morning and still hasn't told us why.'

'Give him time,' says Dani.

'Dani will get it out of him,' says Alice, not looking up from her meal.

I smile at Holly, and she mouths to me, *Always listening*. Behind me, I hear a rattle at the back door. I jump down off my stool and turn the key.

'Dad, where've you been?'

Wearily, he steps into the kitchen.

'Gordon, come and sit down and have something to eat,' says Dani. 'There's plenty left.'

Across the kitchen island, both Alice and Sam eye my father suspiciously.

'I needed time on my own to think,' says my dad, still standing by the door. 'I walked to St Marnham. After the attack, yesterday, I wanted to see the surgery car park.'

'Dad, I told you, it's done.'

'I wish it was,' he replies, walking to the back of the kitchen.

'We should go,' says Holly, quietly standing up.

'No!' cries Alice.

Holly picks up her daughter.

I lift my hand. 'It's fine.'

Alice smiles and slips back into her chair. 'We haven't had pudding.'

My dad slumps onto the sofa. Dani goes to sit beside him.

'Gordon?' she says. 'What's bothering you?'

'I read about the attack online, on the BBC News app.'

Dani nods. 'It must have been a worry for you.'

'Yes, it was. Seeing Ben and Uma together, it brought everything back.'

The kitchen is silent.

'What do you mean?' I say. There must be anger in my voice because Dani turns to look at me.

'Do you know Dr Jha?' she asks quietly, turning back to my father.

He looks up, glancing at all the faces around the kitchen.

'Gordon?' repeats Dani.

He shakes his head. 'No, I don't know her, but thirty years ago, I was in love with her mother.'

CHAPTER 51

Pamela opened the back door of her Haddley Hill home, and then hurried back to the oven, wafting the steam from its open door. Back at her cooker, she lifted the lid on her ancient roasting tin and looked at the crispy roast potatoes inside. She pulled off one tiny corner for a quick taste.

'Delicious!' she said to herself.

She put the roasting tin back in the oven and quickly heated her gravy. With only her fingers, she nipped her broccoli from the steamer, plating it alongside her pork chop. When the gravy was warm, she added the roast potatoes and sat down at her kitchen table to enjoy the meal she most looked forward to each week.

Her favourite radio station was playing quietly in the background. Hearing 'Vienna' reminded her of a time when she was so happy, dancing the last dance with Thomas. When he'd held her in his arms and they'd talked about their dreams for the future. Now, she only ever dreamed of the past. Still, she treasured all her memories.

She found her mind drifting back to Eileen. How

different her life might have been if she'd allowed herself to follow her own dreams. Seeing her now so pale and timid, it was impossible not to want to help her. That must have been how Alaka felt. Questions swirled in Pamela's head. What interested her in Eileen's time at the Mickelside Military Training Centre? And did it somehow link to whoever Alaka met next that fateful Friday evening?

Pamela felt exhausted and couldn't think any more. She put her kettle on to boil and dropped a teabag into the green-and-white china teapot Dani and Ben had bought for her last birthday. She poured milk into a matching jug, and while putting the carton back into the fridge she reached for her Gu chocolate mousse. A Sunday evening treat, even though she knew what Dr Jha would say. Quickly filling her teapot, she placed everything on her tray and carried it through to the living room. After setting the tray down on her small coffee table, she plumped up the cushions on her sofa and eased herself down. She'd saved the last two episodes of her favourite Harlan Coben thriller on Netflix for this evening. But she had barely opened the menu on the screen when her phone rang.

Who was calling at this time? She stepped into her slippers and hurried through to the hallway. Pulling her phone from the pocket of her coat, she saw it was Maggie calling.

'Hello,' she said, 'you've just caught me. I was settling down for an evening of crime.' Pamela stepped backwards and sat down on the second step of her stairs. 'How are you today?'

'Oh, Pamela,' said Maggie, her voice cracking.

'Maggie, what is it?' she replied, hearing her friend struggling for breath. 'Are you okay?'

'No,' said Maggie, sobbing. 'Alan's dead.'

CHAPTER 52

I look up at the ceiling.

'Ben, will you sit down?' says Dani, as I pace our living room.

'I can hear him creeping about upstairs.'

'Give him a few more minutes.'

'He had a shower this morning. Why he needed another after walking to St Marnham and back is beyond me.'

'Perhaps he wanted some time alone to gather his thoughts.'

'Isn't that what he was doing all morning?'

'Ben, you're not being fair.'

'He's just told us he was in love with Alaka Jha and I'm the one not being fair.' After revealing his love for Uma's mother, my father said nothing more and disappeared upstairs. Alice and Sam both devoured sizeable portions of cheesecake, before Holly whisked Alice off home.

'Did Alaka ever mention him?' I ask Sam.

'Not once.' He's sitting in the armchair by the window, a small glass of whisky in his hand. 'When he says he was in love with her, you don't think he was stalking her in some way?'

'Sam,' says Dani, a slight reprimand in her tone. 'Gordon is Ben's father.'

'Who, a few weeks after Alaka's murder, left Haddley, abandoning his wife and family.'

I perch on the arm next to Sam. 'He's my father, but I can't vouch for him. I barely know the man.'

'We shouldn't speculate,' says Dani. 'Let's wait to hear him out.'

The only sound in the room is my father shifting about upstairs. 'This is ridiculous,' I say after a minute. 'I'm going to bring him down.'

'Leave him,' replies Dani.

We fall silent again and I crack my knuckles. Sam puts his hand on my back. 'You should get yourself a drink,' he says, sipping from his glass. 'You're even making me tense.'

I lean back on the arm of his chair. 'While Dani's not drinking, neither am I.'

'Next thing is you'll tell me you've got sympathy pains. You'll be having contractions before Dani.'

She bursts out laughing. 'Sam, don't be mean. Ben couldn't have been more supportive.'

'More thoughtful than you ever were, that's for sure,' I say, gently punching his arm.

'The last thing Madeline's mother would've wanted was me anywhere near the delivery room. It was one of the very few things we agreed upon.'

I listen for any sounds of my father coming downstairs. 'He's gone quiet.'

'Do you think he's okay?' asks Dani.

'I'm going up,' I reply.

'Stay calm,' she says, as I leave the room.

When I'm halfway up the stairs, I quietly call to my father. There's no reply. I go quickly from room to room but find no sign of him. I stand at the foot of the staircase that leads up to my brother's old loft bedroom.

'Dad, are you up there?' I say. When I reach the top of the stairs, the door to Nick's room is standing open.

'Hey,' I say. My father is sitting on the single bed that belonged to his eldest son.

'The room has hardly changed.'

More and more, Dani and I have used Nick's room for storage, but I've left his bed and desk untouched.

'Two days after your brother's death, I came back here. I'd left your mother five years earlier, but she didn't hesitate in inviting me back inside her home.'

I sit beside my father.

'Her grief was so raw, all that had passed between us was briefly forgotten. Even at a time of such horror, it was a kindness I didn't deserve.'

'Why did you leave Mum?'

He sniffs, rubbing his nose with the back of his hand. 'Because she finally realised what a shit I was. Your mum and I had made it to ten years together, but I'd already cheated on her a handful of times. Some she knew about, some she didn't. Each time she did find out, I begged her to take me back. Your mother was the only woman I loved, until Alaka.'

I lean forward on the edge of the bed and stare at the floor. 'What happened, Dad?'

'When your mum and I first bought this house, I sold advertising space in tabloid newspapers. At times it was a brutal job. We had to fill every space, in every edition, whatever it took. It was a young man's game, hard selling and hard drinking. I found it soul destroying, but the bonuses could be huge. Each day, I'd watch journalists go up and down Fleet Street and I convinced myself I could do what they did. I signed up for an evening course in journalism at the university in Oreton.'

'Where Alaka taught?'

My father nods. 'She was a brilliant teacher. After only a couple of weeks on the course, I quit my job. I was nothing if not impulsive. I had no real hope of a job in journalism and instead ended up travelling the country selling sports shoes.

'I did finish the course. Most of the other students were kids, so each week after her lecture Alaka and I started meeting for coffee, or the occasional drink. We became friends, Ben, that's all; shared in each other's dreams. When the course finished, we kept in touch. Increasingly, I could see she wasn't happy.

'She adored being a mum but loved her career as well. If I was being generous, I'd say her husband's family didn't think that was possible. So many times, she told me to follow my dreams and not let anybody stand in my way. It was impossible not to love her, Ben. She was so kind, so special.'

My eyes are still fixed on the floor. I can't bring myself to look at him. I am thinking of my mum, how kind she was, how special.

'Did she . . . ' I begin.

'Did she love me? I don't know. Perhaps I offered her hope, that she might live a different life, but no, I don't think she ever really loved me.'

'I'm sorry, Dad.'

His smile is a wry one. 'A bit like Sylvie, she was too good for me.' He puts his hand on my shoulder. 'And your mum. I've ended up with everything I deserve.'

'You came back now because of Alaka?'

'Like I said, I read all your articles online.'

'Last week you read the anniversary piece.'

Downstairs, I hear our front door open and close and remember inviting Uma over this evening.

'I went to my local Asda to fill up my car with fuel. While I was waiting to pay, in front of me in the queue, were a little boy and his father. The boy might've been eight or nine, I don't know, but he was chatting away about school, and football and playing in goal, and his dad was talking back to him, and the boy was laughing. I never knew how to do that, Ben. We never talked or chatted or laughed, and I feared if I came back, I wouldn't know what to say.'

'But Dad, I'm not a kid any more. We can talk.'

He shrugs. 'Maybe,' he says quietly.

'What changed your mind?'

'I went home. The next day I read about the attack in the

264

surgery car park. That's when I knew, however difficult, I had to come back. For you, and for Uma.'

'She's here now,' I say, 'downstairs.'

'I'd like to see her,' he replies.

'You'll need to tell her everything you know.'

'That's why I'm here.'

CHAPTER 53

I stand with my father at the foot of the stairs.

'Are you sure you're ready to do this?'

He nods.

'Drink?'

'Maybe later.'

He follows me into the living room.

'Hello, Uma,' he says.

She stands to greet him. 'Thank you for coming. Dani told me how close you were to my mother.'

'I've waited far too long to say this, but I'm so desperately sorry about what happened to your mum. She was such a special person.'

I can see Uma is unsure how to respond. 'Why don't we all sit down?' I say. 'Dad, we're all very grateful to you for coming back to Haddley. One of the things we're trying to understand is, could the articles Alaka wrote in the weeks before her death somehow link to her murder?'

'She led so many campaigns. After writing about that poor woman . . . I don't remember her name.'

'Fiona Nicholls,' says Sam.

'Yes, that's her,' replies my father. 'Alaka reported on the trial of her partner. It affected her, especially when so many other women reached out to her, and that led to her final series of articles. She was determined to give those women a voice. The stories felt incredibly personal to her.'

From the corner of my eye, I can see Sam nodding, but he remains silent.

'Those articles did a huge amount of good, but they also created a backlash,' I say. 'Somebody made threats against Alaka. Did she ever talk about the threats or how they made her feel?'

He speaks directly to Uma. 'Your mother spoke openly about the letters she received. Whoever made the threats delivered the first two directly to your parents' home. Another was left on your mother's car. Your parents had an awful argument. Your father was desperately concerned. He wanted Alaka to leave her job.

'I'd never seen her so angry. She felt trapped. She needed time away, time on her own without pressure from family, to think. I said I'd help in any way I could. Two days later, you and your mum moved into the house three doors down from here.'

Uma covers her mouth.

'A retired couple owned the house. They were away for several months, travelling the world, and had left the keys with Ben's mother and me.'

Uma looks at me. 'Holly's house?'

I nod and my father continues. 'You both stayed in the

267

house for a week, maybe a day or two more. The threats continued, but if your mother was afraid, she never let it show.'

'How did she react when the final threat was delivered to the *Richmond Times*?' asks Uma. 'The week before she was murdered.'

'With anger, but also exasperation. She was frustrated by the whole situation. I pretty much kept away from the house. When we did talk, and I suggested one day we might leave together, she told me I was a dreamer. Deep down, I knew it was your father she wanted to be with.'

Uma hesitates. 'Did she ever believe the threats might have come from him?'

'I don't think so, no. She told me she belonged with her husband. We had lunch together the day before she died. She said she was moving back home the following morning. I told her I'd never get over her.'

'I'm sorry, Gordon,' says Dani, quietly.

'When I went into the house the next morning, she was gone. All that was left was her diary, dropped under the dining-room table. I popped it in an envelope and posted it to her home.'

'Her diary?' I ask.

'Where she wrote her appointments, that kind of thing. She'd worked in the dining room and somehow it got left behind.'

'You sent it to Alaka's home?' asks Sam.

'Yes.'

'If only you'd sent it to the paper.'

'I didn't know your address.'

'Dad, that last week, when Alaka and Uma were staying here on the common, the threats became so vile, Sam went to the police.'

'Yes, he did,' replies my father.

'Even at that point, Alaka wasn't afraid?'

'She refused to let anyone intimidate her. Whenever I asked, she dismissed the threats as nothing more than cranks. Her resolve was ironclad. I felt scared, but not her.'

'Why wasn't she afraid?' asks Dani. 'Most people would be terrified.'

Uma looks at her, then back to my father. 'Unless,' she says quietly, 'she already knew who the threats were coming from.'

CHAPTER 54

Alan was dead. Pamela could scarcely believe it. The words echoed in her head as she approached Haddley Hill. Thomas's best man, one of her last connections to him, was gone. She'd promised Maggie she'd be with her as quickly as she could. Her dearest friend, suddenly alone in the world, needed her. Making her way up the hill, she remembered the wonderful times the four had enjoyed together. A picnic on the beach in Malta, swimming in the sea, splashing in the waves. Drinks by the river in Haddley, dancing in the boathouse bar. Every memory filled with laughter.

On the call, Maggie had explained that Alan had become increasingly distracted after their Sunday lunch. Convinced it was nighttime, he'd been determined to get into bed. She'd been unable to persuade him otherwise and joined him in their bedroom. Lying side by side, Alan holding her hand, he'd slowly drifted into a deep sleep. Her husband seemed at peace, so Maggie had slipped her hand away and made her way down to the garden. As she meandered through her favourite place, she'd enjoyed the late afternoon sun as it slowly dropped behind the apartment block. With a slight chill accompanying the rising dusk, she'd headed back inside.

Pamela gave a hurried wave to the security guard when she reached the gatehouse at the entrance to Castle Fields. She followed the pathway around the pond and on to Maggie's apartment building. When she turned towards the flats, she saw her friend coming towards her.

'Thank goodness you're here,' said Maggie, her voice choked with tears. Pamela pulled her into a hug. Beneath the light of the lantern shining outside the building's front entrance, Pamela held her friend close. Maggie began to weep, and Pamela gently ran her hand across her back. 'I'm here now,' she said, softly.

After a moment, Maggie stepped back, her mascara smudged. 'I can't believe it, not now, it's too soon,' she said, her arm linked tightly with Pamela's. 'I went up from the garden and back into our apartment. Since Alan was sleeping, I decided to pour myself a glass of wine. Only a small one, mind you, as I never know when he might wake. I walked through to the kitchen and opened the bottle of red Simon and Louise had left last night.' Maggie paused, turning to Pamela, and rubbing her tear-stained eyes. 'Can you believe it was only yesterday we were all together? I keep thinking it was all too much for Alan. You don't think it was, do you? He was in such a state after the drinks. Of course, you saw him. I thought he was tired, but perhaps it was something more. He was so upset.'

Pamela remembered the horror she'd seen on Alan's face

when Larry stood in the apartment doorway, but feeling this was not the time to speculate, simply replied, 'I think it was lovely that we were all together.'

'You're right, I know you are. So good the old gang got to see him before he passed.'

'What happened after you went into the kitchen?'

'I felt exhausted, so I stood leaning against the side and drank half a glass. Then, I put my glass down and thought I must check on Alan. I popped my head around the bedroom door, and I could see straight away. He wasn't breathing. I dashed over to him, but his hands were cold. I lay next to him on the bed and held his hand. All I wanted was one last hug.'

With their arms still linked, Pamela pulled her friend near. 'I'm glad he went peacefully,' she said.

Maggie sniffed and held her breath. 'In the end, that's all I could've asked for. I don't know what to do.'

'Have you called the doctor?'

'Oh, yes. I don't mean now. I don't know how I'll live my life without him. We've always been together – Alan and Maggie, Maggie and Alan. These last few years have been difficult, but caring for him was all I had left.'

'Give it time,' replied Pamela, as the two women stepped inside the art deco building. 'Is the doctor coming?' she asked again, as they walked slowly across the tiled hallway.

'He's with him now. And so's Susan. I felt I should call her. She's been so good to us both. I don't know the doctor but he's asking all kinds of questions. I suppose he must. I needed to get outside for some fresh air, and I knew you'd be coming.'

Pamela smiled softly and pressed for the lift. From behind, she heard a knock on the building's main door. She turned and saw a young man tapping on the glass panel at the side of the entrance.

'Ignore him,' said Maggie. 'If he's visiting one of the other flats, they can buzz him in themselves; although half the time the bells in this building don't seem to work.'

'Hello!' called the man.

'He can see us,' said Pamela. 'We can't ignore him.' She slipped her arm out of her friend's and walked back towards the door.

'I'm trying to get to flat fourteen,' the man called through the glass. 'I've pressed the bell, but I don't seem to be getting any reply.'

'That's my flat,' said Maggie.

Pamela stepped forward and opened the door. 'Hello, again,' she said. 'It's Dr Lennon, isn't it? Are you with the other doctor?'

'Yes,' the man replied, looking at her quizzically. 'Do I know you?'

'We met briefly, yesterday, at the boathouse. I was with Ben Harper.'

'Yes, of course,' he replied. 'I'm so sorry for your loss.'

'Oh, no, it's not me. I don't live here.' She turned to introduce Maggie, but she'd already hurried back towards the lift.

CHAPTER 55

George Lennon briefly explained he was from the university hospital as he rode up in the lift with the two women. He followed them along the third-floor corridor and into a circular hallway at the entrance to the apartment.

'Whereabouts do I find your husband?' he asked quietly, before Maggie pointed at the left-hand door. 'Thank you, and please do accept my sincere condolences,' he said, as he watched the two women walk through to the living room. Then, he tapped on the door and stepped into the bedroom. With thick rugs spread across the bed, a pile of extra pillows and pill bottles lined up on the bedside table, it reminded him of his grandmother's.

'George, thanks for coming over,' said Graham Foggit, a GP from the local Haddley Park practice.

'No problem.'

'This is Susan Marvis. The deceased's niece.'

Lennon turned his head and froze. His mouth opened but he found himself unable to speak. It must be five years since he'd seen her.

'Good to meet you,' she said.

He paused. 'And you,' he replied, offering only a robotic response.

'I should leave you to it,' she said, fixing her eyes on Lennon as she left the room. 'I must check on my aunt.'

'Yes, thank you.' He watched her go out to the hallway before forcing himself to focus. He closed the bedroom door.

'I'm sorry to drag you out on a Sunday night, especially when it might be nothing, but I wanted you to take a quick look before this went any further. I'm pretty sure it is nothing, but you never can be one hundred per cent sure.'

'What is it, Graham?' Spending four years at university with Foggit had taught him the doctor had zero ability to get to the point.

'The deceased, Alan Atkinson.'

Lennon stood at the end of the bed and looked at the dead man. He appeared peaceful, but most dead men do.

'Go on,' said Lennon.

'He's been under the surgery's care for the past five years. Alzheimer's, with some significant deterioration during that time but no excessive physical decline. Reading through his notes, I wouldn't have expected a sudden death.'

'It's not an exact science,' replied Lennon. 'Cardiovascular?'

'Possibly.'

'I can take a look at him on the table tomorrow, if you like?'

'Yes, I think that would be a good idea, but the reason I called you out now is I noticed a slight discolouration on his lips.' Foggit pointed to a blue tinge around the dead man's

275

mouth. 'And while only very faint, there is evidence of pin-point haemorrhage in the right eye.'

'Not uncommon with severe heart failure. As I said, I'll take a proper look tomorrow. Have you got an ambulance coming?'

'Yes, but blue lips and the haemorrhage combined . . . '

'You're thinking asphyxia?'

'Aren't you?'

'I think it's very unlikely.'

'I shouldn't call the police?'

'Graham, not at this stage, no. I'm pretty certain they wouldn't thank you on a Sunday night. And neither would I, because they'd leave us sitting here for the next three hours awaiting their arrival. Let's get him out of here and let the family grieve.'

'Only if you're sure?'

'Absolutely,' replied Lennon, although the only thing he did know for certain was that he was glad that Alan Atkinson was finally dead.

Seven

Hema Jha

'For three weeks she'd sat, day and night, beside her son's hospital bed. His father visited only once, telling her Ashwin would never improve. She knew he was right, but she stayed with him until he drew his last breath. When he did, she'd held him one last time.'

She felt in her pocket for the key to the apartment building. Two weeks earlier, she'd entered her youngest son's new apartment for the very first time and found herself wondering how he afforded to live in such a place. Like his father, Dinesh was a mathematician. Rakesh's wish had been for him to teach, as he did, but an instinctive ability with numbers was the only thing the two men ever shared. Instead, her son made calculations in the City of London in a manner she had no hope of ever understanding.

Inside the apartment she busied herself picking up food wrappers, beer bottles and cushions from the floor. In the bedroom, she felt the luxurious softness of the cotton sheets before ripping them from the bed and filling the washing machine. From her bag, she took her bathroom spray and attacked every surface with vigour. Then, she pulled out the bottle promising to kill every germ.

The pungent fumes filled the air, and she opened all the windows. While she waited for the laundry, she paused briefly and, sitting on a stool in the kitchen, drank a cup of tea. She smiled at a photograph pinned to the fridge; Dinesh with his two elder brothers. They were together so rarely, and it was two years since her husband had taken the image. With her eldest son, Vikram, living with his family in Newcastle and her second son, Gaurav, in Singapore, only her youngest son remained close to home. Her third son, Ashwin, she thought of every single day. Whenever he rode his bike to school, she'd insisted he wear his helmet but against a speeding motorist the protection it gave was not enough. For three weeks she'd sat, day and night, beside her son's hospital bed. His father visited only once, telling her Ashwin would never improve. She knew he was right, but she stayed with him until he drew his last breath. When he did, she'd held him one last time.

She heard the washing-machine cycle end. She shook the sheets and pushed them into the dryer. Back in the bedroom, she pulled out the spare set of bedding and made up the bed. She kneeled in front of her son's wardrobe and found his dirty clothes, all piled in the back corner. She stuffed them straight into her bag, then rushed into the bathroom for her cleaning cloth and sprays. She scrubbed the bottom of the wardrobe, scouring the floor and the side panel, before sliding the door closed. She wiped the handles and mirror, and, standing in front of her son's wardrobe, she slowly exhaled.

MONDAY

MONDAY

CHAPTER 56

DS Parker walked up the ramp at the back of Haddley police station, scanned his security card and entered the CID offices. Arriving early, he was relieved to find the room deserted. He dropped his bag, opened his phone and clicked on the FaceTime app. On a call last night, as his two daughters battled with their mum over bedtime, he'd promised to show them where he worked. His eldest daughter, Izzy, now answered the call.

'Dad, we're still in bed!' she said.

'I thought Amelia had moved to the top bunk?' he replied, looking at his daughter.

'I decided it was too dangerous for her,' she replied. He laughed. 'It's true, Dad,' she continued. 'You wouldn't want her falling out from up here. Are you at work already?'

'You said you wanted to see my office.'

'It looks quite old fashioned,' said Izzy.

'That's because it is.' Haddley was one of the last remaining Victorian police stations still in operation in London. 'The windows rattle,' he said, scanning his phone around the room, 'and even when the weather's warm the radiators are boiling hot.'

'Dad!' cried his younger daughter, clambering up to appear beside her sister. 'I want to see where you sit.' He walked back to his desk.

'Are you in the naughty corner?' asked Izzy.

'I like being tucked away at the back. Nobody bothers me here. Is your mum about?'

'She hasn't come in yet. We were still asleep.'

'I was awake,' said Amelia. 'I could hear Izzy snoring.'

Her sister pulled a face. 'Dad, my class is going to the Science and Industry Museum today. Can I have twenty pounds?'

'What?'

'I'll need to buy lunch and something from the gift shop.'

'Twenty seems a bit steep.'

'Fifteen?'

'Ask your mum,' he replied. 'Are you doing science experiments?'

'No, it's for history.'

'How is that history?'

'The Industrial Revolution, Dad,' she replied, rolling her eyes.

'I'm glad you're looking forward to it.'

'As long as I don't have to sit next to Claudia Rosen on the coach, I don't care.'

'Dad, who's that?' asked his younger daughter, pointing at the screen.

Instinctively he turned his head. Behind him, coming

through the door at the top of the room, was CI Freeman. 'That's my boss,' he replied, dropping his voice.

'She looks scary,' said Amelia, not dropping hers.

'I've got to go,' he said. 'Tell your mum I'll call tonight. Lots of love.'

The girls waved wildly, blowing him kisses as they did.

'Not too scary, I hope,' said Freeman, standing beside his desk.

'Sorry, ma'am,' he replied.

'You must miss them?'

'I do. It's only been a few weeks, but I can already see a change in them.

'Are you getting home at weekends?'

He hesitated. 'When I can.'

'It's not easy with work, but make sure you get home as often as possible. They grow up very quickly.'

'Do you have a family, ma'am?' he asked, realising he knew nothing of the home life of the station's senior officer.

'A son, Hugo. He'll be sixteen next week. I promise you they don't get any easier,' she replied, holding her hand against the side of her face. 'We spend our whole lives looking out for them, doing all we can, and then suddenly, somehow, that's not enough. I wish there was more I could do for him.' She paused. 'Don't leave yourself with any regrets.'

'No, ma'am,' he replied. 'I'll try not to.'

'Now, we've Cheryl Henry coming up from the holding cells. Shall we see if she feels like being a little bit more co-operative this morning?'

Parker slipped his phone into his pocket, and followed Freeman out of the room and into the claustrophobic corridor outside Interview Room 2. He reached for the door handle.

'Wait,' said Freeman. 'She knows more than she's saying.'

Parker nodded.

'Never get riled or let a witness get under your skin. You need to learn to be patient.'

'Yes, ma'am.'

'Somebody paid Liam five hundred pounds to threaten Uma Jha. Our job is to find out who.'

Inside the interview room, they found Henry already seated beside her solicitor.

'Is it your intention to charge my client?' asked the woman, when they entered the room.

'A charge of assault on Dr Lennon and two charges of carrying an offensive weapon, one for the knife and one for the hammer, will follow.' Freeman took her seat opposite Henry. 'The severity of the charge for stabbing PC Cooke is still to be determined.'

'I didn't stab her. The clumsy bitch fell!' Henry slumped back in her chair.

'That remains to be determined.' CI Freeman opened her notes. 'I know we both want to find whoever killed Liam. Will you help me?'

Pouting like a child, Henry shrugged.

'I want to start by talking again about the argument you had with Liam on Friday night. Having set fire to Dr Jha's car, he came back to the Peacock boathouse, and you argued?'

Henry slowly nodded.

'What time was that?'

'Don't have a watch.'

'How long had it been dark?'

'Long enough for me to have three or four cans. I was up in the space we called the bedroom.'

Parker frowned. The attack on Dr Jha's car had occurred in fading daylight. Liam Kane had not returned directly to the boathouse from Haddley Common.

'Before Liam came back to the boathouse, did he go out drinking?' he asked.

'Don't think so,' she replied. 'But he made up for it when he got back.'

'You argued with Liam,' continued Freeman, 'and eventually you decided to leave the boathouse?'

'Yes. It was too dark to walk along the river, so I made my way through St Marnham and up the hill. In Oreton, when I passed the Rose and Crown, they'd closed up for the night.'

'You slept in the woods by the river?'

'Yes.'

'Why there?'

'I knew a safe spot by the picnic tables. I didn't want anyone to see me.'

'On Saturday morning, when you woke, was it light?'

'Only just. It's not easy sleeping in the woods. You hear lots of noises.'

'Did you head straight back to the boathouse?'

'We still had some food left from what we'd nicked the day before, so pretty much, yes.'

'When you arrived, you found Liam's body by the door.'

Henry nodded.

'Cheryl, from what you've told us, between midnight and eight the next morning, somebody killed Liam. He came down from the room where you usually slept to meet somebody. If that somebody wasn't you, who was it?'

'Don't know.'

'That person took the five hundred pounds Liam had in his pocket. You knew Liam had that money.'

'I didn't take the cash! I would've taken it but some fucker beat me to it.'

'Cheryl, who are you protecting?' asked Freeman.

'Nobody.'

'Is it someone you deal with?'

Henry folded her arms. 'I don't know who killed Liam.'

'I think whoever paid Liam killed him.' Freeman held Henry's eye. 'Who paid him?'

'All I know is it was somebody from the pub, some Indian guy. That's all Liam said.'

Freeman waited. She leafed through her notes before closing the file. She placed her hands on the table. 'Cheryl, I think you do know. Even if Liam didn't tell you exactly who, you guessed pretty quickly.'

Henry looked at the chief inspector. 'Dr Jha's been good to me. I don't want to hurt her.'

'You won't. We're here to help her.'

'Liam told me her dad drank at the Rose and Crown and he was the one who murdered Dr Jha's mum, thirty years ago. I said no way did he kill her.'

'Are you telling us it was Dr Jha's father who paid Liam?'

Cheryl laughed. 'No, he's old. He never comes out into the beer garden, just sits silently inside drinking his beer.'

'So, who?'

'He's always seemed like a nice guy. I think he went to the university but finished two or three years ago. He came back and bought some stuff every few weeks. Liam said she'd be upset if she knew. That's why I had to warn her. He's Dr Jha's cousin.'

CHAPTER 57

'Pamela, can you give me two seconds?' I say, catching my phone in my hand and putting our call on pause. 'She sends her love,' I tell Dani, as I bend to kiss her. 'Promise me you'll call at the first sign of a twinge.'

'Don't worry, we'll be straight on to you,' replies Holly, who is sitting with Dani at the back of our kitchen.

'It's a fifteen-minute walk to East Haddley. I can be back here in less than ten.'

'Go!' says Dani. 'Look after Uma and be careful!'

I smile and hurry from the room. 'Pamela, I'm back with you,' I say, opening the front door. 'I'm so sorry to hear about your friend. It must have come as quite a shock.'

'Sadly, Alan hasn't been with us for many years. It's difficult for Maggie. I had her to stay with me last night.'

I wave to Uma, who has arrived outside our house. 'I'll be with you in one second,' I say, holding my phone away from my ear, as Pamela keeps talking.

'No problem,' Uma replies.

I return my attention to Pamela.

'She's not very mobile,' I hear her tell me. 'If you could come to mine around twelve. It shouldn't take more than fifteen minutes.'

'Happy to help,' I reply. 'I must go now, I've Uma here.'

'Dr Jha? If she's with you, I'd love to see her later.'

'Let me see what I can do.' I disconnect the call and as Uma and I cross the Lower Haddley Road, I explain to her that a friend of Pamela's has passed away.

'I am sorry,' she replies. 'As people get older, it becomes harder and harder as fewer friends remain. I should pop in with you and see how she's coping.'

Uma and I follow a narrow side street, which leads onto the embankment path.

'Still no change with Dani?' she asks.

'Nothing yet. She had a bit of a rough night. I doubt she slept more than a couple of hours. It didn't help having my father creeping about.'

'He's a bit of a night owl?'

'I don't know when he sleeps.'

'He did a kind thing, coming back to Haddley.'

'He should've done it years ago.'

'He's done it now.'

I don't say anything, and push my hands into my pockets.

'It's difficult for you,' says Uma softly. 'But I'm glad my mum had somebody who cared for her.'

We walk on, past the bridge and the modern block of riverside flats, before turning up into East Haddley.

'Did you speak to Edward?'

'I called him late last night. We spoke for more than an

hour. He wanted to come straight home, but that's not what I need.'

Before we enter East Haddley's maze of Victorian streets, I stop. 'Uma, I'm here to help you, but I can't shake the feeling you're not being completely honest with me.'

'Why do you say that?' she replies, stepping back.

'On Saturday, after Cheryl appeared at the farmers' market, Edward accused you of playing a dangerous game. What did he mean?'

'He was upset.'

'I thought he was referring to the threat from Cheryl, but now I'm not sure.'

'He didn't like the risks we were taking.'

'I get that, but on Friday night, after Kane first confronted you and Dani, you were adamant about not calling the police. Why? Were you protecting somebody?'

She shakes her head.

'Whoever is behind the threats, I want them exposed.'

'What you said last night ... how it would make sense that she wouldn't be scared if she already knew who the threats were coming from.'

Uma glances down at her feet.

'You've suspected it all along, haven't you? That the threats against your mother were coming from within your family.'

She is silent, then she says quietly, 'That was always my greatest fear.'

'Not from your father?'

She shakes her head, and we walk slowly on.

'As the eldest son, my uncle Rakesh dominated our family.

Still now, at times, my father struggles to assert his own independence. I've witnessed my uncle's control throughout my childhood, and I'm sure my mother saw the same.'

'Yesterday, at your father's house, I heard your dad talk about the constant pressure from his own family. What did he mean?'

'Even now, Rakesh holds views that would've been out of place a century ago.'

'You believe he was behind the threats against your mother?'

'That is my fear, but I must be certain. It's hard for you to imagine, but when my family closes ranks, however much I push, some things are never spoken of. Listening to Gordon yesterday finally convinced me. My mother knew and refused to be bullied.'

A long row of Victorian homes greets us when we turn onto Nexfield Road. 'Growing up, I loved my aunt and was close to my two younger cousins, but even as a teenager, I understood the grip Rakesh held over our family,' continues Uma. 'Only rarely was my mother's name spoken. Whenever it was, by anybody other than my father, it came with a criticism. Perhaps my intention has always been to provoke Rakesh. That's why Edward spoke of a dangerous game.'

'Even more dangerous,' I reply, 'if it was your uncle who took your mother's life.'

CHAPTER 58

'Maggie,' said Pamela, tapping on the bedroom door, 'it's almost ten.' She pushed open the door to her spare bedroom. 'Maggie,' she repeated, an unease in her voice. 'Are you awake?' With the blind drawn, she had to step closer to see her friend.

Maggie turned on her side and lifted her head. 'What time is it?'

'Ten o'clock,' replied Pamela. 'I was beginning to worry about you.' She sat on the edge of the bed and put a cup of tea down on the small bedside cabinet.

'Thank you,' said Maggie, 'that's kind.' She pushed herself up in bed, before feeling for the switch to light the lamp.

'I hope you weren't too uncomfortable in this little bed.'

'No, not at all, but it did take me an age to get off. In the end, I decided to take one of the sleeping pills you gave me.' Maggie pointed to the bottle next to her bed.

'You took a whole one?' asked Pamela.

'One? I took two!'

The two women laughed. 'No wonder you've slept until this time,' said Pamela. 'A half is the most I've ever taken.'

'I think the sleep did me good.'

'I'm sure it did.'

'Thank you for having me here.' Maggie reached for the cup and saucer and began to drink her tea.

'I wouldn't have dreamed of you being anywhere else. I'm out of the bathroom now, so when you've finished your tea, why don't I run you a nice hot bath? There's plenty of hot water.'

'What would I do without you?'

'I'm sure you'd cope, you always do.' Over the last five years, Maggie's stoicism had never ceased to amaze Pamela. Other than support from Susan, she'd shouldered nearly all of Alan's care singlehandedly. She'd maintained their home, cleaned and cooked, while all the time taking charge of the family finances. Maggie knew all there was to know about pensions, veterans support, home insurance and the best-priced utilities. Pamela felt certain her friend could vie with Martin Lewis as the country's *Money Saving Expert*.

'I struggle to imagine life without Alan. I don't know how I'll find the strength to ever leave the flat.'

Pamela squeezed her friend's hand. 'Perhaps Larry could help?' she said, before getting to her feet and pulling up the blind.

'You guessed,' replied Maggie. 'I should have known you would.'

Pamela turned to look at her friend. 'I understand. It can't have been easy for you.'

'Larry was only ever companionship, nothing more. Somebody to talk to, somebody who understood everything we'd been through.'

295

Pamela couldn't deny her friend that.

Downstairs, while Maggie soaked in the bath, she tidied the living room, plumping the cushions and blowing the dust off her bookshelves. In the kitchen, she warmed the grill and boiled the kettle again. When she heard footsteps on the stairs she called out, 'Walnut-and-raisin toast with orange marmalade?'

'Perfect,' replied Maggie, as she wandered into the living room. 'I forgot what a lovely photograph this is of Thomas. He was such a handsome man.'

Pamela smiled to herself.

'He looks so strong and imposing.'

'Deep down, he was a softy,' said Pamela, joining her friend.

'Now, you are spoiling me.' Maggie sat on the sofa and Pamela placed her breakfast tray on the table in front of her. A moment later Pamela returned with her teapot and rested it by the fireplace to brew. 'He had such an authority,' continued Maggie, still looking at the picture of Thomas. 'Somehow, after the accident at Mickelside, Alan lost belief in himself. Perhaps he never had it, not in the way Thomas did.'

'Alan carried so much, for such a long time.'

'Over thirty years,' replied Maggie.

'Hard to believe.'

'Susan's sixty next year. She's been on her own since the age of twenty-nine.'

'I'd like to get her a little something for her birthday. She's always been so very kind to me.'

'And you to her.'

'I understand what she went through.' During an early morning training exercise at Mickelside, Susan's husband, Mark, had drowned. A second man perished alongside him.

'Those two deaths cast a shadow over the end of Alan's career and so much of his retirement. I don't think Alan was ever able to really forgive himself, even though Susan did.'

'It was never his fault,' said Pamela.

'Overseeing the training centre, he felt responsible. He bore such a weight, so much stress. I've often wondered if it impacted him later in life, with his Alzheimer's. He never escaped a wretched sense of guilt, even though he had such remorse. He'd have done anything for Susan, or for that young widow who lost her husband.'

'A few years later, the poor girl took her own life.' Pamela furrowed her brow. 'Helen something?'

'Helen Lennon,' replied Maggie.

CHAPTER 59

'That's my uncle's home,' says Uma, pointing at a double-fronted Victorian terrace. Standing outside the house is a police car. For a moment we wait, until DS Parker appears leading Uma's uncle, Rakesh Jha, away from his home. 'I didn't think the police would be here so soon.'

'We don't know what Cheryl Henry told them,' I reply.

'Let's talk to my aunt.'

Uma and I cross Nexfield Road, and approaching the Jhas' home, we can see the front door standing open.

'Aunt Hema,' calls Uma, from the open doorway. In the hall, broken pieces of a bright-red floor vase are scattered over the carpet. I follow her inside. She waits in the hallway, where photographs of Uma's cousins cover the walls. Several picture frames hang lopsided. 'Aunt Hema,' she calls again, before stepping over shattered glass and into the kitchen. 'Aunt Hema, it's Uma. Please can we talk?'

Suddenly, a door at the back of the kitchen opens. A grey-haired woman, wearing a buttoned floral housecoat, comes out of a small utility room, pushing the door closed behind her.

'Aunt Hema, what's happened?'

Hema ignores her niece, walking past her and opening the cupboard beneath her sink.

'We saw the police outside,' continues Uma, moving closer to her aunt, 'and then we came inside and found your vase smashed in the hall.'

Hema takes a box of laundry pods from the cupboard. She walks back towards the utility room. Uma reaches for her arm.

'Aunt Hema,' she says, softly. 'Please.'

Hema turns quickly. 'Take your hands off me.'

'I'm here to help you.'

'Help me? You've done quite enough already. All of this is your fault.'

'My fault?'

'The police arrest your uncle for nothing more than pro-tecting his family.' Hema hurries into the utility room, tosses three detergent pods into her machine and starts the wash. 'I didn't invite you into my home,' she says, returning to the kitchen, still holding the box.

'Please can we talk?'

Hema looks at me. 'Is this man your husband?'

'No, this is a friend of mine. I've asked for his help.'

'Not your husband? You invited none of your family to your wedding, not even your cousins.' I hear the disdain in her voice.

'I'm sorry,' replies Uma, 'but please try to understand. Aunt Hema, why have the police arrested my uncle?'

'They came here, demanding to know where to find your

299

cousins. He tells them his sons have done nothing wrong. All he does is protect them.'

'Did he get into a fight with a police officer?'

'A fight, no. The man pushed him. He has no right in our house.'

'What do the police want with my cousins? Surely, it's Rakesh the police wish to speak to?'

Hema shakes her head. 'I am busy.'

'Aunt Hema, somebody paid a man to threaten me and now that man's dead.'

'There is nothing I can tell you.' She turns her back on Uma. 'Please leave.'

'I know how my uncle has treated you.'

'I will not hear such words in my home.'

Uma takes a step forward. 'Please, Aunt Hema.'

'You talk just like your mother.' She faces her niece. 'Still now, she is the cause of this.'

'You blame my mother?'

'You have no idea. The anger Rakesh felt towards her. Not a day went by without him telling me how she brought shame upon our family. I defended her. I told him he needed to accept the world was changing, women worked. Alaka's views were the views of many.' Hema slowly exhales. 'She and I spent time together. I admired her. I confided in her.'

'What changed?'

'Even when she became a mother, she refused to accept her position in life.'

'You mean she kept working?'

'Your father knew what was right, but he was too weak.

300

More and more, she wrote her articles, led her campaigns. Every single week, another cause to make herself the champion of.'

'She gave people a voice.'

Hema's laugh is a bitter one. 'A voice to those women? Really? Is that what you think? I will tell you what happened. On the day she published that first article, on women trapped by their husbands, Rakesh brought a copy of the newspaper home. He burned it.' She crosses the room. 'Here, right here in this sink. He throws in the paper, pours on fuel and lights the fire.' Hema flings her arms in the air. 'The next week he does the same and the week after that.'

Uma shakes her head. 'I'm so sorry.'

'He hated every word your mother wrote. He said these women needed to respect the men they married.'

'What made him so angry?'

'Uma, don't you see? In his mind, if these women were abused by their husbands, then so was I. It felt as if every word your mother wrote was about me.'

CHAPTER 60

I sit beside Uma at her aunt's kitchen table. She reaches out her hand, but Hema locks her fingers together and rests them in front of her.

'Did my mother interview you, for her articles?'

'Directly, no. She named no women, but after reading so much of what she wrote, it might as well have been me.'

'I can't believe she ever set out to hurt you.'

'How does her hope protect me from Rakesh? Inside our family, I'd spoken up for her. He knew how close we'd been. She may not have deliberately written about me, but in his eyes she had.'

'He was willing to do anything to make her stop?' I ask.

Hema doesn't respond.

'I believe my mother knew who made the threats against her. She dismissed the danger; chose not to report the threats to the police. She wanted to protect our family, to protect Rakesh.'

Hema rubs her thumbs together. She looks towards the sink. 'The third time he burned the paper, he said to me there wouldn't be a fourth. He told me the next time he would burn me.'

Uma briefly closes her eyes.

'I begged him,' Hema continues. 'I swore not one word Alaka wrote had come from me. He simply repeated his threat. I had no choice but to act.'

'What did you do?' asks Uma.

'When I wrote the first note, my hand shook; such horrible words. I pushed the paper through your parents' letterbox. When she saw it, perhaps she knew immediately, but if she did, she didn't stop writing. I became more desperate. I wrote a second letter, and then a third to leave on her car. And then finally I sent one to the newspaper. All I knew was I had to make her stop.'

Sitting beside me, I feel Uma tense. 'Aunt Hema, do you know who killed my mother?'

'Uma, no, never. Despite all the threats I made, I would never have hurt her. You must believe me.'

'And Rakesh?' I ask.

'He had no idea.' Hema drops her head into her hands and covers her face. 'Still now, he has no idea.'

'What about the new threats against me?' says Uma, quietly.

Hema presses her fingers into the corners of her eyes. 'Last week, Rakesh brought the newspaper home, pointed at the story. He said now you were the one to bring shame on our family. I had to make it go away.'

'What did you do?'

Hema turns away. 'Many times, when I see your father,

he talks about a man in the pub where he drinks. He says he sells drugs. I found the man and paid him.'

Hema's words don't ring true. 'Can I ask where you met him?'

'In the garden, the garden of the pub.'

'Where in the garden?' I ask, pushing her.

'I don't remember, at one of the tables.' She edges back her chair. Her voice becomes desperate. 'You must believe me. Uma, please, you must believe me.'

I rub my hands across my face. 'Mrs Jha,' I say, 'the police will very quickly identify who paid Liam Kane. It'll be better for you if you tell them the truth.'

'No,' she replies.

'Aunt Hema, from his time at university, Dinesh knew that pub.' Uma's voice fades in disbelief.

Hema's face drains. She is exhausted. 'I should never have asked for his help.'

'Dinesh paid Kane?' I ask.

She nods. 'Kane went further than we ever agreed. To set fire to your car, Uma. I would never do such a thing. That night Kane came to this house, boasting. I couldn't believe what I was hearing. He tells me he wants another five hundred pounds. He is blackmailing me. I tell him Rakesh will be home any minute, but he refuses to leave.'

'What happened?'

'I had to make him go away. I said he would have the money the following day.'

'You met him on Saturday morning?'

'Dinesh and I went to the abandoned boathouse. Kane

304

appeared from a room upstairs. He told us today the price is now one thousand. I tell him no, but he then threatens us with the police. He will tell them we paid him to burn your car. In my head, all I can hear is Rakesh's rage, him screaming at me, lecturing me on the shame I have brought upon our family. I tell Dinesh to give Kane the money, but instead he picks up the hammer.'

Hema rests her head on the table and begins to sob.

CHAPTER 61

George Lennon looked at the man's decrepit body, lying naked on the table. For the first time ever, he found himself alone with the man who had stolen away so much of his life. A childhood filled not with joy, but a wretched sense of emptiness.

He picked up a blade.

He held no truck with the military's official investigation. As Mickelside training centre's senior officer, he believed Alan Atkinson responsible for his father's death. That was the conclusion he'd reached at a young age and one he'd clung to ever since. As soon as he understood the events surrounding his father's drowning on a cold January morning, he regarded Atkinson's conduct as a dereliction of duty. Two men sent out alone, unprotected, to hike over exposed hills and dive through icy waters. Atkinson defended it as commando training, but how was that training? It was nothing more than torture.

He paced the room before bending to observe the man's face. He lifted his eyelids and photographed his mouth. Touching the man's nose, he felt a small fracture.

He'd never understood the ability of Atkinson's niece to forgive. Three times he'd met with her. They shared their stories and the last time they were together he'd asked her directly – *how could she forgive?* Her family was a military one, she'd told him, and she accepted duty meant sacrifice. He vehemently disagreed and they never spoke again.

Until last night.

In his mind, Atkinson deserved to die. Had something changed in hers? More than three decades after her husband's death, what had finally made her feel differently? Was George now here to pass judgement on her?

He moved around the table, but he had no need to look at the body any further. He ripped off his gloves and tossed them on the floor. He grabbed his jacket from beside the door and felt for his phone. Quickly, he typed a message to Ben.

I need your help.

CHAPTER 62

'It's very good of you to do this,' I say to Uma, as we drive up Haddley Hill.

'I'm not due at work until five. If Mrs Cuthbert requested us both to attend, who am I to deny her?'

Opposite Pamela's row of small terrace houses, I pull into a thirty-minute parking bay. I switch off the engine.

'Tough morning?'

'When he was a baby, I helped my aunt bathe Dinesh; as a toddler, I chased him around the garden.'

'I'm sorry.'

'I can't help thinking how desperate Hema must have been.'

'She's done the right thing now, speaking to the police. Better they hear the truth from her. Dinesh will be picked up from his office in the City.'

'Perhaps he acted in self-defence.'

'Let's hope so. He was protecting his mother.' Uma looks towards Haddley Hill Park. 'Despite all he's done, my uncle goes free.' She sighs. 'We've come so far, but all of a sudden I don't know if we're any closer to finding who killed my mum.'

'Don't give up yet,' I reply. 'It's hard, but once they start, secrets have a habit of unravelling. The threats made against your mum might not have played a direct part in her death, but we're building a picture of the last days of her life.'

There's a tap on the passenger-side rear window.

'It's open,' I call, and Pamela climbs into the back seat.

'I saw you both chatting away,' she says, reaching for her seatbelt, 'and thought I'd come over. I don't want us to be late.'

'I'm so sorry for your loss,' says Uma.

'Thank you,' says Pamela, reaching forward and touching her shoulder. 'All in all, probably a blessing. Alzheimer's is such a cruel disease.'

I look across the road, towards Pamela's home. 'Is your friend with you?'

'Who?'

'Maggie, wasn't it?'

'No, she's walked home.'

Now I'm confused. 'I thought we were . . . '

'That's my fault, Ben, I should have explained myself better.'

Or, I should have listened.

Pamela continues. 'I've a friend coming for lunch, and she struggles on her feet. I need you to run her up the hill.'

I glance at Uma. 'Where are we heading?'

'Beyton Road.'

I pull into the traffic and in my mirror catch Pamela's slightly triumphant smile. 'You have been busy,' I say.

'I can't take all the credit. It was you and Sam who brought her to my attention.'

'Who are we talking about?' asks Uma.

Pamela leans forward. 'Eileen Blenkhorn. Ben said she had a story to tell, and I think he might be right.'

We travel onto the high street. 'How did you meet her?' I ask.

'Let's just say I bumped into her.' Pamela rests her hand on Uma's seat. 'She was most fond of your mother, and I suspect your mother felt the same way about her.'

Pamela proceeds to tell us the truth behind 'Mrs Cooper's Cookery Course' and the kindly interest Alaka took in Eileen.

'Each time they met, your mother must have witnessed how much Eileen suffered in her marriage. I wonder if she might even have been one of the catalysts for her articles. She would've known Eileen's marriage quite intimately.'

'On the afternoon of my mum's death, did they meet?'

'Yes, Eileen's confirmed that. Now Ben, you're our expert, but after seeing Eileen almost every week for several years, it seems odd to me that, with only one more day to complete her article, Alaka rushed to see Eileen again. Unless, of course, she wanted to ask her something more specific, something which couldn't wait until their usual Wednesday-afternoon meeting.'

I smile at Pamela. 'You wouldn't have any inclination as to what that might've been?'

310

'As a matter of fact, I do. Alaka wanted to ask Eileen about her time working in the kitchens at the Military Training Centre in Mickelside.' We turn onto Beyton Road. 'We're here now to find out exactly what she wanted to know. Dr Jha, if you don't mind, I think it best if you wait by the car. Too many new people at once might overwhelm Eileen.'

Pamela leads me through the unkempt gardens at the front of the tower block. We arrive at the lift and find the doors open. 'Hold your breath, Ben, it's only the fourth floor.'

I look briefly at my phone and see a message from George Lennon.

You okay? I reply.

Can you come to the hospital? is his immediate response.

Give me an hour

Outside Eileen's flat Pamela stops and takes hold of my arm. 'When we're inside, I want you to follow my lead.'

'In what way?'

Pamela knocks on the door. 'You'll see.'

The door opens and Pamela steps quickly inside to greet her new friend.

'You're early,' says Eileen.

'Are we?' replies Pamela. I'm not sure she ever does anything by accident.

311

'I'm not quite ready. I've made a Black Forest gateau for dessert.'

'How wonderful! Your first ever recipe from your cookery course. I am honoured.'

'I just need to box it up.'

'This is Ben,' says Pamela, ushering me inside. She moves us quickly into the living room.

'It's so very kind of you to come and collect me.'

'Whenever Pamela issues an instruction, it's best to simply follow her orders,' I say.

Eileen laughs. 'What power.' She disappears into the kitchen.

'Ben's the partner of my goddaughter, Dani,' calls Pamela. I look at her quizzically. 'Ben, why don't we sit down for two minutes until Eileen's ready?'

Pamela joins me on a small sofa. 'I didn't know you were Dani's godmother?' I whisper.

'Shh,' she replies, 'I'm not, but I helped raise her, so I'm as good as. You're lucky I didn't call you her husband.' She winks at me. 'Remember what I said: follow my lead.' She leans towards the kitchen, where we can see Eileen busy packing up her cake. 'Ben attended the Military Training Centre in Mickelside, when he was younger,' she calls. 'Sadly, he didn't make it past his first six weeks.'

'It was good that you gave it a go,' says Eileen, popping her head out of the kitchen door, 'but it's a physically demanding place.'

I try to hide my confusion. 'It was a tough regime,' I say, hesitantly.

'The military's loss is our gain,' Pamela adds. 'How long ago was it, Ben, when you were there?' She turns to me with an exaggerated stare.

'Difficult to say. Ten years?' I reply, raising my eyebrows.

'Would that have been when you were there, Eileen?' she asks.

Eileen comes out of the kitchen, precariously carrying a box and laughing to herself. 'Pamela, you forget how old I am. It'll be over thirty years since I worked in the kitchens. I'm ninety this year.'

'How stupid of me!' replies Pamela. 'Ben, you take Eileen's arm, and I'll take the box. I've lunch in the oven, and I don't want it to spoil. Eileen's a professional cook, so it needs to be my best efforts.'

'I wouldn't say professional,' she replies, as she feels in her pocket for her door key. 'I was a very good amateur.'

'Amateur? Feeding all those military boys?'

'All you do is double your ingredients and keep doubling until you have enough.'

'I wouldn't know where to start. How long were you there, at the training centre?'

'Only eight months,' replies Eileen, turning the key.

'I bet they all missed you when you left.'

'I doubt that. I only ever worked because Dennis said we needed another wage coming in before he retired. Not that my little earnings made much difference, I'm sure.'

'Why did you leave so soon?'

Eileen is silent. Pamela goes to press for the lift but stops.

'Eileen, that last afternoon with Alaka, is that what she wanted to understand?' Pamela looks at her friend. 'Please, Eileen, I think it might be very important.'

CHAPTER 63

We step out of the lift and Eileen takes hold of my arm. I can feel her hand shake.

'I don't want to let anybody down,' she says, 'but I swore to Dennis I'd never talk about it again.'

Ahead of us, Pamela stops. 'Eileen, Dennis can't hurt you any more. Alaka was your friend. Thirty years ago, somebody killed her. It's time that person paid for what they did.' She walks on and, standing at the roadside, waits for a refuse truck to pass. 'There's somebody I'd like you to meet,' she says.

I move to cross the road but feel Eileen hold me back.

'No,' she says, shaking her head. 'It can't be.'

'There's nothing to be afraid of,' replies Pamela, taking a firm hold of her other arm and leading her across the road. 'Eileen, I'd like you to meet Dr Jha.'

Uma, who is waiting beside my car, holds out her hands. Eileen clasps hold of them both.

'It's as if your mother was standing here right now.' Her hand trembles as she gently touches Uma's cheek. 'I could be looking at her from thirty years ago. You are just as beautiful as she was.' Eileen takes a deep breath. 'I was so very fond of her.'

'I feel certain she felt the same way about you.'

Eileen dabs a tear from her eye. 'She was so very kind to me. I was devastated by what happened to her but my husband, Dennis, had no idea we were friends. I did all my grieving alone. I would've loved to watch you grow up, but I had no idea how.'

'I'm here now,' replies Uma.

I open the back door of my car. Holding my arm, Eileen slowly climbs in before Pamela slides in beside her.

'Eileen, I know you want to help both Alaka and Dr Jha,' says Pamela. 'Why don't you tell us more about your time working at MTC Mickelside?'

'It was all Dennis's idea. I think he wanted the money to spend at the pub. I signed up with a local agency, and within a couple of days they'd found me a job at the Military Training Centre. Along with three other women, I was employed to cook breakfast before helping in the preparation of lunch. Each morning, I left home before four to catch the night bus.'

Uma turns in her seat. 'That really was an early start.'

'It didn't worry me. If I felt tired later in the day, I'd have a nap on the bus travelling home. Most mornings, I was in the kitchen before five. I was always first in and at that time I hardly ever saw anybody up and about on the base. From around six-thirty, we'd see some of the boys and girls heading out on training runs. I don't know how they managed, weighed down with heavy boots and equipment. Those not out on exercises would come in for breakfast. I enjoyed serving up, everyone was so friendly. I always felt they missed their mums. Whenever I was on my break, I'd sit with some of the younger ones, listen to their troubles. There were one or two I became quite close to. I found a friend in a woman named Fiona. We tried to look out for each other and we even met briefly after she'd left.'

'That's nice,' replies Pamela, with a hint of impatience, 'but what we need to know, Eileen, is were you on the base on the day of the accident, when the two men drowned?' asks Pamela.

Eileen can barely bring herself to answer. Hesitantly, she nods.

'You were in the kitchen by five?'

'On that day, before five,' replies Eileen. 'Dennis snored terribly whenever he'd drunk too much. I'd hardly slept, but rather than lying awake in bed, I caught an earlier bus.'

'What happened when you arrived at the base?'

'Nothing out of the ordinary. I let myself into the kitchen as I always did. There was a room at the back, only small, where we stored tinned foods, jars of sauce, that kind of thing. It was where we hung our coats. I looped my bag on a hook behind the door and as I did, I heard a noise outside. At first, I thought it was a cat or a fox rattling amongst the bins. But then I heard the stomp of boots. The room only had one window. I saw three men leaving the barracks. I can still see their faces now.'

Eileen stops, her eyes flitting from Pamela to Uma, and finally to me.

317

'What happened next?'

'As soon as they disappeared, I went back into the kitchen and looked at the clock. It was one of those digital ones where the numbers clicked over. The time was four forty-one. In all the reports which followed, it said the men left the camp at five-fifty, but there's no doubt in my mind they left over an hour earlier. Dennis told me he didn't want me getting involved, so I gave my notice to the agency and left at the end of the week.'

'Did anyone ever come and ask you about that morning?'

'Alaka was the first. We'd spoken about Dennis sending me out to work before, but that Friday afternoon Alaka wanted me to talk through my time at Mickelside one more time.'

'Did anybody else ever interview you?' I ask.

'Why would they?' she replies. 'I was nobody.'

CHAPTER 64

I leave Pamela and Eileen to their lunch. After dropping Uma back at her rented car, I drive to the university hospital in Oreton. Three times I circle around the car park searching for a space, and all the time my head is filled with thoughts of MTC Mickelside. On the morning Eileen found herself alone in the kitchens, two men drowned while diving in a deep-water lake. One of those men was David Lennon, George's father. From the moment I met him, George has maintained a steely conviction that there was a cover-up surrounding his father's death. Listening to Eileen, I'm beginning to wonder if he might be right. Finally, I find an empty space on the top floor of the multi-storey. I hurry from my car, click on my parking app as I go, and pay eleven pounds.

Inside, I follow a dimly lit staircase down into the hospital's basement. Staff give little attention to me as I walk quickly towards the morgue.

'George,' I call, knocking on his office door.

'I'm in here,' he replies, from his examination room. He

hears me hesitate. 'Don't worry, all the bodies are covered over.'

I push open the door. Dressed in his medical scrubs, he's scribbling notes on a clipboard as he leans against a stainless-steel countertop. He turns. 'Thanks for coming.'

We shake hands and half hug with a brief shoulder pat. 'Whatever you need,' I reply. I glance towards a dead body, draped with a light blue sheet, in the centre of the room.

'It's Alan Atkinson,' he tells me.

'Fuck, no, of course,' I reply. I suddenly realise Pamela's friend, who died last night, was at one time the senior officer at MTC Mickelside. 'Please tell me this has nothing to do with you.'

I was seventeen when George first told me of his intention to kill a man named Alan Atkinson. After three pints of Thatcher's cider, he told me why. In George's mind, Atkinson will always be responsible for the death of both his parents.

'A local GP called me yesterday evening. Atkinson was well and truly dead by the time I arrived.'

'Thank God for that.'

'He deserved to die. I'm only sorry it didn't come sooner. Alzheimer's might have robbed him of his dignity, but bizarrely it probably eased his guilt.'

Despite an official inquiry, George always refused to accept his father's death as an accident. What did happen at Mickelside that cold January morning? And what part might it have played in Alaka's death less than a year later? I look at the body on the table and wonder if the only man who knew the truth is lying right there.

'He wrote me a letter, after my mum died.'

'I know,' I reply, quietly, as George continues.

'To a seven-year-old boy, a formal letter on military writing paper, telling me what a brave man my father had been and how it was to him I should always look for my inspiration. My mum's body was barely cold.' George rubs his face. 'I'd tried so hard to make her happy, but without my dad life proved too much for her. The day I discovered her body, I sat with her for ten, fifteen minutes until an ambulance arrived. I gave her one last hug and then I pissed myself.' George laughs at himself. 'Can you believe that?'

'George, you were seven.'

'I ran upstairs and changed my clothes. I stuffed my school trousers into a green-and-white Asda carrier bag and hid them at the back of my wardrobe. My nan kept me off school for a month. When I went back, she bought me new trousers. I might not be perfect, but he deserved to die.' I hear George's voice break. 'I only wish it had been me who'd killed him.'

'Are you telling me somebody else did?'

He nods. 'Yes.'

'Are you sure?'

'One hundred per cent. What do I do? If I say nothing, nobody will ever know, and the bastard can be sent to burn in hell.'

'George, the one thing I know for certain is you're a far better man than Alan Atkinson ever was. You know what you have to do.'

CHAPTER 65

'All I have to do,' said Pamela, opening her phone, 'is type in your postcode, click on search and your driver is on his way.'

'That's it?' asked Eileen, watching in amazement as her friend ordered her an Uber.

'Four minutes and Vlad will be here,' replied Pamela, delighted by her own technical ability. 'If you give me your phone, I can download it for you.'

'I don't have a phone, except for the one in my hallway.'

Pamela laughed. 'You have so much to learn!'

'I'm so glad you found me,' said Eileen, smiling, 'however it might have happened.'

'Why don't we call it destiny' replied Pamela. 'Let's get your jacket on before the car arrives.'

Pamela helped Eileen to the door. 'Thank you so much for a lovely lunch. I think you're a wonderful cook.'

'From you, I will take that as the ultimate compliment.' She opened the front door and waited with Eileen for the car. She refreshed her phone and saw Vlad was two minutes away.

'You can see where he is?' asked Eileen, in total amazement.

'Coming over Haddley Hill as we speak.' Pamela turned to look for the car, but when she did, she spotted a fancy little sports car coming over the brow of the hill. Immediately she recognised the driver. When the car was opposite her home, it pulled into the 30-minute parking bay. Larry lowered his electric window, and Maggie called from the passenger seat.

'Pamela, I need to speak to you.'

'What is it?' she replied, but her friend was already climbing out of the car. Behind Larry's Porsche, Simon and Louise's very practical Volvo was already pulling up. 'All the gang,' she muttered.

Maggie pressed the button at the pedestrian crossing, and as she did so, a black Mercedes slowed at the lights allowing her to cross. Maggie hurried over but the lights changed before the others could follow. The Mercedes cut across the traffic and stopped in front of Pamela's home.

'Look at you, travelling in style,' said Pamela, opening the car door for Eileen. She gave her a brief hug, and her friend eased herself inside. With the door closed, Pamela knocked on the window to wave goodbye, but Eileen's head had dropped. She smiled to herself and imagined Eileen falling asleep on the short journey home.

'Thank God you're here,' said Maggie, hurrying towards Pamela. Behind her the other three friends followed.

'What is it?' asked Pamela.

'You won't believe what's happened. The police have arrested Susan.'

Eight

Susan Marvis

'At twenty-nine she'd buried her husband, with a Union Jack draped over his coffin. The sound of the Last Post echoed as his colleagues lowered his body into the ground.'

The thin blue mat placed on top of the custody suite's wooden bench reminded her of the ones handed out at the start of her yoga class. With no pillow, she rested her head on a folded towel. Yesterday afternoon, arriving at the bank, she'd felt a rush of adrenalin. Waiting in line, her heart pumped; it was years since she'd felt so alive. She'd approached the window with an absolute calm and confidently made her withdrawal request. After keying her details, the teller had invited her to take a seat. That was her moment to leave, but instead she'd done as the man suggested, her mind suddenly in a fog. Minutes later, the branch manager appeared and sat beside her. When she did get up to leave it was already too late. A police car was outside the front of the building. A police constable entered through the main door, and she'd begun to shake. Asked to put her hands behind her back, she'd closed her eyes. Her wrists cuffed, her humiliation was complete.

At twenty-nine she'd buried her husband, with a Union Jack draped over his coffin. The sound of the Last Post echoed as his colleagues lowered his body into the ground. Not once had she come close to marrying again. As the years passed, she'd spent more time with her aunt and uncle. Always close, it was they who'd first introduced her to her husband, Mark, and her uncle Alan who'd walked her down the aisle at her wedding. Her happiness with Mark lasted two years until one January morning when an officer arrived at her door to inform her Mark was dead.

She accepted the findings of the official investigation into her husband's death. Although her uncle served as MTC Mickelside's most senior officer, not once did she doubt his exoneration. Her aunt and uncle supported her in every way possible. Over recent years, as her Uncle Alan's life had slipped away, she'd been able to repay their kindness. When he'd begun to fade, together with her aunt, she'd trawled through the endless documents of his life. At first her discovery had left her bewildered, but over time she'd seen the opportunity. Everything she did felt so easy, but now, staring at the light creeping under the cell door, she realised how stupid her actions had really been. She knew she was faced with only one choice. She would plead guilty.

TUESDAY

CHAPTER 66

DS Shawn Parker stood inside the disused bus shelter at the back of Haddley police station. Heavy clouds swirled above the town, with a strong breeze beginning to clear an early morning mist. Beside him, George Lennon sucked on a cigarette before crushing it beneath his Adidas trainer.

'Thanks for coming over,' said Parker. 'I'll give you a call if I need anything further.'

His hands in his pockets, Lennon nodded. 'You'll have the official report this afternoon.'

'But in your mind, there is no doubt?'

'None. Suffocation was the cause of death and Atkinson suffered injuries consistent with a physical assault.'

'With you attending the crime scene on the night of his death, I'm going to need you to make a short statement as to your conversation with Susan Marvis. Any time this afternoon is fine.' Parker stepped out of the shelter.

'Detective,' said Lennon, 'I know how she's suffered. I'd be lying if I didn't say there were times I've thought about killing him myself. I don't believe she's a bad person.'

Parker turned away, quickly ran up the ramp at the back of the building and entered the CID offices. In desperate need of his morning coffee, he walked straight through to the narrow kitchen at the top of the room.

'Kind of you to join us,' said CI Freeman, putting a milk carton back into the fridge.

'I was just—'

Freeman held up her hand. 'Let's talk in my office,' she replied, opening the opposite door that led out to the narrow corridor.

'Yes, ma'am,' replied Parker, searching in the cupboard for a clean mug. He ran the hot water to rinse one from the sink.

'Whenever you're ready,' she added, before leaving the room.

He turned off the water, rubbed his hands down the sides of his trousers and followed her. Outside her office, he tapped on the door.

'Yes, come in,' she said, already seated back behind her desk. 'Have you raised charges in the Liam Kane murder?' She pointed to a chair, and he sat.

'Dinesh Jha's got himself a decent solicitor. He claims Kane threatened him and his mother, and the first physical attack came from Kane.'

'Anything in it?'

'It doesn't fully tally with his mother's statement, but there's a grey area. Murder or manslaughter; either way he'll be charged today.'

'And the mother?'

'Hema Jha,' he replied. 'She spent yesterday morning

cleaning her son's flat and washing the clothes he wore on Saturday morning. We'll charge her as an accessory.'

'Any link to the murdered journalist?'

'Alaka Jha was her sister-in-law. Hema orchestrated a hate campaign against her, but we can't find any link to the murder.'

'I think we'll leave that one to Ben Harper for now.'

'Yes, ma'am.'

Freeman sipped on her tea. 'Cheryl Henry?'

'Charged last night.'

'Aggravated assault on Dr Lennon and PC Cooke?'

Parker nodded in response.

'How is Cooke?' asked Freeman, holding his eye.

He hesitated. 'Recovering I think, ma'am. I'll give her a call later to check in.'

'Be careful,' she replied. 'In the month you've been here, you've done good work. Your first murder and you laid a significant blow on the Baxters. I think we can work well together. Don't let station gossip undermine you.'

'No, ma'am,' he replied, feeling uncomfortable and getting to his feet. At the door he stopped. 'One other thing, ma'am.'

'Go ahead.'

'Yesterday afternoon, following a call from the manager of the NatWest Bank, we brought in a woman for attempting to fraudulently access her late uncle's account.'

'And?'

'The man only died on Sunday evening. I met with the medical examiner this morning and his finding is suffocation as the cause of death.' Parker explained the events surrounding Alan Atkinson's death. 'When Dr Lennon attended the scene, the niece was already present.'

'Really? Two murders in a week. You're going to send my conviction rate through the roof. The following day the niece hurried off to the bank to collect her winnings. How much are we talking?'

'Atkinson had an account untouched for over thirty years. Each month the account received an anonymous deposit of two thousand pounds.'

'I don't do mental arithmetic.'

'With interest, just over a million pounds.'

CHAPTER 67

Sam let the side door of his apartment block swing closed behind him. He hurried across the tarmac driveway towards a row of sixteen single garages. Beneath a decaying terracotta plant pot, he found the key for garage number 3, the garage he rented from his friend, Mrs Wasnesky, to store his *Richmond Times* archive. Bending to lift the rusty door, he let out an audible groan. He really wasn't getting any younger. When the door was halfway up, he ducked inside and fumbled for the light switch. He rifled through three different years of newspapers until eventually he came across the edition he'd published the week of Alaka's murder. He'd forgotten he'd devoted eight pages to the horrendous crime on Haddley Hill, but it wasn't the report he was searching for. Following the details of the crime, he'd written an obituary to his friend and colleague.

> Four weeks after she first joined the team at the *Richmond Times*, Alaka Jha pitched me a story on the ill treatment of patients at a local psychiatric

hospital. Her article became a campaign ushering in nationwide reforms and new levels of patient protection. At the regional press awards that year, her series of articles won the newspaper Campaign of the Year award, and the voting panel named Alaka Specialist Journalist of the Year. Working with Alaka on the series, I quickly realised I'd been fortunate to employ a colleague of rare talent. At the same time, witnessing her care and compassion for the victims, I felt certain I had discovered a friend for life.

Last year, her reporting on the murder of Fiona Nicholls shone a spotlight on the merciless tactics abusive partners use to trap survivors inside a controlling relationship. After reporting on the trial and conviction of Fiona's partner, Evan Littlewood, Alaka helped so many other women find the courage to make their voices heard.

Wiping his hand across the corner of his eye, Sam closed the newspaper. He planned to rerun the obituary in next week's edition. He tucked the paper under his arm, reached to close the garage door but then stopped. He thought of what Gordon had said on Sunday evening. Fiona Nicholls's murder had made Alaka angry. She wanted to help bring change. Sam scurried back inside his archive and rifled through the editions from the year before Alaka's death. He pulled two copies from the pile.

After locking the garage, he headed down the driveway.

He waited for a group of cyclists to cross Richmond Bridge before dodging between the traffic and entering the Rich Café. He waved at the owner, Woody, before piling an extra cushion on his favourite corner seat.

'Usual?' called Woody, from behind the counter.

'Poached eggs, please,' he replied, deciding to add a marginally healthier element to his full English.

'No Mrs Wasnesky today?'

'Hoping to meet her for lunch,' Sam called in reply, before holding up his A4 notepad. 'Work to do this morning.'

After Woody delivered his Americano to his table and Sam had added a splash of milk, he started scrawling his article. He'd missed the deadline for this week's edition, but he'd run the full story of Dinesh and Hema Jha next week. Although still no closer to identifying Alaka's killer, he was determined the article would serve as full redress for both Alaka and Uma. When Woody returned with his breakfast, he piled his sausage and eggs between two slices of toast and congratulated himself on a most excellent sandwich. He ordered a second cup of coffee and continued writing until a man arrived at his table and pulled out a chair. Sam pointedly looked across the café at two empty tables.

'Can I help you?' he asked.

The man placed a padded brown envelope down on the table. 'I'm Manish Jha,' he said, offering Sam his hand. 'Alaka's husband.'

Sam stared at the envelope and then at the man's hand. He shook it briefly before Manish sat opposite him.

337

'I went to your office, and they told me I might find you here.'

'I guess I'm getting predictable in my old age.'

Manish smiled. 'I thought you should have this,' he replied, resting his hand on the envelope. When he lifted his hand, he nodded, inviting Sam to look inside the package.

Hesitantly, Sam opened the envelope and pulled out a thick red leather diary. He recognised it immediately.

'My wife's,' said Manish.

'You kept this to yourself for thirty years?' replied Sam.

Jha shook his head. 'Until late last night, I had no idea it existed, even though it was sent to me.'

Sam curled his nose. 'How?'

'Thirty years ago, after my wife's murder, Hema came briefly to stay at my home, to help care for Uma. She received the delivery and kept it, without telling me. Had I known, I would have told the police at once.'

Sam turned over the envelope and looked at the handwritten address. 'Gordon,' he said, quietly.

'Who?'

'It doesn't matter now.'

'Hema was scared. She is sorry for what she has done.'

'Does Alaka reference the threats from her aunt?'

'Not from what I can see.'

Sam shrugged.

'You cared for Alaka,' said Manish, 'but so did I. I loved her. I tried my very best to support her but, if I look back now, I should have done more. Sadly, for me, it's now too late.'

338

Sam shook his head. 'We both have daughters of whom we are very proud.'

'Uma means everything to me.'

'You should start by telling her that,' replied Sam.

Manish Jha nodded courteously. His head bowed, he walked slowly towards the door.

'Wait!' called Sam. Hurriedly pushing his breakfast plates to one side, he reached for the newspapers he'd brought from his archive. He spread them across the table and Professor Jha returned to stand beside him. 'Do you remember Alaka working on this story?' he asked. He pointed at a headline reporting the guilty verdict on Fiona Nicholls's partner, Evan Littlewood.

'Of course I remember it,' replied Manish. 'Littlewood was such a vile man. The jury could see he was guilty from the very first minute.'

Sam nodded and scanned the report. 'Alaka was so relieved when they found him guilty.' He pointed at a paragraph in Alaka's report. 'DNA evidence at the trial proved Littlewood was not the father of Fiona's unborn child.'

'Yes, that was his motive. He killed her in a jealous rage. It made Alaka so angry. She despaired at a woman like Fiona Nicholls being left so vulnerable. Only weeks before, she'd resigned a promising naval career, leaving her trapped inside such a brutal relationship.'

CHAPTER 68

Inside Interview Room 3, Parker sat opposite Susan Marvis.

'Mrs Marvis,' he began, 'I'm interviewing you under caution in relation to the Fraud Act of 2006. Before I begin, I want to repeat the law entitles you to legal advice, either from our duty solicitor or by asking us to contact a solicitor of your own choosing.'

The woman shook her head.

'For the recording, please, Mrs Marvis.'

'I don't need a solicitor. I want to make a full statement.'

Parker glanced briefly towards the police constable seated beside him, before asking, 'Are you certain?'

'One hundred per cent,' replied Marvis.

'Why don't you talk me through what happened prior to your attempt to access your late uncle's bank account?'

'I've worked hard all my life. I receive a small military pension and work as a secondary-school teacher. I'm not pretending I'm poor, but I've never been well off. I live in a nice cottage, but I don't go on expensive holidays.'

'What can you tell us about your aunt and uncle?' Parker glanced down at his notes. 'Maggie and Alan Atkinson.'

'For as long as I can remember, we've been close. Their apartment in Castle Fields is a twenty-minute walk from my home. My uncle passed away on Sunday night.'

Parker nodded in response but said nothing.

'He suffered from Alzheimer's for several years. At first his deterioration was gradual; he became forgetful, repeated himself. Then, three years ago, his decline became more rapid. Together with my aunt, I began to work through all his papers, life insurance, bank accounts, those kinds of things. We worked on transferring everything into my aunt's name. Quite unexpectedly, and in all innocence, I stumbled across an account untouched for more than thirty years. Aunt Maggie was completely unaware.'

'The natural thing would have been to inform her. Is that what you did?'

Marvis briefly closed her eyes. 'No,' she replied, her voice quiet. 'Don't ask me why, but I didn't.' She paused and looked at the detective. 'I didn't have a plan, but my overriding urge was to keep it secret. There was a lot of money. I never planned on taking it all, but somehow it was reassuring to know it was there.'

'You set yourself up as a signatory on the account?'

'I did.' She pressed her hand against her neck. 'I wanted the control. It was quite easy to do. Uncle Alan would sign anything I put in front of him. I didn't desperately want the money.'

Parker opened his folder and slid a copy of a bank

statement across the table. 'At the start of last year, using a cash card, ten multiples of two hundred pounds were withdrawn from the account.'

'I planned a trip to the French Riviera and Monte Carlo; funny thing is, I never even went.' She passed the statement back across the table. 'I think Uncle Alan would have wanted me to have the money.'

'Yesterday, you returned to the bank for more. Twenty thousand pounds.'

'With Uncle Alan's passing, I thought it'd be nice to visit a German market this Christmas.'

'That's a lot of shopping. Twenty thousand now, before you took the rest?'

'No, never,' replied Marvis. 'I knew the money would pass to Aunt Maggie.'

'Putting the money to one side, can you talk us through what happened on the evening of your uncle's death?'

She paused and looked quizzically at the detective. 'I received a call from my aunt a little after seven.'

'On your mobile?'

'Yes, on my mobile. My aunt was distraught. I drove straight over to her flat.'

'You have your own key to your aunt's building?'

'The door downstairs doesn't always open. It's easier for me to have a key, to save her coming down. What's that got to do with anything?'

'On Sunday night, did you let yourself in?'

'I might have done,' replied Marvis. 'Yes, I think I probably did.'

'Was the doctor in attendance when you arrived?'

'Yes.'

'A short while later, the medical examiner arrived?'

Marvis hesitated. 'Yes,' she said.

'Dr George Lennon. Do you know him?'

For the first time, Marvis edged back in her chair. 'I've met him two or three times.'

'So, you are acquainted with him?'

'Yes.'

'In fact, your husband and Dr Lennon's father, David, drowned in the same military training accident,' said Parker, repeating the information George Lennon had shared with him.

'Yes,' replied Marvis.

'Why then, on the evening of your uncle's death, did you feign not knowing Dr Lennon?'

Marvis put her hand to her face. 'In the spur of the moment, it was a stupid thing to do.'

'That doesn't tell me why you did it.'

'I didn't want to compromise Dr Lennon in any way. If I suggested he was somehow connected with my late uncle, I realised it might make things difficult for him, professionally.'

Parker shook his head. 'Or was it because you were desperately seeking Dr Lennon's help?'

'I don't know what you mean.'

'Mrs Marvis, you were already fraudulently taking money from your uncle's bank account and now had a plan to take more. You were the only person with access to the account, and not only that, as you've told us yourself, the only person with knowledge of its existence. I spoke to your aunt this morning and she confirmed she was unaware of this money. On Sunday evening your aunt went down to her garden, leaving your uncle sleeping in bed. You arrived at their home and, as on many occasions before, let yourself in. You found your uncle alone and suddenly an opportunity presented itself.'

'No.'

'Yes, I think it did. You saw your uncle sleeping, thought of the money, picked up a pillow and suffocated him.'

'No.'

'You held him down, but despite his illness he was still strong. He struggled, fought hard, but you kept pressing down with enough force to break his nose, until eventually he stopped breathing.'

'No.'

'By the time Dr Lennon arrived, you realised Dr Foggit already suspected something, and in an act of desperation you signalled to him your need for help.'

She looked at Parker. 'I want a solicitor.'

CHAPTER 69

'Wait until you see this,' says Sam, pushing past me when I open my front door.

'Hang on!' I call, as he starts down the hall.

'Leave the door open,' he replies. 'Uma's on her way over.'

'What's going on?' I ask, following him into the kitchen.

Sam deliberately places a brown envelope in the centre of the kitchen island. 'Just wait,' he says.

At the back of the room, my father is dozing with the morning's paper laid across his chest. Sam tells me of his meeting with Manish Jha, and at the mention of his name my father stirs.

'You saw Alaka's husband?' he asks.

'He kind of found me.'

I hear a knock on the front door and move back into the hallway.

'It's open,' I call, and Uma steps inside. As she does, Dani appears at the living-room door.

'Hello again,' she says, surprised at Uma's arrival.

'I received a summons from Sam,' she says.

'He's with me in the kitchen,' I reply, 'preparing for his great reveal.'

We all stand around the kitchen island, except for my father who has returned to reading his newspaper. With the precision of a bomb disposal expert, Sam deliberately opens the brown envelope and carefully slides out a red leather diary.

'Alaka's appointment book,' he proudly tells us.

Uma slowly rests her hand on top of the diary. 'I have so few things that were hers.' Gently, she turns the first page. The inside cover is full of pencil drawings of bright-red poppies. Uma touches the flowers. 'My mum drew these,' she says, smiling softly.

My father comes to stand beside her. 'Alaka's diary,' he says, looking over my shoulder. 'That's the one I put in the post. Where did you find it?'

Sam rolls his eyes. 'Uma's father.'

'Am I stupid in wishing he'd come to me?' asks Uma.

'He knows he could have done things differently,' replies Sam. 'Maybe give him a chance.'

Uma nods but remains silent.

'I'm sure you've looked through it already, Sam,' says Dani, 'so does the diary actually tell us anything?'

Sam starts to turn the pages of the book, flicking past different dates and pencilled appointments. 'Each Wednesday afternoon she wrote the initials EB.'

'Eileen Blenkhorn,' I say, 'but we know that's when Alaka met her for "Mrs Cooper's Cookery Course".'

'Yes,' replies Sam, 'but on the Friday afternoon of her death she also wrote *EB 3 p.m.*'

'Exactly as Eileen told us,' says Uma.

'But,' replies Sam, flicking to the back of the book, 'in the days before mobile phones, Alaka also kept a handwritten list of her key contacts.' He points to the last name on the list – Eileen Blenkhorn. 'Easy enough to put two and two together and conclude Eileen was the last person to see Alaka alive.'

'Which is exactly what Aunt Hema did.'

'From there all she had to do was share the name anonymously with the Sunday newspaper and Eileen became the media story, never her.'

'What about the week of Alaka's death? Is there anything to help us understand what Alaka was working on?' I ask.

Sam flicks through the pages. 'Other than Eileen, on Wednesday and Friday afternoon, there are two other entries. The first is a woman called Susan Marvis on Tuesday morning.'

Dani lifts her eyes to mine. She is aware of my conversation with George in the morgue.

Sam continues. 'The second is on the Thursday. Alaka blocked out the whole afternoon and wrote the address, *375, Rossett Drive, RH 24.*'

I reach for my phone and type in the address. Looking at the search result, I realise Alaka's diary has given up its secrets.

'The Military Training Centre, Mickelside,' I say.

CHAPTER 70

'MTC Mickelside again,' says Uma, an urgency in her voice.

'I feel certain it's connected to your mum's murder,' I say. 'Now we have to understand why.'

'Should I know the name Mickelside?' asks Sam.

'The military base where two naval officers drowned.'

'Of course.'

'And where Eileen Blenkhorn worked in the kitchens,' I explain. 'She saw the men leave the base early that January morning.'

'The inquiry never interviewed her?' asks Sam.

'I doubt they even knew she existed.'

Dani moves to sit on the sofa at the back of the room. 'When I spoke with Auntie Pamela last night, she told me the police had arrested the niece of her friend Maggie, after she tried to access a one-million-pound savings account. Her niece is Susan Marvis.'

Sam rapidly taps his finger, pointing at the name in Alaka's diary. 'It's here, look, Susan Marvis! Alaka met with her the week of her death.'

'Her uncle was Alan Atkinson, the commanding officer at Mickelside when the two men drowned. Atkinson died on Sunday night.'

'How?'

'According to George, and I have no reason to doubt him, he was suffocated.'

'Ben!' says Sam, grabbing me around the shoulders. 'You've done it!' Hopping from one foot to the other, he can barely contain his excitement. 'This is it. Mickelside is the key.'

'But who killed Alaka?' asks my father, impassively. 'It sounds to me like you've got a million and one pieces but no idea how to put them together.'

'Ben?' says Sam, desperately wanting me to provide the answer.

'For once, Dad, I think you're right.'

'Alan Atkinson,' replies Sam, beginning to pace the room. 'It's him, it has to be. Two men drown at Mickelside. He instigates a cover-up and the official inquiry exonerates him, when in reality he was negligent. Alaka realises this and follows up the story. On the Thursday afternoon, she visits Atkinson at Mickelside and he's spooked. He fixes to meet her again the following day and kills her.'

'I can buy that,' says Dani, 'but who killed Alan Atkinson?'

'His niece, for the money,' replies Sam. 'For a million quid, I'd have finished him off myself.'

'Sam!' says Dani.

'Sorry,' he replies, 'but we're so close.'

'The problem is the one man who could have told us the truth died on Sunday night.'

Uma moves to stand by the window. 'In all honesty, I doubt he's been in a fit state to tell us anything for the past three years.'

'Maybe he's not the only witness. We should talk to his widow.'

Dani smiles at me. 'Pamela's the one who can make that happen. The other person we need to speak to is Susan Marvis.'

'Isn't she under lock and key at Haddley police station on suspicion of murder?' asks Sam.

'I'm sure there are ways around that,' replies Dani, a glint in her eyes.

'No, absolutely not,' I say, sitting beside Dani. 'You cannot be getting involved, not in your condition.'

'My condition?' replies Dani, laughing.

'You know what I mean. You could go into labour at any moment.'

'I'm not ill. Dr Jha, will you tell him?'

'This isn't an argument,' I say, before Uma can reply.

'We need to speak to Susan Marvis, and I'm the one person who can make that happen.'

'What if Uma goes with her?' says Sam.

I turn in his direction. 'You keep your nose out.'

'I'm happy with Uma coming along. There's somebody who I know will help us.'

I slouch down on the sofa. Dani leans across and kisses me on the cheek. 'That's settled then.'

'What about me?' asks Sam.

'You can stay here,' I reply. 'Get on my laptop and find

350

everything you can on the drowning deaths of Mark Marvis and David Lennon.'

'I'm not the online guy.'

'You are now.'

CHAPTER 71

When Dani and Uma arrived at the coffee shop on the Upper Haddley Road, they found PC Karen Cooke already seated at a corner table.

'Dani, you sit here,' she said, springing to her feet as soon as her colleague arrived. 'It has a nice, cushioned back. You'll be much more comfortable.'

Dani smiled before introducing Uma.

'Let me get these,' said Uma, taking requests from the two women, and joining the queue at the counter.

'I brought you this,' said Karen, pulling a green dragon from her bag. 'I couldn't resist him.'

'He's so cute.' Dani sat the soft toy on her knee. 'I will put him next to the baby's cot.'

'We couldn't give you just vouchers. There's four hundred quid's worth in there,' said Karen, passing Dani an envelope. 'I always said you were one of the boss's favourites. She topped up the collection with a hundred quid of her own money.'

'Very generous.'

'I put in fifty.'

'You shouldn't have.'

'Honestly, don't worry,' she replied, waving her hand away.

'How's the arm?'

'Bit sore, but fine. Shawn's nailed two murders since I've been off. He'll be getting all the glory. I can't wait to get back.'

'At least you and he are working well together. Don't forget without Cheryl Henry, he'd have never got to Dinesh Jha.'

'With a little help from Ben,' replies Karen.

'Let's not shout too loudly about that at the station. I'm sure Ben's happy to leave the credit with you.'

'Shawn called around to my new flat on Sunday morning, to see how I was doing.'

'Nice of him. Have you moved?'

'I bought a place in the block by the tube station.'

'Fancy.'

'My parents sent me the money from Dubai. I'd rather one of them came to visit. They don't take me seriously.'

'You've got a serious job.'

'My dad called to ask if I was done playing police and wanted to go and work for him.'

'That's shit.'

'All my mum ever wants to know is if I'm dating.'

'Are you?'

'Kind of.'

Dani smiled. 'What does that mean?'

'Shawn came back for dinner on Sunday night. He stayed over.'

'Karen!'

'I know, I'm bloody stupid. I'm a fool to myself but it wasn't the first time.'

'I didn't know he was available.'

Karen raised her eyebrows.

'Is he available?'

'His wife lives in Manchester. I suppose you could say he's got to fill his evenings somehow.'

Dani clicked her tongue. 'That didn't take him long. Karen, you always tell me you want to be taken seriously but you're sleeping with a senior officer.'

'Yes, but one that's pretty cute.'

Dani smiled before raising her finger. 'Time and again, you've told me you want your career to progress. Is sleeping with a married senior officer the way to go?'

Karen shook her head. 'I don't know why I do it.'

'You like playing games. If you really want to progress, that needs to stop.'

Before Karen could answer, Uma returned to the table.

'PC Cooke, a flat white for you, and Dani, a pot of tea for us to share.'

'Karen, we need your help,' said Dani, as Uma poured her drink. 'We believe the murder of Uma's mother is linked to two drowning deaths that occurred at MTC Mickelside in the months before her death.'

'I want to help. What do you need?'

'There was a woman brought into the station yesterday, Susan Marvis.'

Karen nodded. 'Bank fraud, but Shawn now likes her for killing her uncle.'

'That's what it looks like,' replies Dani, 'but Susan Marvis is the widow of one of the two men drowned at Mickelside.'

'We believe my mother met with her during the week of her death. I realise we're asking a lot, but if we knew what my mum asked her, it might help us unlock the story she was chasing.'

'And if the pursuit of that story ultimately cost Uma's mother her life,' added Dani.

CHAPTER 72

I stand in Pamela's living room and look at the photograph of her late husband, Thomas, standing proudly on her bookshelves. Over forty years since his death and he is still in her life every single day. That's real love.

'I'll be with you in a minute,' she calls, from the top of her stairs.

For the last half hour, I've sat with Pamela. I shared with her my fears surrounding the accident at MTC Mickelside, and Alan's links to Alaka's murder. With her sharp mind, Pamela had many questions, but seeing her contemplate Alan's death, I realised with his passing she has lost one of her last remaining links to Thomas. The gang of four, Thomas, Alan, Larry and Simon, played such an important part in her life.

'Ready,' she says, appearing at her living-room door, with her jacket fastened. 'Are you sure you'll be warm enough? There's quite a breeze blowing.'

'I'll be fine,' I reply, before we begin a steady walk up Haddley Hill.

'I've been so stupid,' she tells me, after a minute. 'I should have seen the link to Alaka's murder.'

'How could you? It was thirty years ago.'

'You're right, Ben, of course you are, but her murder is a crime which lives on through all its victims. Your friend George, your father, Alaka's husband, even Dr Jha's poor, tormented aunt. All of them have suffered. If only Alaka had been allowed to uncover the truth, so many lives would've been so very different. I didn't realise how much Eileen had told us.'

'About the morning of the accident?'

'Well, yes, at some point she sparked Alaka's interest, or confirmed something she already suspected. Her telling Alaka the reported time was wrong convinced Alaka to start asking questions.'

'Do you think Alaka met Alan?'

'Absolutely, yes. That's what Eileen told us.'

'Did she?'

'We both saw it, Ben. The moment Eileen saw Dr Jha, it took her breath away.'

'Yes,' I say slowly. 'It was as if she'd seen a ghost.'

'Not a ghost, but Alaka. Eileen couldn't believe how alike mother and daughter were. It was the same with Alan at the reunion of our little gang on Saturday night. I even said it myself, how he could have brief moments of lucidity. Of course, they were very rare and enormously unreliable. He became convinced he'd recently seen Thomas. *Thomas is back*, he told me. But how could he be? In reality, he'd seen Larry creeping back into Maggie's life, making Alan even more confused.'

357

For a moment, listening to Pamela, so am I.

She smiles at me. 'I should explain myself better. Saturday night, after the reunion drinks, I took Alan upstairs to his and Maggie's flat. Outside his neighbour's apartment, a small group of us gathered in the hallway. With the sudden recollection of a deep-seated memory, Alan became terrified. He said something garbled about changing the time. My instinct told me the arrival of Larry triggered his reaction. I was wrong. Coming out of the neighbouring flat was Dr Jha. In Alan's confused mind, Alaka had returned to haunt him.'

CHAPTER 73

Pamela and I walk through the imposing wrought-iron gates at the entrance to Castle Fields. She leads me to her friend's building and presses the door buzzer. A moment later, a male voice appears over the intercom.

'Is that you, Larry?'

'Pamela? We weren't expecting you.'

'No, I don't suppose you were,' she replies. 'I won't take up too much of your time, but can you let me in.'

The lock clicks but the door remains fast.

'Press it again, Larry,' says Pamela, not hiding her frustration with him. He does as she instructs and we enter the building.

When we arrive at Maggie's flat, the door is open, and she is waiting to greet us.

'I feel like I know you already, Ben,' she says. 'Pamela's mentioned you so many times.'

'Should my ears be burning?'

'Only good things,' replies Pamela, as I follow the two friends through to the living room.

Larry appears from the kitchen, wearing a cooking apron. A dismissive glance crosses Pamela's face.

'We're about to have lunch. Would you like to join us? I think I've got enough.'

'No, no,' replies Pamela, 'we'd hate to intrude.'

He disappears back into the kitchen.

'Have the police spoken to you any further about Alan's death?' asks Pamela, taking a seat beside her friend.

'Is that why you're here?' Maggie replies. Pamela looks in my direction, but her friend keeps talking. 'I've heard nothing more since I spoke to the police yesterday evening. They told me about all this money.'

I sit opposite the two women. 'Have you any idea where it came from?'

'That's what the police asked. Alan looked after all our finances. All I can think of is another pension, but in all honesty I've no idea.'

'And they've said nothing further on Alan's death?' asks Pamela.

'No. Why?'

Pamela takes hold of her friend's hand. 'Maggie, the police now believe somebody else was involved with his death.'

'Not Susan? No, that can't be true.' Maggie's eyes are wide. 'She loved her uncle. I wouldn't have coped for these last five years without her. Larry!' she calls. 'You won't believe what the police are saying.'

He hurries into the room.

'The police think Susan killed Alan. It's just not possible.'

Larry sits on the arm of the sofa, next to Maggie.

'We don't know anything yet, and we've heard nothing official from the police,' I say, 'but whatever happened to Alan, I'm certain it links back to the drowning deaths at MTC Mickelside over thirty years ago.'

Maggie is silent.

'How can that be possible?' asks Larry.

'We need to understand what happened the morning those two boys died,' says Pamela.

'We already know,' replies Larry. 'It was a terrible accident.'

'That was the verdict of the navy's own inquiry.'

'What are you saying?'

'The military's instinct is always to protect their own,' she replies.

'Ridiculous.'

'Larry, it's Maggie we came to see.'

'I can remember it like it was yesterday,' she says. 'We were all devastated. Alan felt responsible, he was the senior officer, but there was nothing he could have done.'

'Can you tell us what happened that morning?' I ask.

'Alan was asleep. We'd been out the night before, a dinner of some sort. We were still living on the base. I heard somebody knocking. I told Alan but by the time he stirred, I'd answered the door and invited the young officer in. Two men were dead. The news shook Alan. He dressed almost in a trance. Of course, he'd lost men in action, but this was different. There was no reason why they should have died.'

'What time was this?' asks Pamela.

'Alan was a good man. You know that, Pamela.'

Pamela says nothing, and Maggie looks at the floor.

'Sometimes good men do bad things, but I don't believe this even was a bad thing.'

'What are you saying, Maggie?' asks Pamela.

'Fifteen minutes after the officer arrived, Alan left the house. I made myself some breakfast and sat drinking a cup of tea. An hour later, Alan was back. The two men had drowned, a terrible accident. He sat me down in the living room and told me there would be an official investigation to follow. He told me the time of the accident was six-thirty and that the officer arrived at our house at seven-thirty. I knew he'd arrived at our house before seven, but we never spoke of it again.'

Pamela looks at me. Both of us are thinking what Eileen told us, and the time she saw the men leave the base that morning. Thirty years ago, the day before her murder, when Alaka met Alan Atkinson at MTC Mickelside, she knew he was lying.

CHAPTER 74

Lunchtime crowds packed Haddley high street. Approaching the Chicken Joint restaurant, Cooke hesitated, but she was too late. Shawn had seen her.

'Barbeque sandwich?' she said, stopping outside the entrance.

'You know me too well,' he replied. 'You're not back at work already, are you?'

'Heading in now,' she replied.

'Didn't the boss sign you off until the end of the week? I'd stay home in my flash apartment with my feet up if I were you.'

'No point me sitting around at home watching paint dry.' She moved past him, but as she did, he reached for her hand.

'I'll be interviewing a suspect most of this afternoon, if the bloody solicitor ever turns up,' he said, 'but I'm at a loose end tonight if you fancy a drink?'

Thinking of what Dani had said, she smiled. 'Sorry, no, I'm working.'

Inside the station, the desk sergeant welcomed her back

as if she'd been away for a month. It felt nice having the officer show concern. With the corridor outside the interview rooms deserted, she walked quickly to the end. She tapped her pass on the security door and followed the steps down into Haddley's holding cells. Rarely used to detain suspects longer than twenty-four hours, she found the stone cells depressing.

'If you've come looking for revenge, you're too late,' said Trevor Barnes, the custody sergeant, with a wink. 'Cheryl Henry departed for Silvermeadow early this morning.'

She laughed. She was fond of Barnes, a man who remained perpetually positive despite his bleak surroundings.

'Rest assured, Trevor, I'm happy for due process to run its course.'

'She'll be looking at a few years,' he replied. 'What can I do for you?'

'I'm working with DS Parker on the Susan Marvis case.'

'Smothered her uncle for a million quid.'

'She's requested a specific solicitor and we're having trouble getting hold of them. Can you give me a couple of minutes with her?'

She followed Barnes down the short corridor and waited while he unlocked the cell door.

'Two minutes is all I need,' she said, and Barnes stepped away.

At the back of the small cell, Susan Marvis sat with her legs crossed, a tattered paperback novel resting on her knee. Trevor always tried to make anyone in his cells as comfortable as possible. Cooke introduced herself, before shifting a neatly folded towel and sitting at the opposite end of the cell's wooden bench. She explained there was a delay in the arrival of Mrs Marvis's solicitor, but once they did arrive, she'd be given the opportunity to meet with them in private. Nothing she said was untrue.

'I did a stupid thing,' said Marvis, 'but I didn't kill my uncle.'

'You should wait for your solicitor and talk to them.' Karen smiled. 'Reading the case notes, I recognised your uncle's name. Wasn't he involved at MTC Mickelside?'

'That was a long time ago.'

'My father spent four years in service. I'm pretty sure he was at Mickelside.'

'Really,' the woman replied, but she didn't hide her lack of interest.

Cooke persevered. 'He has his own security company now, in Dubai. Last weekend, a reporter called me wanting to get in touch with him. Something about the murdered journalist Alaka Jha. I told her she had the wrong man. My dad's too young.'

Marvis simply nodded and picked up her book.

Cooke stood at the side of the bench. 'Did you ever meet her, Alaka Jha?'

Marvis raised her eyes. 'I don't know why you're here, PC Cooke, but I'd like you to leave.'

She knew it was a risk, but Cooke persisted. 'Mrs Marvis, did Alaka Jha contact you in the week of her murder, asking about MTC Mickelside and your husband's death?'

'Get out.'

Cooke stopped at the cell door. 'Please, if you can tell me anything.'

'Get out, before I call the custody sergeant.'

'If we can understand who Alaka Jha spoke to before she was murdered, it might take us to whoever killed her.' In the corridor, she saw Barnes approaching. 'One second, Trevor,' she called, smiling. 'Please,' she said, turning back to Susan Marvis.

'She did contact me, but not about Mark's death. She asked me if he knew a woman named Fiona Nicholls.'

CHAPTER 75

Sam stretches out on the sofa at the back of our kitchen. I tell him and Dani of the conversation Pamela and I had with Maggie.

'That confirms it,' says Sam. 'It must be Alan Atkinson. He met with Alaka, and she caught him in a lie. His wife as much as told us. Mark Marvis and David Lennon drowned due to his negligence. Alaka discovered the story, went after him and he killed her.' Sam reaches up and takes a mug of coffee from Dani. 'Has it got any sugar in?'

'You don't take sugar,' I reply, from across the kitchen.

Sam taps his head. 'I need the energy to help me think.'

'Get your bloody own, then. I think there's some in the cupboard, above the coffee machine.'

'Ben, I might not look it, but I'm seventy-five next year.'

'Good for you to keep active.'

He snarls and Dani pats his arm. 'I'll get it for you.'

'Alan Atkinson killed Alaka to cover up whatever really happened at Mickelside?' I say.

'Yes,' replies Sam. 'I just said that.'

'Why lie about the time?' asks Dani. 'How did that help?'

Sam stirs his coffee and passes her his spoon. 'To cover up his own failings on diving safety.'

'I'm not sure,' replies Dani. 'Did you find anything online?'

'The official report into the drownings is one hundred and seventy-eight pages long,' replies Sam, 'but reading its conclusion, both men suffered from oxygen poisoning.'

'How's that possible?'

'Too much oxygen in their air tanks. Both men experienced convulsions and drowned.'

'Awful.'

'Faulty equipment was blamed,' continues Sam, 'and Atkinson was exonerated.' He sits up and flips open my laptop. 'I googled the two men who drowned.'

'Who says you aren't the *online guy*?' I say.

'Don't push your luck,' he replies. 'David Lennon was an officer recruit, yet to see active service. He left a wife and a two-year-old son, George.'

Dani's phone rings.

'It's Karen,' she says. Picking up the call, she wanders out into the garden.

'Keep going,' I say to Sam.

'Mark Marvis served on a peace-keeping mission in Bosnia and later in Northern Ireland. He transferred to a training position at MTC Mickelside, as a diving instructor.'

I turn in my chair and look out into the garden. Dani is sitting on the brick wall built by me and my mum a lifetime ago. When she stands, she bends and struggles to catch her breath.

I run outside.

'Just a twinge,' she says, holding up her hand and breathing deeply.

'Not a contraction?'

She breathes again. 'No, not a contraction.'

'Are you sure? Shall I call Uma?'

She shakes her head and stretches her back. 'I'm fine,' she says, stepping inside.

Sam's on his feet. 'Come and sit here,' he says, ushering her to the sofa.

'Don't you start, Sam,' she replies, smiling.

I sit beside her. 'Can I get you anything?'

'Cup of tea?' asks Sam.

'Stop it, the pair of you!'

Sam chuckles to himself. 'Did Karen Cooke have anything useful to say?'

Dani tells us of Karen's conversation with Susan Marvis. 'Alaka didn't ask her about the drownings at Mickelside. Her interest was in a woman named Fiona Nicholls.'

Sam rushes across the kitchen and grabs his bag. 'There, there!' he cries, pointing at Alaka's obituary in a thirty-year-old edition of the *Richmond Times*. 'Fiona Nicholls was the trigger for the articles Alaka wrote before her death.'

'How does her death at the hands of her partner link to Mickelside?' asks Dani.

'She was in the military,' Sam tells us.

I think of our conversation with Eileen in my car yesterday afternoon. She briefly mentioned a woman named Fiona, who she'd befriended at the training base. Could it

369

be the same woman? I flip open my laptop. Googling the name Fiona Nicholls delivers me pages of reports on her death and the trial of her partner, Evan Littlewood. I search for details of her life.

'Sam, you're right,' I say, clicking on a report on her early life. 'Born in Stoke-on-Trent, after college she joined the Royal Navy. Before leaving the force, she spent nine months as a trainee diving instructor at MTC Mickelside.'

'Mark Marvis and Fiona Nicholls worked together as diving instructors,' he says. 'At Littlewood's trial evidence showed he was not the father of Fiona Nicholls's unborn child.'

Dani leans on my shoulder and looks at my screen. 'Could Mark Marvis have fathered the child?'

'That would explain a lot,' I reply.

'No, no, no,' says Sam. 'He can't be.'

I stop reading, and both Dani and I raise our eyes to him. 'Why?'

'While serving at Mickelside, Mark Marvis was briefly recalled to Northern Ireland. He couldn't have fathered the child, and he couldn't have killed Fiona Nicholls.' Sam winks at me. 'Turns out I *am* the online guy.'

I smile at him before clicking open Alaka's final report on the trial. 'You might be right, Sam, but why did Marvis attend every day of Littlewood's trial?'

CHAPTER 76

Pamela walked home alone. She needed time with her thoughts and, leaving Castle Fields, she hurried Ben back to Dani.

She felt certain, like so many men, Alan had done stupid things. On the morning of the drowning deaths at Mickelside, for a reason she was yet to fathom, he'd asked Maggie to lie. What a foolish thing to do, but she knew someone must have placed enormous pressure on Alan. Alaka Jha caught him in that lie. When she did, did he decide to kill her? To Pamela, Alan had always been a gentle giant. Caring and thoughtful, the compassion and tenderness he'd shown Thomas would stay with her until she drew her own dying breath. It gave her such comfort to know Alan had been with him at the very end. She refused to believe he was a cold-blooded killer.

Having not eaten lunch, by the middle of the afternoon she felt peckish. She brewed a pot of tea and cut herself a generous slice of Eileen's Black Forest gateau. While she sat in her chair by the window, she watched the traffic on

Haddley Hill and let her mind wander. She thought of Alaka's final days. What story might they still tell? Alaka had seen Eileen on the Wednesday afternoon, just as she always did. What did she want to hear again, which made her return on Friday afternoon? What more did she want to know beyond the change of time? Pamela sipped on her tea and eased back in her chair.

Just as her head began to drop, she sat bolt upright. Had she been dreaming, or had she somehow missed what Eileen told them in Ben's car the previous afternoon? On that cold January morning, Eileen had seen three men, not two, leaving the base.

'How could I have been so foolish?' she said to Thomas. Hurrying into the kitchen, she couldn't stop herself from smiling. She was in pursuit of the third man.

'Damn,' she said, opening her mobile and realising she didn't have Eileen's telephone number. She clicked on her Uber app and within three minutes a car had stopped outside her home.

'Good afternoon, Haroon,' she said, climbing into the car after reading his name on the app.

'Good afternoon, Pamela,' he replied, and she thought how polite he was.

'Just a short trip, to the flats on Beyton Road, although I am in quite a hurry.'

'Don't worry, I know the flats well. My mother lived at flat number four until the end of last year. We will race through the back streets.'

'It is a small world,' she replied, as Haroon's quick

acceleration pushed her back in her seat. 'Did your mother move on somewhere nice?' she asked, still struggling with her seatbelt.

'Very sadly, she passed away. However, she was seventy-three, so she had lived a good, long life.'

Pamela wasn't sure seventy-three was a good, long life.

At the junction with the Upper Haddley Road, with the traffic lights turning red, she covered her eyes as they flew across.

'Do not worry,' called Haroon, looking in his mirror. 'I drive for over twelve hours each day. I know the sequence of every set of lights in Haddley.'

She nodded and half smiled, just as outside the railway station Haroon slammed on his brakes.

He lowered his window. 'Keep crossing after the lights and you'll never make it to the end of school,' he shouted at a group of teenage boys. He turned and smiled at Pamela over his shoulder. 'No consideration for others,' he said, before taking a sharp turn followed by another quick right.

'You must be exhausted by the end of each day,' she said, her hand held tight around her seatbelt. 'Pedestrians and cyclists coming at you from every angle.'

He laughed at himself. 'I always try not to react. It's bad for my blood pressure.'

They turned onto Beyton Road and Haroon brought the car to a sharp stop. 'Number four on the ground floor,' he said, pointing towards a corner flat. 'She always had a basket of flowers hanging outside her door, but look at it now.'

'You should try and remember it as it was,' she replied,

touching his shoulder as she climbed out of the back seat. She always left her Uber drivers a tip on the app – fifty pence – but she didn't have time right now. She'd do it at home this evening.

The stench in the lift was worse than ever. Riding up to the fourth floor, she kept her mouth covered. When the door opened, she hurried towards Eileen's flat. She thought it odd when she found the door ajar and called Eileen's name. There was no reply. Pushing the door further open, she saw the Yale lock smashed from its latch.

Her heart began to race. 'Eileen,' she called, stepping inside. 'Anyone home?'

The only response came from voices talking on the radio. She walked into the living room, where she found Eileen sitting in her high-backed tartan chair. She was asleep.

'Eileen,' she said, softly. She moved closer, but before she could reach for her hand, Pamela's heart seemed to stop in her mouth. Eileen's eyes were wide but unseeing; the bruising around her neck already starting to show.

'How horribly, horribly cruel,' she said, before gently closing Eileen's petrified eyes.

Nine

Alaka Jha

*'Leaving Eileen's home, she'd felt so
certain. Mark Marvis and David Lennon.
Two deaths to conceal another.'*

She sat at her desk and stared at the phone in front of her. She lifted the receiver from its cradle, only immediately to drop it back down.

What if she was wrong?

Leaving Eileen's home, she'd felt so certain. Mark Marvis and David Lennon. Two deaths to conceal another. She thought of what Fiona Nicholls had confessed to Eileen. A senior officer, a pattern of sexual abuse and intimidation that had led to the woman's resignation and return to Evan Littlewood, a man who, with his history of violence, had been all too easy for a jury to convict.

Yesterday, Alan Atkinson had lied to her. Now, she must confront the man who'd stolen so many lives. She picked up the receiver and dialled the number Atkinson had written on a scrap of paper.

'Come on, come on,' she said, waiting nervously as the phone rang and rang. And then she heard his voice.

CHAPTER 77

Pamela stood at her living-room window and watched the police car turn quickly in the road. The driver, PC Higgins, had talked throughout the ride home. He'd been full of his own theories on the dreadful crime, but to her none of them appeared to hold much water.

On discovering Eileen's body, she'd called the police from her mobile phone while the man next door had brewed her a cup of tea. He'd invited her to sit with him and his wife, but she'd preferred to stand outside on the walkway. Within minutes, two police constables had arrived at the scene and two detectives soon after. DS Parker had stood beside her.

'Mrs Cuthbert, why were you visiting Mrs Blenkhorn this afternoon?' he'd asked.

'After walking home earlier in the day, I sat by my living-room window and dropped off to sleep. When I woke, I said to Thomas how foolish I'd been.'

'Who's Thomas?'

'My husband.'

'Where is he now?'

'An Argentine missile killed him in the Falklands War.'

DS Parker smiled a sympathetic smile, and she worried she wasn't making sense.

'Haroon brought me here as quickly as he could,' she continued, trying to improve the officer's perception of her as a credible witness. 'I'm only sorry I was too late.'

'You were later than your arranged time with Mrs Blenkhorn?'

'No, detective, we'd arranged nothing. I'm sorry I was too late to save her.'

He'd patted her hand before asking PC Higgins to drive her home. He'd said she should try and get a good night's rest. He'd invited her to visit the station the following morning to make a statement. If it wasn't for such tragic circumstances, she'd already be looking forward to it.

In the early evening with the light beginning to fade, she reached for the cord and pulled the blinds down over her window. She felt for the switch on the lamp, which stood beside her television, before crossing the room and picking up her favourite photograph of Thomas. She placed it on the small table next to her chair.

'I should have seen it sooner,' she said, sitting down and looking at the picture. 'The moment Eileen climbed into that Uber with Vlad, I fear her fate was sealed. I hate to think it was me who put her in danger.'

Thomas would tell her not to blame herself. She'd done nothing wrong, but she couldn't shake the image of poor Eileen from her mind. If only she hadn't become so distracted. She hated to admit it, but someone had misled her.

If that hadn't happened, perhaps she'd have got to Eileen sooner.

Hearing her back gate bang shut, she sat upright and cursed the wind. The gate rattled again, and she snuck her feet into her slippers. Stepping into the hallway, she saw the bright security light, which Dani had insisted she installed, illuminating her kitchen. For a moment the light dazzled her, forcing her to squint. From the hallway, she tried to peer through the kitchen window and out into her back garden. When her eyes focused, she watched a figure move forward. He pulled on the handle of her back door.

She didn't hesitate. She marched into the kitchen, found the key she kept hidden on top of her microwave and unlocked the door. Startled by her appearance, the figure took a brief step back towards the swinging gate.

'Simon, if you'd wanted to come in, all you had to do was knock.'

CHAPTER 78

'A year before her own death,' I say, 'Alaka reported on the attendance of Mark Marvis, a fellow Mickelside diving instructor, at the trial of Fiona Nicholl's partner. Three months later, when Mark Marvis drowns in a tragic accident, Alaka remembers his name.'

'Suddenly she realises there is a link between the deaths,' says Dani.

'Mickelside,' I reply.

'She begins to suspect the drowning deaths were not an accident.'

'Mark Marvis ended up dead to conceal the truth behind Fiona Nicholls' killing?' asks Sam.

'Exactly,' I reply. 'When Eileen tells her story of the men leaving the base at an earlier time than officially reported that January morning, Alaka's suspicions only grow.'

'Ultimately, that's enough for her to visit Alan Atkinson at Mickelside, the day before her death.'

'A visit that haunted Atkinson until the day he died.'

'What made him so terrified?'

'Somehow he became embroiled in a cover-up,' replies Dani.

'I should've listened more closely to Eileen in the car,' I say. 'When she told us about her time working at the kitchens at Mickelside, she wanted to talk about her friend, Fiona. She even told us they'd met up again after Fiona had left the military.'

'Fiona Nicholls?'

I nod. 'Alaka went back to Eileen on the Friday afternoon, not to hear again about Mickelside but to understand about her friend, Fiona. At the training centre she'd confided in Eileen. Eileen saw how afraid she was, but didn't know how to help her.'

I open my laptop and read again Alaka's final report on the trial of Evan Littlewood. At the bottom of the page is a photograph of Fiona's friends and family outside the court after the jury had delivered its verdict.

'Shit, where's my phone?'

Dani grabs my phone from beside the coffee machine. I call Pamela's number. Immediately I hear her voice. *If you are listening to this message, I'm probably asleep. Leave me your number and I'll call you back.*

'Fuck,' I say, and snatch my car keys. I point at a photograph on the screen and read the caption below. 'Supporting Fiona's family is senior officer, Simon Carmichael.'

CHAPTER 79

'Pamela, I wasn't sure you were home,' said Simon, taking a step forward.

She dropped her hands and invited him in.

'I was passing and thought I'd call by to see how you were,' he continued, his voice calm.

She'd already left the kitchen. Behind her, she heard him close the back door and turn the key. She returned to her favourite armchair. 'You can see I'm just fine,' she replied, when he stood in the living-room doorway.

'I'm pleased. It's been a shock for us all, losing Alan; let alone Susan becoming entangled in his death. I'd never have thought it possible. I always thought of her as such a timid little thing.'

'Sometimes, Simon, you really can't tell.'

His face hardened as he sat on the corner of the sofa closest to Pamela. In the hallway she heard her phone ring in her jacket pocket.

'Somebody's eager to get hold of you,' he said.

'I'm sure they'll call back.' She wrinkled her face. 'Louise not with you?'

'Helping out with the grandchildren.'

'I'm sure they'll be of some solace to her.'

He laced his fingers and stretched his hands across his knee.

She touched the photograph of Thomas on the table beside her. 'Do you remember the night we all first met?'

'Such a long time ago,' he replied.

'I can remember it as if it was only yesterday. Maggie and I were at the bar inside the Royal Navy boathouse. We were both so young. You boys had won the fours race. Larking around with the trophy, you dropped it on the floor. We both giggled. You were the first to speak to us.'

'Two pretty girls.'

'Thomas followed you over and offered to buy me a drink. You didn't like that. He whispered to me, *One drink from Simon and he thinks he owns you for the night.* I saw then you were someone who thought you could control people, manipulate them. Other people were something to be used for your benefit. Thomas told me you led your men in the same way.'

'Your beloved Thomas.' He reached forward and snatched hold of the frame. 'Saint Thomas, trapped in time, always perfect.'

'He'd have stood up to you in a way, I fear, Alan never could.'

'But he couldn't because he was dead.' Simon dropped the frame onto the floor and smashed his heel into the glass.

Pamela held his eye. 'You can destroy as many photographs as you like, but this is where Thomas lives,' she said, her hand touching her heart.

385

He was fast to his feet. 'Shut up!' he yelled. He raised his hand and without hesitation struck her across her face. Her head thrown to one side, her hand shook as she raised it to her mouth. Her fingers came away stained red; blood mingled with the lipstick Maggie had given her for her last birthday. She swallowed hard.

'It was you who drowned those two poor men at Mickelside. I just don't know why.'

'Marvis knew too much. Lennon was nothing more than collateral damage. I picked him at random. Somebody had to dive with Marvis.'

Her cheek stung and Pamela pressed her palm against her face. Even now, hearing Simon say the words, she still struggled to comprehend his callous approach to human life.

'When you saw Eileen leaving my house yesterday, you realised she could place you at Mickelside that morning.' He began to pace the room, but Pamela pressed on. 'You employed Alan in your cover-up. I doubt he ever knew you deliberately killed the men. I'm sure you spun him a story – a senior officer, with ambitions to move into the security services, couldn't be caught up in a scandal, however much a tragic accident.'

'I paid him handsomely.'

Pamela nodded. 'Two thousand pounds a month. He never touched a penny of it.'

'More fool him, but once he'd taken the money, he was guilty by association. That guaranteed his silence.'

'He did talk to Alaka Jha, and after that you agreed to meet her, in the layby on Haddley Hill.'

Standing directly in front of her, Simon towered over Pamela. With a single pull, he snapped the cord from her window blind.

'Her problem was she had a habit of asking too many questions, just like you.'

CHAPTER 80

Avoiding the traffic on the Lower Haddley Road, I race through the town's Victorian side streets. When an Uber pulls out in front of me, I accelerate past and hurtle towards the junction with Haddley Hill. I think of the people killed when they came too close to revealing the horrendous crimes Simon Carmichael committed against Fiona Nicholls. Thirty years ago, it cost Alaka Jha her life. Now, I have an agonising fear it might cost Pamela the same.

I fly through a set of changing traffic lights, swing across the road and abandon my car behind a Volvo SUV. I can see a light illuminating Pamela's window. I rattle the brass door knocker on her front door. There is no reply. I hammer my fist against the wooden door.

'Pamela,' I yell. I move to her living-room window. With the blinds down, it's impossible for me to see inside. I bang on the glass. Still there is no response. I take a step back. An alleyway runs along the side of the house. I decide to run to the back. Before I do, I pound again on the window.

'Pamela,' I shout.

Her hand slams against the blind, before slowly sliding down the glass pane.

CHAPTER 81

I crash my boot against Pamela's front door. A crack ripples up the side of the wooden frame. I slam my shoulder against the damaged door, and it flies open. I charge into the hallway.

'Pamela,' I shout. From the living room, I hear her howl. Racing into the room, I'm confronted by Simon Carmichael. Instantly, he shapes to hit me. I duck and hurl myself forward. I can feel his strength but the weight of my frame bowls him over. He falls backwards, crashing through Pamela's coffee table.

'Ben!' she cries.

For a split second, I turn. She is lying on the floor, beneath the window. In that moment, Carmichael scrambles to his feet. He flings himself forward, wrapping his arms around my legs. He drops me to the floor. I fall backwards, my head slamming against the wall.

Dazed, I look up and see him looming over me. He bends, grabs my shirt and swings a furious punch. I throw myself sideways. Clutching my collar, he swings again, catching me with a glancing blow on the side of my face. I stagger to my feet, but as I do, he jumps over my legs and flies out of the room.

I turn to Pamela. She's hauling herself up into her armchair.

'Are you okay?'

'Yes, fine,' she replies. 'Stop him!'

I run out of the room. I see Carmichael charge through the open front door. Car horns blare as he scurries across Haddley Hill Road. I tear after him, but as I do the lights of the Volvo SUV flick into life. He scrambles inside the car. I grab at the handle of the driver's door, but the car is locked. I bang my fist on the window.

Carmichael fires the engine. He rams the Volvo into reverse and slams into my car. Standing in the middle of the road, I jump backwards. He races forward, oblivious to the white transit van speeding over the brow of the hill.

The two vehicles collide, flipping the Volvo onto its side and then over onto its roof. I stand and watch as, sparks flying, the car slides down the hill.

I run forward. An exploding airbag briefly traps Carmichael behind the steering wheel. He wrestles it to one side and, on his knees, scrambles out onto the road. I grab his jacket, haul him to his feet and before he can react land one clean strike against his jaw. As he drops, I hear police sirens racing up Haddley Hill. Clutching her phone, Pamela hurries from the front of her home. She stands beside me, and I wrap my arm around her.

'It's over,' I say.

CHAPTER 82

'You really are a wonder, coming out so quickly,' I hear Pamela say to the carpenter working in her hallway.

'All part of the service,' he replies.

'Are you sure I can't make you a cup of tea, with a slice of cake?'

'That's very kind of you, but I stopped for a chicken sandwich on the way here.'

'As long as you're sure,' she says, before joining DS Parker and me in her living room.

'Now I understand why you told me you wished you'd arrived sooner at Eileen Blenkhorn's flat,' says Parker. 'You already had your own suspicions.'

'I wanted to know if the third man might have been Simon. I knew whoever it was had such control over Alan. If only I'd asked sooner.'

'You can't blame yourself,' he replies. 'I should have listened to you.'

Pamela sits on the corner of the sofa. She bends forward

and picks up the broken photograph frame from the floor. 'We'll need to buy you a new frame,' she says.

Parker smiles. 'Nice to meet you, Thomas.'

'What I still don't quite understand, Ben, is why? What was Simon hiding?'

I tell both Pamela and DS Parker of the murder of Fiona Nicholls.

'Little more than a girl herself,' replies Pamela. 'Simon would be terrified of anything or anyone that might interrupt his relentless rise through the ranks, or equally his enjoyment of Louise's wealth. To him, people are as disposable as a bottle of water.'

'He abused her when she was in the military but feared reprisals even after she'd left?' asks Parker.

'I'm afraid so,' I reply. 'Mark Marvis, David Lennon, and of course, Alaka Jha. He couldn't risk anyone exposing his secrets.'

'Poor Eileen became his final victim. I'd like to make sure she receives a good send-off.'

'Dani and I can help with that.'

'Afterwards, I'd like to place a bench, with her name on, by the river.'

'That's a lovely thought.'

'I think she'd enjoy the company,' replies Pamela.

I smile. 'Come and have dinner with Dani and me tonight,' I say.

'That would be nice. I've one last thing I must do, so shall we say I'll wander over in an hour or so?'

CHAPTER 83

In the early evening, Haddley Hill remained closed. Simon's upturned car still blocked the road. Pamela slipped on her jacket and hurried past the policeman tasked with diverting the traffic. It was PC Higgins, the officer who'd driven her home earlier in the day, and she had no desire to listen to any more of his chatter.

When she passed through the gates of Castle Fields, she felt more nervous than a young child arriving for her first day of school. Over the entry intercom, she heard Maggie's surprise. Her stomach fluttered as she rode up in the lift. Reaching Maggie's apartment, she found the door standing open.

'You've got me worried, turning up unannounced again,' said her friend, who was waiting for her in the hallway. 'You look exhausted.'

'It's been a long day,' replied Pamela, 'but I needed to see you.'

'Let's have a glass of wine,' said Maggie, leading the way into the living room. 'I've still half the bottle Simon and Louise brought at the weekend.'

'God, no.'

'What's wrong?'

The two women sat at the small dining table and Pamela explained.

'I can hardly believe it,' said Maggie. 'Simon was always domineering, but a killer? That poor girl and all those people since. How much do you think Alan might have known, about Mickelside, I mean?'

Pamela reached across the table. 'Alan was a good man. If he'd known the truth of Simon's actions, I feel sure he would have come forward.'

'But the time changes on the morning those boys drowned?'

'Simon persuaded him of the need to protect him. Perhaps Alan was foolish enough to delete an exit record from the base or change the time. Whatever he did, Simon compounded his collusion by paying him the money and ensuring he was guilty by association.'

'That's where the money came from?' Maggie pushed her chair back and disappeared into the kitchen. Pamela followed and watched as she drained half a bottle of red wine down the sink.

'I think I'd choke on it,' said Maggie. She opened the corner cupboard and reached for a bottle of Glenfiddich whisky. 'This was always Alan's favourite. Why don't we raise him a toast?'

She poured two small servings, and Pamela added a touch of water to hers.

'To Alan,' she said.

'And Thomas,' added Maggie,

The two women sat together on the living-room sofa. Maggie sipped on her drink. 'Pamela,' she said, 'I've something I'm almost too afraid to ask.'

'Go on.'

'I've been thinking about Saturday and Simon's time with Alan.'

'I did wonder myself,' she replied. 'That evening I told both Simon and Louise how Alan could have brief moments when he was suddenly his old self.'

'Could that have been too much for Simon to risk? A fear Alan might let something slip about what happened thirty years ago. He did try and tell us about the change in time, but of course he confused Larry with Simon.'

'Ben is so very bright, but I think he could be persuaded to believe that's what happened. Of course, he doesn't know everybody in quite the way I do.'

'I'd almost rather it was the case. I do so hate to think of Susan somehow being involved.'

'Susan wasn't involved.' Pamela slowly finished her drink.

'You don't think so?'

'I'm certain,' she replied.

'Simon did come back here on Sunday night?'

Pamela shook her head. 'I wish you weren't so organised and efficient, Maggie. Whatever Susan stumbled upon, I'm sure you'd already done the same.'

'I don't know what you mean.'

'Larry's lovely little sports car. It's almost as if he knew a windfall was on the way.' Pamela brushed her cheek. 'Alan

396

so adored you, Maggie, trusted you with every ounce of his soul. He remained such a strong man, physically, I mean. Of course, if he was sleeping nothing was impossible.' When tears began to well in her friend's eyes, Pamela took hold of her hands. 'He relied on you. You're the only person he'd let get so close to him.'

Maggie swallowed a sob and sniffed. 'I loved him so very much, but I was exhausted. When Larry came back, suddenly I had one last chance at life.'

'Why didn't you use the money to put Alan in a home?'

'It would have broken his heart. And, if I'm completely honest, I wanted the money to really live. For once in my life, to do something for me. I wanted to be the one sending postcards from far-flung places.' She squeezed Pamela's hand. 'Every single day, the same conversation, over and over and over. Everything was about me taking care of Alan. Not just for the last five years, but my whole married life.'

CHAPTER 84

'Are you sure you won't join us?' I say to Uma, as I open a carton of sweet-and-sour chicken.

'There's loads,' adds Dani. 'Ben has a habit of ordering far too much.'

'I'd love to stay, but Edward's home this evening and we're taking my father to the pub, although probably not the Rose and Crown.'

'He's holding up okay, your dad?'

'He needs to hear everything from me. I realise now how much he loved my mum.'

I open a carton of white rice and spoon it onto my plate.

'Go easy with that,' says Dani.

'What are you saying?' I reply, laughing. 'I've earned it today.'

'You most definitely have.' Uma steps down off a kitchen stool. 'My mum fought for justice for so many people, and now, finally, she has her own. I'll never be able to repay you.'

Uma hugs me close. We walk out into the hall, and I call upstairs.

'Dad, dinner!'

'I'll be down in a minute,' he replies. 'I like it cold.'

I shake my head.

'Your father is unique,' says Uma, 'but he's a kind man.' Uma turns to Dani. 'Call me any time,' she says, before they head outside.

'Get yourself a plate,' I say to my father when he appears in the kitchen.

'Uma is so much like her mother,' he says, standing by the window. 'For a long time, I missed Alaka. I missed her so much I ran from Haddley and simply kept running. That was wrong of me because it meant I ran from you and your brother.'

I pass my father a plate. 'I'll let you help yourself,' I say, reaching for a fork.

He puts the plate down on the island. 'I'm sorry, Ben, I really am.'

I look at him. It's the first time he's ever said those words to me.

'Family's important to you and that's why I'm such a dis-appointment. I'm sorry I ran and I'm sorry I never showed up on the day Nick died.'

I've always told myself I'd never forgive him. 'When I was a kid, I'd sit for hours thinking of that day. I'd imagine it so you did meet Nick off the bus before the two of you spent the afternoon swimming at the lido. Occasionally, I'll still find myself doing it now.'

'Don't you think I do the same? I know you've never forgiven me, but I've never forgiven myself and I never will. I lost both my sons on that day.'

I take a deep breath. 'Come and get yourself some food.'

He spoons out his meal and for a moment we sit in silence, both of us listening to the voices outside the front of the house.

'Dad,' I say, as he mixes rice in with his pork, 'why don't you stay on a couple more days?'

'No, I'll be gone in the morning. I'd only get in the way.'

'Please,' I reply. 'You could use Nick's room.'

Dani reappears at the kitchen door. 'Look who I found arriving in an Uber.'

'Pamela, you made it,' I say, jumping off my chair to greet her.

My father steps down from beside the island. 'Mrs Cuthbert, I'm honoured to meet you. You are the hero of the day.'

'Pamela, please,' she replies, slightly flustered by his gallant welcome.

'Come and sit down,' he says, offering her his arm and helping her up onto a high kitchen stool. 'Ben, a plate please.' He smiles at Pamela. 'It'll be my privilege to serve you.'

I catch Dani's eye, and she grins. We all sit at the island and Pamela tells us of her conversation with Maggie.

'I'm so sorry,' says Dani, finishing her meal. 'I know what a good friend she's been to you.'

'If only I'd realised how desperate she was.'

'Pamela, you mustn't blame yourself,' says my father.

'He's right,' I add. 'You couldn't have done anything more.'

Dani stretches her back and stands behind Pamela. She wraps her arms around her and kisses her on the cheek. 'I'm going to go upstairs and lie down. Ben will run you home when you're ready.'

'Can I make you a cup of tea?' asks my father, as Dani disappears out of the room.

'That would be lovely,' replies Pamela.

My father busies himself clearing our plates before filling the kettle.

'I spoke to Sam,' I tell Pamela. 'He wants to interview you tomorrow. He's planning on running a feature piece in the *Richmond Times*.'

'On me? Most definitely not,' she replies. 'I couldn't think of anything worse.'

'I don't know,' says my dad, bringing Pamela her drink. 'You could do a nice photo shoot, perhaps out on the common. It'd give you an excuse to get your hair done and the paper might even pay for a new outfit.'

'Gordon, I'd be so embarrassed.'

'Dad, I think Sam might want to talk to you as well.'

'A profile piece on me?'

'More like a couple of quotes.' I turn to Pamela. 'Sam's planning on rerunning some of Eileen's old recipes, as a tribute.'

'She'd like that,' she replies. '"Mrs Cooper's Cookery Course" was important to her. It was one of the few things that made her feel valued.'

401

My dad brings Pamela two chocolate mints, which he's placed on a saucer. 'A little something sweet.'

Suddenly, we hear a cry from upstairs.

'Ben!' shouts Dani. 'My waters have broken!'

CHAPTER 85

'There's no need to panic,' I hear my dad say, as I sprint up the stairs.

'Gordon, nobody is,' replies Pamela. 'Why don't you finish clearing up and I'll pop upstairs with Ben to check on Dani?'

I find Dani sitting on the edge of our bed. 'It's time,' she says.

I sit beside her. 'Are you okay?' I ask.

She turns to me and raises her eyebrows. 'We're about to have a baby.'

We both smile. 'I won't suggest doing your breathing exercises, not just yet anyway.'

Dani cries a low, guttural scream. She grabs hold of my hand and bends forward in pain.

'That sounds like a contraction,' says Pamela, standing at our bedroom door. 'Have you packed a bag?'

'We did that a month ago,' says Dani, desperately catching her breath.

'I'll get it,' I say, jumping to my feet.

'Ben, we're not leaving yet,' says Dani, as I hurry into the spare room. Pamela sits beside Dani on the bed.

'I can't help but think of your dad,' says Pamela, a man she and Dani both loved. 'He'd be so proud of you.'

I stand in the doorway. 'Shall I put this in the car, so we're ready?'

'No harm in being prepared,' replies Pamela.

I run outside. I look out onto the common and remember my own mum. With the imminent arrival of her first grandchild, her excitement levels would be off the scale. Like every grandmother, she'd fuss but I know how much she'd share in our joy. When I head back inside, I hear Dani cry out again. I scramble up the stairs.

'You shouldn't be having another contraction now!'

Bent double, Dani is clutching Pamela's hand.

'I think this baby might be coming quite quickly,' says Pamela. 'Breathe through it,' she tells Dani. 'When you're ready, let's get you downstairs.'

Dani blows out her cheeks.

'Shall I call Uma?' I ask.

'I think it's the hospital we need,' replies Pamela.

With Dani holding my arm, we move slowly down the stairs. My father is standing in the hallway. 'I've cleared the kitchen,' he tells us. 'How else can I help?'

'You stay here and look after the house,' replies Pamela. 'We'll call you as soon as there's any news.'

'I'll grab some towels and clean up the bathroom,' he says, as we leave through the front door.

'Don't put them back in the cupboard!' yells Dani, over her shoulder.

In the car, Dani and Pamela sit together on the back seat. We turn away from Haddley Common and follow the road through the woods towards St Marnham. We stop at the traffic lights at the edge of the village and a BP tanker rumbles past. When the lights change, we follow in a slow procession up the hill towards Oreton.

Dani cries out again, a longer and more strangled cry.

I glance over my shoulder and see the fear in her eyes.

Pamela is holding her hand, while dabbing her forehead. 'Ben, the baby's coming. Can we get there any quicker?'

I duck out from behind the BP tanker, but the brow of the hill obscures my view. Finally, at the top of the hill, the road is clear, and I race past.

Dani howls in pain. She lies across the back seat.

'Remember your breathing,' says Pamela.

Outside the university hospital, I run a red light. We speed into an ambulance bay at the front and I charge inside.

'Somebody help, please,' I say. 'My girlfriend's having a baby in our car outside.'

Two nurses hurry out. When they open the car door, I hear Pamela say, 'One more push and the baby's here.'

I stand frozen as the two nurses deliver our child from the back seat of our car. From behind me another nurse appears and cuts the cord. I clamber in the opposite side and hold Dani in my arms. Together, we watch as two nurses race back inside the hospital carrying our tiny son.

WEDNESDAY

CHAPTER 86

Late in the afternoon, Vlad drives us along the Lower Haddley Road before turning onto the common. He slows Madeline's Mercedes outside the front of our house. Sitting on the back seat, I lean across and kiss Dani.

'Welcome home,' I say.

'It's good to be back.' She smiles and unbuckles our baby seat.

I hurry around the car and open Dani's door. By the time we've manoeuvred the baby carrier out of the car, Pamela already has the front door of our house wide open.

'Look at him sleeping,' she says, as we approach. 'He's so beautiful.'

In the hallway, my father stands awkwardly at the foot of the stairs.

'Gordon, come and say hello to your grandson,' says Dani, softly.

He takes two small steps forward and looks inside the carry seat. He stares open mouthed.

'Meet Jack Nicholas Harper,' she says. 'Jack, say hello to your granddad.'

My father's eyes swell with pride. I put my arm around him and for the first time since I was a three-year-old boy, I hug him close. For a moment, I don't want to let go.

'Come through to the living room,' says Pamela, where we find a giant helium balloon and several familiar faces.

'Congratulations,' says Sam, his hand on my back.

'Make sure he does his fair share of nappy changes,' whispers Madeline, as she greets Dani.

'Good to see you, boss,' I say, a wide smile lighting my face.

'If you're willing to go to such extremes to have a couple of days off, I had no choice but to come back and take over the reins.'

'I couldn't be more delighted,' I reply.

From the back of the room Alice creeps forward, tightly holding her mother's hand. She peers at Jack.

Dani crouches down to speak to her. 'He's sleeping at the moment, but when he wakes you can hold him if you like.'

Uncharacteristically shy, Alice takes a step back behind her mother's legs. Holly embraces both me and Dani. 'He's gorgeous,' she tells us. 'If Alice doesn't want to hold him, I will.'

Madeline and Sam soon slip away, and when they do my father follows.

'Dad, you don't have to go,' I say.

'I'll be back later tonight, but I want to give you some time as a family.'

'Thanks, Dad.'

'Also, I'm buying Pamela supper, so don't wait up.'

'It's only supper,' Pamela adds, flushing, before she hurries out of the door.

When we're left with only Holly and Alice, Dani and I sit with Jack on the oversized sofa.

'Alice, come and sit on here with us,' says Dani. 'Why don't you open that big present?' she continues, pointing at the largest parcel among a stack of gifts.

Alice carries it across the room and tears open the paper. Inside is a personalised teddy-bear blanket and a soft, black-and-white puppy wearing a *Jack* jumper.

'Somebody moved quickly,' said Dani, looking to the gift tag. 'Love from Uncle George.'

'He might have had some insider knowledge on the name.'

Dani smiles. 'Perhaps we should make him an official uncle as Jack's godfather?'

'I'm not sure he'd be one hundred per cent the best influence.'

'That might be good for Jack, and George.'

'I think he'd love it.'

Alice clambers onto the sofa and sits beside Dani. She peers again at Jack sleeping in his carry seat.

'Why are you so quiet?' asks Dani.

Alice stands up and cups her hand around Dani's ear. 'I said we wanted a girl.'

Dani laughs and hugs Alice close. 'For the next one, I promise we'll try.'

ACKNOWLEDGEMENTS

Writing the end of this story, I imagined a good number of readers rolling their eyes at the speed with which Dani and Ben's son made his appearance in the world. But, in the spirt of truth being stranger than fiction, the final culmination of the story is based exactly on what happened with my own birth, right down to the BP petrol tanker.

I was born somewhere between my parents' home and the old Harrogate hospital. My dad drove my mum to the hospital just after midnight, with my 'auntie' Pamela sitting in the back seat supporting my mum. When we arrived at the hospital, nurses rushed outside and I was taken into the hospital first. My mum, dad and auntie Pamela followed.

This book is dedicated to Pamela, who has been ever present throughout my life. From the day I was born she's been like a second mum to me. For thirty years she and her family lived across the road from my own family home and she was part of my life almost every single day when I was growing up. She was my mum's very best friend, and to me she was, and remains, someone who I love like a mum. She's a great listener, and talker; she cares, is funny and wonderfully kind. Now in her nineties, she's still as sharp as ever and I will for ever adore her.

Nine Hidden Lives is also dedicated to my sister, Katie. Katie is an amazing human being. She has an inner strength and determination to tackle any problem in life that I have never witnessed in anyone else. She is the most brilliant and loving mother; a most caring and generous parent. Throughout our lives we have been incredibly close, at various times sharing a home and often travelling together. She is the person to whom I am closest in the world. When I'd finished writing this book, I received some devastating news. From nowhere, I was diagnosed with stage four cancer. In the weeks following, Katie has been by my side every step of the way. Going through treatment without her would be impossible. I owe her everything.

My diagnosis has made me appreciate how important friends and family are as we all face life's challenges. So many people have rallied to my side following my diagnosis. Their kindness sustains me every day. Without my closest friends Oli and Lee-Anne I wouldn't have made it through the early days of my diagnosis. My boss, Tom, has been as unflinching in his support of me as he was throughout the decade we worked closely together. We share so many fond, and at times challenging, memories.

All of the children in the Ben Harper series are inspired by my two 'godless' children, Max and Emilie. Their brilliant personalities are the inspiration for so many of the lines spoken and I am so incredibly proud of them both.

Special thanks and love, as always go to O, H and W for the loan of the name. Each of you mean so much to me.

My agent, Juliet, is amazing in every situation and simply never misses a step. My editor, Rosanna, is my partner in all things Ben Harper and I love working with her. I hope one day we can work together on another book.

With such wonderful support from so many readers, it had always been my hope to continue the Ben Harper series for a number of stories more. However, with Ben, Dani and baby Jack happy at home this now feels like the perfect place to rest the series and let them enjoy their time together. If I'm lucky enough to write another book in the future, I think it might be time for some new characters, new stories and new twists.

Finally, my thanks go to you, the reader. Your support of the Ben Harper series has been amazing. It's impossible for me to thank you enough for choosing my book to read when so many books are published every single year. Thank you for taking the time read *Nine Hidden Lives* and I hope the twists and turns kept you entertained to the very last page.

Robert Gold

December 2024

Revisit the first Ben Harper mystery . . .

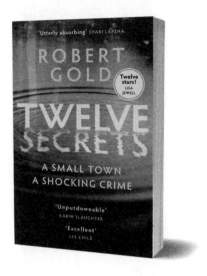

A SMALL TOWN. A SHOCKING CRIME.
YOU'LL SUSPECT EVERY CHARACTER.
BUT YOU'LL NEVER GUESS THE ENDING.

Ben Harper's life changed for ever the day his older brother
Nick was murdered by two classmates. It was a crime
that shocked the nation and catapulted Ben's family and
their idyllic hometown, Haddley, into the spotlight.

Twenty years on, Ben is one of the best investigative
journalists in the country and settled back in Haddley,
thanks to the support of its close-knit community. But
then a fresh murder case shines new light on his brother's
death and throws suspicion on those closest to him.

Ben is about to discover that in Haddley no one is
as they seem. Everyone has something to hide.

And *someone* will do anything to keep the truth buried . . .

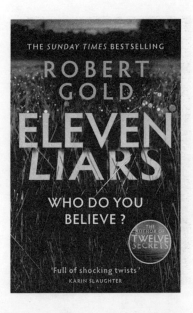

'Packed with explosive twists and impossible to put down' *WOMAN & HOME*

Journalist Ben Harper is on his way home when he sees the flames in the churchyard. The derelict community centre is on fire. And somebody is trapped inside.

With Ben's help the person escapes, only to flee the scene before they can be identified. Now the small town of Haddley is abuzz with rumours. Was this an accident, or arson?

Then a skeleton is found in the burnt-out foundations.

And when the identity of the victim is revealed, Ben is confronted with a crime that is terrifyingly close to home. As he uncovers a web of deceit and destruction that goes back decades, Ben quickly learns that in this small town, everybody has something to hide.

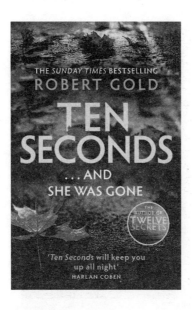

**The third thriller from *Sunday Times*
bestseller Robert Gold is a race-against-the-clock
mystery and his most compelling yet.**

After a tense birthday celebration in Haddley, journalist
Ben Harper watches his boss, Madeline, get into the car that
has come to collect her. He walks home, never imagining
that by the next morning, Madeline will be missing.

To find Madeline, Ben will have to return to the
now infamous murder case that made her journalism
career over a decade ago. A case which, Ben quickly
discovers, was never as simple as it seemed.

But time is of the essence, and soon it's not
just Madeline's life on the line ...